He smiled, rising. "Don't worry. I've got you."

When he returned, her eyes had closed again already, and her breathing had smoothed and lengthened. He spread the cover over her, leaning close to tuck it carefully behind her shoulder. And pausing, before he could stop himself, to gently touch his lips to her temple before slipping away.

Outside on the porch he stood for a few moments, wondering whether he'd done what he had only because he didn't yet dare to kiss his children. But in his heart, he knew this was nothing like that, just as he knew he was playing with fire by giving in to his need for her approval, his desire for her touch...

You have no business wanting any woman right now, he reminded himself sharply, *and this one least of all*. Instead, he needed to stay focused on his duties as a father, the first of which was making certain his kids were well and truly safe.

Dear Reader,

In my latest story, I'm excited to introduce you to a section of the beautiful Texas Hill Country that I've come to know quite well. Though I've taken a handful of geographic liberties and altered a few of the locations and individual names for privacy reasons, the area is every bit as stunning and the animals just as fascinating as those you'll read about within these pages—from its crystal clear rivers to its mountains and right down to the boxing jackrabbits sometimes spotted on the dirt roads as they violently compete for love.

Unlike the hares, however, it isn't a jealous rival that stands between resort owner Mac Hale-Walker and his chance to find lasting love. Instead, it's his own ability to trust himself, not only as a man but as a father to the children stolen and hidden away from him for eight long years in a foreign country. At first resentful and suspicious of the young social worker sent from the state capital to assess his parenting abilities—and help him translate for the twins he can no longer even speak with—Mac soon discovers there's a great deal more to Sara Wakefield than he first imagined...

But even as Sara is called upon to pass judgment on the handsome but world-weary father, she sees the danger in him—and the twins she's all too quickly growing attached to. For like Mac, she fights a battle against her own secrets...

Along with a deadlier opponent hidden by the stunning scenery.

Colleen Thompson

DANGER AT CLEARWATER CROSSING

Colleen Thompson

HARLEQUIN
ROMANTIC
SUSPENSE

Recycling programs for this product may not exist in your area.

ISBN-13: 978-1-335-75963-4

Danger at Clearwater Crossing

Copyright © 2022 by Colleen Thompson

This edition published by arrangement with Harlequin Books S.A.

For questions and comments about the quality of this book, please contact us at CustomerService@Harlequin.com.

Harlequin Enterprises ULC
22 Adelaide St. West, 41st Floor
Toronto, Ontario M5H 4E3, Canada
www.Harlequin.com

Printed in U.S.A.

The Texas-based author of more than thirty novels and novellas, **Colleen Thompson** is a former teacher with a passion for reading, hiking, kayaking and the last-chance rescue dogs she and her husband have welcomed into their home. With a National Readers' Choice Award and multiple nominations for the RITA® Award, she has also appeared on the Amazon, BookScan and Barnes & Noble bestseller lists. Visit her online at www.colleen-thompson.com.

Books by Colleen Thompson

Harlequin Romantic Suspense

Lost Legacy
Danger at Clearwater Crossing

First Responders on Deadly Ground

Colton 911: Chicago
Colton 911: Hidden Target

Passion to Protect
The Colton Heir
Lone Star Redemption
Lone Star Survivor
Deadly Texas Summer

The Coltons of Mustang Valley
Hunting the Colton Fugitive

Visit the Author Profile page at Harlequin.com for more titles.

To Mike, who never tires of trekking down yet another unmarked country road to help me chase down stray plot bunnies...

Chapter 1

Real County, Texas
Sunday afternoon

Sweat-soaked, shirtless and coated with a layer of the same muddy grime he had just wiped from his face, Mac Hale-Walker looked down from the debris heap on the rocky, tree-lined bank where he stood to the still-swollen Frio River. As a tangle of tree limbs wrapped up with barbed wire rushed past on the current, he weighed whether it was safe to risk a quick swim or if anyone—other than the gray-muzzled Labrador retriever who watched over him from the pile of old feed sacks Mac had stacked up for her—would give a damn if he were finally well and truly washed away.

His body ached with weariness after days of back-breaking labor in the June heat working to repair the flood-damaged river resort with its dozen rental cabins, days that only added to the weight of eight long years of grief and anxiety, bitterness and anger over losses beyond measure. What if he finally quit fighting so damned hard just to keep his head above water? What if, at long last, he quit worrying about whatever might come hurtling downstream next, waiting—

Mac scowled, cutting off the thought cold. Hell with that idea, since he knew all too well his death would, in some circles, be a cause for celebration. He would never give his enemies the excuse to host a grand fiesta, no matter how many bleak years he had to keep on spitting in the wind to spite them.

His thoughts were interrupted by a clunking sound, one loud enough to carry over the rushing water. Recognizing it as the slamming of a nearby car door, Roxy gave a gruff alarm-woof and attempted to raise herself from her nest before apparently deciding that her heart—or her hips—weren't in it at the moment.

"I know, old girl," he said as he attempted and then gave up on shaking out the filthy shirt. If these trespassers were going to drive right past the Closed Due to Flooding—Keep Out signs without reading, they'd have to deal with the sight of him looking like Sasquatch's river rat cousin. "Some folks just aren't worth the effort of climbing up out of your hammock."

Tossing aside his crumpled shirt, Mac grabbed the same ax he'd been using to deal with some warped and splintered decking. Then he clambered up the bank, eager to eject what he figured were either gawkers or more of the thieving scavengers who'd been making off with whatever they could grab and flee with from the only property left to his name.

In most cases, his fearsome scowls and a few choice words would be more than enough to send them scurrying away. If not, however, he was perfectly prepared to resort to harsher methods—methods that might not earn him any five-star reviews for hospitality but would go a long way toward allowing him to vent the frustrations he'd been carrying around for far too long.

Ten minutes earlier...

After a struggle to suppress a yawn, Sara Wakefield wriggled in the driver's seat of her Honda then pinched the inside of her lip with her teeth—anything to keep herself awake as she negotiated the bumps and ruts of a muddy, washed-out road between two walls of green so thick that she felt almost crushed between them.

Though she found the Central Texas Hill Country beautiful with its tree-clothed slopes, its flower-strewn pastures and its boundless wildlife, the thirty-one-year-old was a city girl at heart, who'd happily made her home near the heart of Austin since completing her degree in social work there. After an hours-long drive, following a seemingly endless international return flight home to the States in the wake of her Buenos Aires errand, she found herself fantasizing—or most likely hallucinating—about returning to the small apartment she'd only recently moved into with its amazing city views, exposed brick walls and, most important, her comfy bed.

This place shouldn't be much farther. Then I'll have done right by my charges and I can find a place to grab some sleep... Maybe at that mom-and-pop motel she'd spotted in the last little town she'd passed through because there was no way she would safely make the three-hour drive back home without first catching some shut-eye.

At the sight of the sign she'd been anticipating for so

long, Sara wanted to whoop with joy but kept buttoned up so as not to wake the children riding in her back seat.

Clearwater Crossing River Resort
Rio Frio, Texas
Welcome to Your Hill Country
Home Away from Home!

Her grueling, weeklong journey, a trip that had spanned not only counties but continents as she'd worked, at the personal request of one of the governor's top aides, to reunite a broken family, was finally at its end.

Slowing for the turn, she allowed the fantasy of a joyous, tearful reunion with decorated cakes and streamers to spin out in her sleep-deprived brain. But reality caught up moments later, her stomach twisting with the memory of how the eleven-year-old twins had been crying themselves to sleep each night since they'd been torn from the arms of the loving grandmother who had doted on them since they were three and a half years old, when their mother had brought them to her native Argèntina for a visit with her parents.

The children's mother's tragic accidental death abroad had set off an eight-year battle when her grieving parents—who were apparently wealthy and powerful enough to pull a lot of weight in their home country—had refused to turn the twins over to their American father. A father who had spent every dime he could come up with and pleaded for help from every government official he could persuade to listen as he'd fought a one-man war to win them back.

She only hoped he had plenty of patience and enough resources remaining to pay for the counseling they'd surely need to put this Humpty Dumpty of a broken family back together. Because they were going to need all of that, and plenty of love and luck besides.

As she turned into the drive, she mashed down on the brakes, eliciting startled cries from just behind her.

"¡Lo siento!" she apologized, automatically using her Spanish, the only language to which the twins now responded. Apparently, whatever English they had spoken before leaving had been lost during their years abroad.

"Look out the front," she urged, continuing in the same tongue, which she had learned at the knee of the grandmother who had helped to raise her—though her fluency often surprised fellow Texans because of her fair skin, green eyes and blond-streaked, sandy-brown hair.

"Deer, and with a baby, too," exclaimed the girl, Silvia, for once not sobbing and pleading to be taken back to the place that she considered home. *"¡Que bonita!"*

They certainly were pretty with their white-spotted golden hides glistening in the dappled sunlight. Sara wondered if they might be one of those exotic species she'd read about, imported by ranchers and then accidently released to breed freely in the region.

"They're twins, like us," said curly haired Cristo, shaken from his long sulk by what sounded like pure wonder as the second fawn stepped out from behind its mother.

All three of the car's passengers held their breath, but a moment later the beautiful doe led her two fawns into the heavy brush, where they melted away into the shadows.

"Now that you're both awake," Sara told the children, "I need to let you know we've just pulled onto the property. I know it's been a long time since you've seen your father, and you're probably a little nervous—"

"I don't feel so good," Silvia fretted, once more sounding on the verge of tears.

"I won't let him hurt you," Cristo insisted, his own

Spanish edged with pride and anger. "The first time he tries anything, I'll knock him right out. Grandpa taught me how a real man protects his family."

"Your father *is* your family, and he wants you, desperately. He's always loved and wanted you, no matter what you have been told," Sara repeated, knowing the words were even less likely to sink in right now, with both of them scared to death, than they had the last ten times she'd said them. The grandparents had really done a number on these children with their stories. Worse yet, they'd flatly refused to allow their son-in-law any contact with his children whatsoever, giving him zero opportunity to counter their poison.

Sara was aware of the couple's claims that Mac Hale-Walker had been physically abusive to his late wife. The children's mother had supposedly tearfully told her parents, before the snorkeling accident that took her life, that she'd planned to file for divorce immediately upon her return to the US. But an investigation here in Texas had turned up no evidence that Analisa Rojas-Walker had ever consulted with any attorney, sought medical help for any injuries or spoken to any of her friends in less than glowing terms about what had appeared to be a loving marriage.

It was enough to make Sara confident that she was helping to right a tremendous wrong by bringing the twins home to their sole living parent—a restoration that had only been made possible after the recent death of the children's powerful grandfather. What was making her nervous, however, was the governor's aide's failure to return her calls since her return stateside. He was to have worked through this county's social services department to make sure the transition into the children's new home went as smoothly as could be reasonably assured, and she didn't like arriving without knowing they would have clean, welcoming rooms of their own set up and warm, smiling faces to greet them and help put them at ease.

But between her hit-or-miss cell service overseas and the terrible reception out here in the sticks, which had caused an issue for her phone as it attempted to download all her stacked-up messages and e-mails, she had no way of making certain.

Don't fret so much. Paul Barkley's surely got it covered, she told herself, thinking what a stickler the veteran aide was for details—and how personally concerned for the twins' welfare he'd seemed during their in-person briefing. But she hadn't driven another twenty yards before she stopped to read a large hand-painted closed sign.

"What does it say?" Cristo asked her of the black block letters.

"It's nothing to do with us," she assured him as the Civic wallowed through an especially deep puddle on its way past. But her dreamy fantasies of crawling into a clean bed vanished, giving way to a gnawing in the pit of her stomach.

She only hoped they didn't end up stuck on the godforsaken excuse for a dirt driveway before she had the chance to figure out what her instincts were rattling on about. So what if the resort's rental cabins had been affected by the recent storms she'd read about in news updates in those odd moments when her phone had been working right?

Surely, the owner himself would have a nice, dry home—one he'd spent the past joyous week preparing for the miracle of this sudden reversal in fortune after so many years of foot-dragging by the authorities overseas?

Turn around now, a small voice inside her whispered. The sensible, no-nonsense voice of her better judgment.

Drive back to town. Check into that motel with the kids and don't go anywhere until you've made some phone calls.

A sensation of icy dread crept up into her throat like bile, another nudge from instinct. This time, however, she decided to listen to her social worker's intuition. She'd turn around for certain. The only problem was, she had no choice except to move forward far enough to find a spot that looked wide and firm enough to hold her tires so the Civic wouldn't get stuck when she tried to turn around.

Gritting her teeth, she continued until the gravel driveway finally opened up directly ahead and to their left.

From the back seat, Silvia gasped in horror at the sight that greeted them. "Is this really where we have to live?"

"No, Silvia," Sara told her, stopping for a moment to stare at the ruin of what appeared to have recently been a lovely, if rustic-looking, cabin. "You two won't be living in *this* house, I promise. I'm sure this is just an old guest cabana, and there'll be a nice home somewhere you can—"

"We would run away first," Cristo vowed, managing to sound both fierce and solemn, though beneath the veneer of his bravado, the eleven-year-old's voice was trembling. "We'll run all the way back to Abuelita!"

Sara's heart squeezed over how much they missed the grandmother they had come to think of more as a mother. But with Silvia still going on about how she needed to go home *now*, Sara needed to keep focused on the cabin, which must have been washed off of its posts by the force of the water. Poised near the edge of a slope, the structure had collapsed on one end, its timbers buckling. In its collapse, all of the windows had been shattered, as well, giving the place the empty-eyed look of a desecrated skull.

Before she could attempt to calm the children, a tall, powerfully built man appeared on the slope's edge, quickly striding toward them. Shirtless and smudged with grime, he had a mane of thick, dark blond waves and a fierce expression—one underscored by the item he was hoisting, an honest-to-goodness Paul Bunyan, or maybe serial killer, styled ax.

Alarmed by the sight and the speed of his approach—both of which had the children screaming—Sara dropped her Civic into Reverse, thinking, *This isn't right. Get out now!*

But in her haste, the rear tires rolled up over something—a big rock, maybe? Whatever it was, she felt the car's front end literally lift up as the vehicle tipped backward, and after that, nothing she did, from stomping the accelerator to wrenching the wheel back and forth to yelling, "Go, go, *go!*" made a single bit of difference.

She double-checked the locks and then reached for her phone as the man strode nearer.

No bars of service. At all. Sara would have screamed or cried or cursed a blue streak—she wasn't entirely sure which—had the children not been with her, so terrified that they'd gone silent.

"Is he going to kill us?" Silvia finally whispered, her small voice shaking.

"Abuelita said he would!" insisted Cristo.

"No one's killing anybody," Sara assured them, but it wasn't until she had looked over at the man approaching that she gusted out a sigh of relief, seeing that he'd dropped the ax he had been carrying when she'd initially spotted him. "And I'm not entirely sure who this is, but I'm going to get out and talk to him, and you two are going to lock the doors after me and—*promise me you're listening*—stay inside no matter what. Do you understand?"

After both children gave their word, she took a deep breath, donning her professionalism like a suit of armor, and climbed out of the car.

The first thing she did afterward was turn and point to Cristo, who reached over from the back seat to lock the doors before giving her a nervous-looking thumbs-up.

Only then did she turn around to face the tall man who'd stopped within six feet of her, a pained look creasing his dirt-coated forehead and an apology in his blue-gray eyes.

"I'm sorry for frightening you and your children, miss." He grimaced, looking stricken. "When I heard the—the screaming, I realized what a sight I must be after all day working on this mess the flood's left." He gestured toward the cabin.

"Then you're the...the *owner*?" she asked, peering harder at the lean but handsome face, though it certainly needed not only a washing but a good shave. And trying to come to grips with the stunning possibility that the impeccably organized Paul Barkley might have somehow left one absolutely essential detail off of his to-do list.

How could such a thing have possibly happened?

Nodding, the man continued speaking. "Only reason I came boiling up here like a thunderstorm in the first place is on account of the thieves who keep driving past my closed sign and making off with whatever they can steal out of the damaged cabins. As if I haven't lost enough here, having to shut down for what might amount to half the season—but I'd never intentionally scare anybody's kids."

"So you're really Mac Hale-Walker?" she tried to clarify, noticing that beneath all that sweat and grime, there was a tanned, work-hardened body with an honest-to-goodness six-pack. When was the last time she'd seen one in the wild, especially on a man nearing forty who'd apparently earned his muscles through honest work rather than a gym?

"I am," he admitted, raking back the thick mane, which fell to his shoulders. "But you seem to have me at a disadvantage—and I feel rude as hell, standing here half naked while your poor kids are stuck in the car, which, excuse me for noticing, isn't going anywhere until I help you get it down off that big log you're hung up on like some kind of seesaw."

Without correcting him about the children, she said, "It's Sara—Sara Wakefield—and is *that* what I hit?" Her face heated with the appalling memory of her panic...because he no longer seemed so terrifying at the moment—just completely unprepared.

She felt for him, too, realizing that, as crazy as it seemed, some bureaucratic snafu had messed up what should have been the biggest moment of his life. But that empathy didn't mean she didn't also have concerns—and huge ones—about what she was seeing.

"If you'll give me just five minutes, ten tops, *Miss Wakefield*," he emphasized, as if to prove he had been listening, "I'm going to ride over to the house in that little utility cart I have parked there, grab myself a clean shirt and come back in my truck to pull you out of trouble. Meanwhile, you're welcome to take the kids out, let them stretch their legs a little. You can show them the river down that slope there, if you keep a careful eye on them. The water's up, and it's running fast right now, with way too much debris in it to want to let them play near."

"We'll be fine," she assured him, grateful for the thought of a respite.

"Oh, and if you see a big black Lab down there," he told her as he started toward the utility cart, "that's just my Roxy. She's getting on in years, but she's super friendly and she lives to love on kids."

"Before you go, please," she said, her heartbeat picking up speed as she asked the question that had been weighing on her since leaving Argentina. "I have just one more question for you. It may seem a little odd, but…" She hesitated long enough for the moment to grow awkward before blurting, "How's your Spanish, Mr. Walker? Would you, by any chance, be fluent in the language?"

Stiffening, he very slowly turned back toward her, the hospitable look on his face hardening into something far more guarded. Or maybe hostile was the right word. "I can't help but wonder why you'd ask me such a question. Especially when the two of us have just spent the past few minutes communicating in English with no issues."

"You're absolutely right. But believe me, I have my reasons. Reasons, I assure you, are for your benefit as well as mine. Now, please tell me, Mr. Walker, *habla español*?"

"Just about enough to understand your question and order off the menu at the nearest taco stand without straining my brain too hard," he told her, his face darkening with anger. "Now, *you* answer a question for *me*, Miss Sara Wakefield. Just what the hell are you doing snooping around my closed property, asking questions about my abilities with the Spanish language? And why on earth would you drag along your kids on your little spy errand—because that's what you're here for, isn't it? Digging up dirt on me for someone, aren't you? You have that look about you—some kind of two-bit bureaucrat, or maybe you're another reporter crawling out of the wood-work after all these years, looking for a new angle on a half-forgotten story—hoping to crack open this damned chest of mine—" he thumped it with his knotted hand "—and tear open the scar tissue. Because nothing sells a blog or whatever crime TV docudrama you might be shopping to the cable networks like a victim's bloody-fresh pain, does it?"

"I'm not here to hurt anybody," she argued, though inside she was shaking, every part of her wanting to re-coil from this man's fury.

"The hell you aren't," he countered, clearly in no state of mind to listen. Nor to do anything but further trauma-tize the children witnessing his outburst. Children who were already more than half convinced he was a madman.

"We're done here, Mr. Walker," she told him, forc-ing her voice to icy coolness. "When you return to your house, I'll thank you to stay inside. But if you'll call a tow truck to assist me, we'll be off your property as soon as possible."

"That's ridiculous. A tow truck around these parts could take hours and I'm just up the—"

"Out of the question," she said, cutting him off crisply. "If the tow truck's not a practical option, then a call to the police will do—"

"We don't have police here in Rio Frio."

"Then the sheriff or whatever kind of hayseed brigade you do have on duty."

"*Hayseed* brigade?" He made a huffing, half-amused sound. One that wasn't at all friendly. "But sure, all right, if you're certain that's what you want."

"I've been awake and traveling for so many hours by

this point that I barely know what day it is, but there's one thing I am absolutely sure of," she insisted. "I have nothing more to say to you until *you* get some more clothes on and *I* get some official guidance on how I'm to proceed."

Chapter 2

"This is outrageous—sending armed men in the dark of night to steal away those children from Don Roberto's grieving widow, without a single word to me about it!" Slapping his desk, the cabinet minister pushed to his feet, glaring at the secretary who had had the misfortune to bring him the morning's news.

In all the years she'd worked for the government, Dolores had handled many crises and broken more bad news to ill-tempered men than she cared to remember. But she could think of nothing she had dreaded more than being forced to tell him of the grave insult to the memory of a revered—and in some circles, feared—figure in Argentinian affairs, a wealthy shipping magnate the minister had been honored to count among his closest compatriots.

Worse yet, the beloved twins, the lights of their grandmother's eyes, had somehow been smuggled to the airport before the minister could be apprised of the calamity, much less have the opportunity to prevent the pair from being returned to the home country of their father. A father whom Dolores had heard whispered had subjected Don Roberto's only daughter, herself now in the arms of the angels, to unspeakable cruelty.

"Where did this order come from? And why was I not notified?"

Dolores waited for a moment to make certain the minister was finished shouting. "You did lock your cell phone in your desk drawer and specifically asked not to be disturbed this weekend, on pain of your extreme displeasure. Your *family time*, if you remember, sir..."

As the minister's most senior secretary, Dolores was aware that, in fact, the minister had been with his latest mistress and no one had wished for his wife, who was naturally sensitive on the subject, to be embarrassed by having to track him down while he'd spent a few days in their love nest on the other side of town.

"Very well. Just tell me. Who is it I have to *thank*?"

She drew a tremulous breath, well aware that she might be about to pronounce the death penalty on a man's career. Or perhaps the undersecretary in question, an ambitious younger man said to be obsessed with Argentina's prospects in an upcoming trade deal he was negotiating with the US—even if he had to upset the current domestic status quo to do so—would lose more than his job.

"Who?" the minister repeated. "Or must I find a new chief secretary, one with a better understanding of her loyalties?"

Blood running cold, Dolores thought of her beloved children and what would become of them if she, a widow of many years, were to suddenly lose her position. She didn't have to long consider before stammering the undersecretary's name.

"Ah... I should have guessed," the minister said, nodding with a look of grim satisfaction. "Very well, then. I wish for you to go directly down to his floor—no phone calls or any e-mails—and bring the undersecretary to me. Bring him right now. No excuses. But you are not to tell him why nor allow him to stop to speak with anyone. Do you understand this?"

"I—I do," Dolores told him, backing toward the door with her knees quaking beneath her skirt. Because the look on the minister's hawklike face now terrified her, his pupils dark as her deepest fears.

Once he had dismissed her, she rushed to do his bidding, her heartbeat a deafening drumbeat in her ears. Passing another secretary, she tuned out the younger woman's cheery hello and then only shook her head when someone else asked if she might be feeling ill today, since she was looking so pale as she scurried to the elevator.

Down on the second floor, she passed the undersecretary's clerk's empty desk. Seeing no one else nearby, she headed straight for the closed door of the office of his superior.

Drawing a deep breath, Dolores knocked once and then again. When the undersecretary failed to answer, she tried the knob, deciding that the safest course of action might be to wait for his return inside, even if she had to stay there, trembling as she tried to piece together what she'd say to convince him that they must make haste.

But after opening the door, it took her only seconds to spot the pool of blood...

It had started from behind the desk, where she found the once ambitious body lying facedown. Yet it wasn't until she spotted the child's toy—a stuffed bear soaked in crimson—that Dolores's screams rang out, frantic cries that brought the others running and soon threw the entire compound into chaos.

Tuesday afternoon
Real County, Texas

Less than forty-eight hours after her arrival in Real County, Sara found herself closeted inside a tiny, musty-smelling storage room off the judge's chambers in the local county courthouse, in the midst of a furiously whispered conversation with her boss back in Austin.

"I thought you told me that you *cared* about these children? That you were so concerned about their welfare, you just had to involve the governor's office to get this emergency custodial hearing?"

"Of course, I care about them, deeply," Sara said.

"And you've established a bond of sorts, have you not?" Regina Browning went on. "After all, the three of you *have* spent the last full week together."

The truth was, Sara had found herself becoming so emotionally invested in the twins' well-being that it had begun to scare her. For all their sakes, she told herself, it would be best if she moved on now before they became too dependent on her...*or I start daydreaming about a future I can never have.*

"I'm trying my best to help them. It's what I do—as a *social worker,*" she told Regina, more forcefully this time, "but not a foster mother." Even saying the word *mother* out loud, imagining it used to describe her, brought back memories so painful that it made her throat tighten and her eyes burn.

Can you confirm for me that you're the child's mother?

she still heard the officer asking, and probably always would, until her dying day. Just as she would carry the mix of sorrow, judgment and disgust she'd seen on his face forever.

"Why are you not getting this?" Sara demanded, her frustration mounting. "What about all my cases piling up in Austin?"

Desperately understaffed and chronically under-funded, her department was struggling, Sara knew from those e-mails she'd managed to get to, to deal with her week's absence.

"It's not going to be a foster situation, exactly," the older woman explained. "It's an emergency extension of your temporary guardianship to ease the children's transition—"

"This is highly irregular," Sara pointed out, as if Regina didn't know it.

"I told you, these kids are special."

"Aren't *all* the children and vulnerable adults we serve?" Including those now getting short shrift while she was away.

"You know what I mean," her supervisor argued, sounding especially exasperated. "The media's been following this family's story for the better part of a decade, and people want a happy ending. The *governor* himself wants a win on this, but he wants to see it done right—and he believes that having continuity will be best for—"

"You've spoken to him personally?"

"Oh, no," Regina admitted, "but that aide, the one you've been dealing with—"

"Paul Barkley," Sara said, her stomach flipping at the thought of the distressing news she'd received after trying his office number rather than the cell phone contact she'd been given. "You heard about his accident?"

"Of course, I did." Regina's tone turned somber. "I could scarcely believe what happened to the poor man. But people drive like maniacs on those roads out near the lakes—and they never watch the roads for bicyclists. I'm always afraid I'll be run down and left to die like that someday myself."

"You haven't heard any more about how he is, have you?" Sara asked. "I mean about whether or not they think he'll pull through?"

"They're saying 'grave condition,'" Regina told her, "which usually means they aren't expecting good news. Unfortunately, the area where he was hit had no cameras, so it's not even likely that they'll find the culprit, unless the guilty party grows a conscience and turns himself or herself in."

"I feel just terrible about this." Sara felt her throat thicken. "He seemed like such a good man...so concerned with getting the children through their ordeal with as little emotional fallout as possible."

"The woman who called from his office, Madeline Herrera, tells me everyone's in shock there," Regina said.

"They must have been," said Sara. "Otherwise, someone surely would have handled the call he was meant to make to Mac Hale-Walker regarding his children's recovery in Argentina."

"That was horribly unfortunate," Regina agreed, "but let's get back to your situation."

"Yes, please," Sara said.

"While you're away in the Hill Country, we'll be dividing up your cases here and seeing that they're covered until our staffing increase comes through."

"Staffing increase? You're finally getting that bump you've been begging for for ages? But *how*?" Their annual budget wasn't due for review for months. "What magic wand did you wave?"

"Actually, it was Ms. Herrera from Paul Barkley's office. She's stepped in for him to handle the situation with the Walker children," Regina told her. "The state's coming through with a special emergency allocation. After I explained how we really couldn't afford to lose one of our best bilingual workers for weeks or even months—"

"Months?" Sara's heart sank as a halcyon vision of her Austin neighborhood with its cute corner coffee shop, her favorite bookstore and the great walkable shopping popped like a soap bubble in her imagination. Because she understood now, her services had been part of some unholy bargain, part politics and part expediency, since, as a single, childless woman who lived alone, the truth was, no one else back in Austin would really miss her that much. She didn't even have so much as a goldfish to worry over, thanks to her apartment's ridiculously strict no-pets policy. "You're telling me I'll have to stay for *months* in a place where all five hundred residents—if there are even that many living in this little Wild West town—glare at me like I'm the embodiment of evil every time I set foot in the café or what passes for a grocery store around here?"

"I'm sure you're just imagining that," Regina said. "Why would anyone care that you're doing your sworn duty?"

"Are you kidding? I've overheard the whispers. To them, I'm a walking, talking symbol of government overreach, keeping a poor, beleaguered father from his children after all these years," she whispered. "Do you know the Hale-Walker brothers had to sell off a ranch that's been a fixture here for generations because of all the legal costs? I gather they barely speak to each other now on account of their brother running a tab against the ranch's line of credit until—"

"Forget the local gossip," Regina pleaded. "I was promised this new staffing could become a *permanent* line item on our budget. Do you know how many at-risk adults, how many more children will be helped—not to mention those poor, motherless twins—by your unselfish sacrifice?"

Sara groaned, hearing in Regina's voice that the deal had already been cut without her. If she refused to go along with it, she had zero doubt that her boss would make her life at work unbearable. She'd seen Regina in action before when she'd wanted to run off an employee, and Sara shuddered to imagine enduring the overloading of her schedule with the most soul-crushing of cases, after-hours callouts when there was no budget left to pay her overtime, and hypercritical remarks designed to chip away at her desire to come to work each morning. As much satisfaction as she'd gotten over the past six years out of helping people, her job had always been a pressure cooker. With the additional stress, Sara knew she'd crack like an egg in no time and be forced to quit.

Besides, she told herself, as strange as the judge's proposed arrangement had been, she truly did want to be certain the children were protected—not simply kept fed and clean, but counseled in their native language and eased into the idea that they had a loving biological father who was even now preparing his home to receive them…and preparing himself, she hoped, for the great challenges he had to face.

"All right. I'll do it," she blurted before she could change her mind.

"That's wonderful!" said Regina, sounding so relieved that Sara wondered how much pressure had been placed on her to make this happen. "Be sure to tell the judge that I'm signing off on this for however long you will be needed."

"But what about my clothes and things?" Sara asked. "I only packed for a brief trip, not an extended stay."

"I'm sure you have some friend or family member who'd be happy to make a weekend drive out to the country to drop off a few things for you. But meanwhile, don't keep the judge waiting, Sara. And please be sure to tell her, you absolutely have my blessing to stay right there and help the children with this transition, if it takes all summer, or even longer if you're needed."

"Longer?" she asked, her mind boggling at the idea. But it was too late. She was speaking only to dead air.

So she put away her cell phone, wondering how long she'd be stuck here, but vowing that as long as she was, she would fight tooth and nail to be the advocate that a pair of scared and lonely kids deserved.

As Mac sat in the hearing room waiting for the judge to return from her chambers, his heart was pounding wildly and he was sweating in his suit. Emotions tumbled through him, so jumbled he could not begin to sort one from the next.

Where are my kids right now? Waiting in the next room? Or have the powers that be already spirited them off to some foster home across the county? If they think for one damned minute I'll stand for it—

"Easy there," urged a deep voice beside him. A voice he hadn't heard much from in months, since the last time he and his brother Hayden, who looked especially sharp today with his sheriff's uniform freshly pressed and his often unruly dark brown hair neatly combed back, had interacted. He had taken time out from his duties this afternoon to show support for his older brother on the day when Mac had been promised he would at last get real news about the children.

"Focus on taking deep, steady breaths there, brother," Hayden advised, "and keeping your reactions nice and fatherly-like for the judge."

"What do you mean 'fatherly-*like*'?" Mac snapped, his nerves strained to the breaking point at being treated like some abusive monster when he'd done absolutely nothing wrong. "I *am* their father, and they're being kept from me for no damned reason. No dog and pony show is gonna change that."

"You need to calm down and cool that temper," whispered Ryan, the youngest of the three Hale-Walker brothers. A ranch foreman who competed on the rodeo circuit on weekends for prize money, the tawny-haired bronc rider looked even more stiffly unnatural than Mac did in his suit—which was usually reserved for attending funerals only, since around here, even weddings tended to be casual denim-and-lace affairs.

After a cautious look around, Ryan surreptitiously pulled out a scuffed and slightly dented silver flask that Mac recognized as having belonged to their late father. Though Ryan hadn't willingly sat in the same room with Mac for maybe two years, he said, "Here you go, bro. Maybe a little nip of this'll help to take the edge off?"

Bristling at the sight, Mac said, "For heaven's sake, put that away before someone reports me as an unfit drunkard." He had no doubt that everyone in the courtroom would be watching to see the three, mostly estranged brothers, one-time heirs to a thriving ranch legacy, in such a rare show of solidarity, all for the sake of the children whose abduction had torn their family apart.

Before he could decide whether the looks he was receiving were damning or supportive, the diminutive yet commanding figure of Judge Willa Cartwright finally returned from chambers, her age-lined face stern but her dark gaze filled with compassion.

Neither eased Mac's anxiety a bit, but all three brothers rose as one, only to have Judge Cartwright cluck at them, "Sit please, everyone."

As they did, another arrival caught his eye: *her* again, that little snoop of a social worker who had submitted a report to the court. He'd been shown a copy, whose words were now branded painfully into his soul—suggesting that *until his housing situation, mental stability and support system may be properly assessed and remediated if necessary, Mr. Hale-Walker should not be allowed unfettered access to the minor children, at the risk, in my professional opinion, of doing them irreparable emotional harm.*

Wearing a softly feminine blue shirtdress and with her hair pulled up to reveal the elegant column of her neck, the young woman, who had signed her full name as *Sara Chavez-Wakefield*, cast what he could have sworn was an apologetic look in his direction before averting her distinctly nervous-looking gaze.

"As sworn enemies go," Hayden whispered gruffly, "at least you picked a looker…with a pretty blush, too."

"If you need somebody to *seduce* her into changing that report she sent the judge," Ryan offered, cocky as only a bronc buster could be, "I believe I'd like to throw my hat in the ring for a crack at that job."

When the bailiff cleared his throat and sent a disapproving scowl in their direction, Mac was grateful for their sudden silence. Because he didn't like the two bachelor reprobates he called brothers cracking wise on Sara Wakefield's appearance, or anything else about the do-gooder, no matter how much he'd railed about her interference.

Once the preliminaries had been dispensed with, Judge Cartwright got straight down to business, explaining, "After taking Ms. Wakefield's report into consideration, along with your responses to my questions, I have decided that a delay is definitely in order to allow the children time to—"

Unable to restrain himself, Mac came to his feet to get in a detail he had not been allowed to share while being questioned earlier. "My brothers have volunteered to help me out the next few days around the house," he said, feeling bolstered by the fact that they had both stepped up to do so, considering how furious they had both been with him for years. And not without good cause. "We'll get fresh flooring laid down in all their bedrooms and the new furniture I've ordered for them set up."

He'd had to dig into money he needed for resort repairs to do so, but he wasn't bringing his kids home after living in their grandparents' luxurious compound to rooms they'd be anything but proud to call their own.

"You may be seated, Mr. Walker," the judge said, her voice both cool and firm.

"But they're my children, Your Honor, and I've had more than eight years of their lives stolen from me already. Do you understand what that's like? Can you begin to imagine—"

The gavel came down hard three times before Hayden's restraining hand on Mac's arm and Ryan's urgent, "You're making it worse, man!" finally sank into his overheated brain.

"Yes, I can, Mr. Walker," Judge Cartwright told him, "and I do assure you that I am most sympathetic to your suffering during this long separation. Sympathetic enough that I'm inclined to ignore this *one last outburst* before having you removed from my courtroom. Do we understand each other?"

"Yes, ma'am," he said before thinking to drop in an additional "Your Honor" for insurance.

"I'm glad to hear it," she said, nodding sagely. "But regardless of any compassion I may feel for your situation, the responsibility of the family court is to prioritize the needs of the children first and foremost, and after speaking with your son and daughter—"

"You've spoken with them?" Mac blurted, forgetting himself once again before Hayden's fingers dug painfully into his arm. "Ow! Sorry."

"I have, through a court interpreter," the judge said, looking annoyed but somehow restraining herself from bringing down the gavel she had once more raised. "Which is why I'm convinced Ms. Wakefield is right—and that her temporary guardianship is best continued. She has generously agreed to remain in the community, off-property, but as close as may be arranged to your resort with the two children for the next thirty days, to begin with, and work out arrangements with you privately to effect a smooth and gradual transition. But these children are *absolutely* not to be rushed or forced or further traumatized with any undue pressure. Do you understand that?"

"What? For thirty days?" Mac had imagined five days, or maybe a week, tops, to let everyone get used to the idea. It would give him time to get the kids' rooms painted, as well, and maybe take them out for ice cream or on a couple of day hikes at the state park where they used to go when they were little. Maybe he'd even bring Roxy, whom they'd played with when she had been a glossy, ink-black puppy, fat and wriggly, and later, an energetic young dog. Surely, that would jog some memories. Memories of them squealing, laughing, all of them and their mother so happy together, back when they'd still been living on the ranch.

"We'll reevaluate where we stand after that, Mr. Walker," the judge said, "but for now, that's what we're looking at. Thirty days, or possibly longer, depending on Ms. Wakefield's weekly check-ins and her next full report to me."

He shot a furious look in the social worker's direction. A look that, unfortunately, Judge Cartwright didn't miss.

"Or would you rather *permanently* lose custody of your children?" she threatened, clearly at her limit with him.

"Absolutely not, Your Honor," he said.

"Then, I'm asking both of you, before the court, are you willing to work together to help restore this family to wholeness?"

"I certainly am, Judge Cartwright," Sara Wakefield said in a voice that shook a tiny bit but still managed to sound both resolute and forthright. "And I'm committed to continuing with the same security precautions as outlined on my temporary guardianship, for the children's safety."

What security precautions? Mac restrained himself from blurting, despairing that, as the children's father, he'd been left out of so many fundamental decisions regarding his own kids.

The judge nodded in agreement. "I'll be adding the same requirements to your new paperwork. And what about you, then, Mr. Walker?" the judge asked him. "Can you give me your absolute assurance that you're willing to make a good-faith effort, no matter how unfair this additional delay might seem at the moment?"

He hesitated, thinking about how the same report had

also pointed out that the twins now understood little to no English and that it seemed likely they had been told *a number of unfortunate falsehoods regarding their father's propensity toward violence.*

Maybe he really would need help—as well as a translator—if he really wanted to get this right. And maybe he would need to work on the crusty attitude he'd developed a little—okay, a lot—before bringing two terrified kids back into his life.

"All right," he promised. "Yes, I'm willing to do whatever's best for Silvia and Cristo."

Even if stepping back and watching this interfering stranger playing mother to his children shattered what was left of his heart.

Chapter 3

Sara had to admit that she'd had reservations about taking the children to meet with their father for the first time at a location referred to as "the motorcycle bar."

But Judge Cartwright had approved Mac Hale-Walker's surprising suggestion, assuring her, "That place is as family friendly as can be, and they have the best burgers." Sure enough, when Sara arrived, it turned out that the sign in front of the metal building, whose huge bay doors were open to let in the fresh air and an eye-popping viewing across a valley expanse, actually named the place Bent Rim *Grill*.

"Look at all those motorcycles!" A skinny boy with a mop of honey-brown curls that threatened to obscure his warm brown eyes, Cristo forgot his nervousness long enough to point out one of a half dozen chromed-out specimens as she parked the car. "I'm going to get a blue one just like that when I'm old enough."

"Maybe I'll steal that one," Silvia told her brother, joining in the fantasy as she pointed out a stretched, red chopper-style cycle with especially shiny silver forks. "You can jump right up behind me and we can race all the way back home to Abuelita! *Zoom!*"

Sara arched a disapproving eyebrow at the girl, whose hair streamed in glossy dark brown waves behind the hot-pink headband holding it back—a match to the equally vibrant flutter-sleeve T-shirt she'd chosen to wear with her floral skirt and sandals for court.

"No one is stealing anything today, but we *are* having hamburgers with your *papá*," Sara said, trying out the more familiar term rather than the formal *padre*.

The twins let it pass, distracted when a dark gray F-250 pickup pulled in beside them and their father, whom they hadn't gotten a good look at since that frightening afternoon at the resort when he'd shown up shirtless with his ax, climbed out.

"There he is now," Sara said, once again impressed by how well the man had cleaned up since their alarming initial meeting. Since leaving the courthouse, he'd removed the tie and jacket he'd worn, unbuttoning his collar before rolling up his shirtsleeves, too, against the June heat. Clean-shaven, he'd recently gotten his hair trimmed, as well, though the thick, dark gold waves remained on the long side, now crowned with a wide-brimmed Western hat that served as a perfect counterpoint to his neatly buffed leather boots.

As their gazes came together, she felt a little tug beneath her stomach and quickly looked away, half afraid he'd see how ridiculously attractive she found him in that get-up. It must be the Hill Country getting under her skin, because until that very moment, she'd never imagined that cowboys were her catnip.

"That's *him*?" Silvia piped up. "Are you sure? I thought our *padre* was a wild man."

Biting her lip to keep from smiling, Sara shook her head. "I told you. That day he was just finishing some very hard and dirty work." *The kind that builds up six-packs...*

"This is his *disguise*," insisted Cristo, his skinny shoulders stiffening as his eyes narrowed. "He's just trying to fool us, like that evil guy on the cartoon this morning."

Sara sighed, regretting having chosen today to introduce the kids to a certain crime-fighting Great Dane and his teenage pals after the motel manager had kindly offered her a Spanish-language DVD. But since that ship had sailed already, there was nothing to be done but model her best manners in the hopes the twins would follow her lead.

Moving toward Mac, she switched to English. "Hello again, Mr. Walker. Please allow me to reintroduce this fine young lady, Silvia, and the gentleman at her right, Cristo Rojas-Walker." Looking to the twins, she reversed the introduction. *"Hijos, estes es su padre."*

"Hello—*hola*," Mac said, staring from one child to another as if he wished to drink in their beautiful young faces. "I—I'm so happy to finally— To see you both again. You…you've gotten so grown up! Both of you… and you look— You both look so much like your—"

As the children shifted their feet, glancing nervously at one another, he cut himself off, looking to Sara, his blue-gray eyes shining. "I'm sorry. I know I need to slow down and let you translate, don't I? And I didn't mean to come on so strong. It's just that—"

"It's been eight years," she said, her heart going out to this man who didn't even yet dare to gather his long-missing, much-loved children in his arms or so much as touch them. "If you weren't at least a bit emotional at seeing them, I might have to wonder."

After holding up her index finger in a *wait a minute* gesture, she relayed his greeting to the twins, stopping after the part about looking grown up before adding, "He is *very* glad to finally see you."

"Shall we go inside and order?" Mac invited before assuring Sara, "Yours is on me, too."

"You don't need to—I have a per diem from the state that I can put in."

He waved off her offer. "No need to bother with all that paperwork over just your lunch. I insist."

She thanked him and they walked inside an enclosed grill area to look at the short menu. After getting the twins' orders squared away—despite Silvia's telling her she wasn't hungry and Cristo's complaining there were no empanadas on the menu—and choosing a salad with grilled chicken for herself, the four of them filled their own drinks before heading back outside, where a handful of other diners, including a young family and a group of jovial-looking older men in jeans, leather vests and T-shirts, all of whom had helmets close at hand, sat at widely spaced tables.

As Mac led them past a small bar area, currently unstaffed and devoid of customers, Sara caught the twins' heads swiveling to take in the decor, from the slightly moth-eaten stuffed animal mounts to the old movie posters from vintage motorcycle-themed films, including several featuring leather-jacket-clad tough guys gritting their teeth as they gripped their handlebars, and one with a pair of bad-girl biker babes, their backs arched to display their impossibly pointy bosoms.

"Let's head out back, where it's more private." Mac

gestured toward the currently vacant outdoor pavilion with its picnic benches.

"With this amazing view, I'm surprised that everyone's not out here staring," Sara said as they headed that way, looking out across the sunlit valley to the gorgeous tree-cloaked hillside beyond. Or maybe it was even a mountain—her imagination, captured by a pair of soaring raptors, didn't stop to ask for measurements.

"It *is* beautiful, isn't it?" Mac sounded almost surprised as he, too, stared out. "Thanks for reminding me to notice. A man can get so caught up in his work and worries that he neglects to look up every so often if he isn't careful."

She wasn't certain why, but she stopped walking for just a moment as the twins took a detour to check out a rusty antique motorcycle frame left propped beneath a decorative gate.

When Mac looked back at her over one broad shoulder, she couldn't resist asking, "Is that what you've been doing here these past eight years, just working, worrying…and biding your time waiting?"

He grimaced. "I didn't have a lot of choice in the matter, did I? Not after I ran my family's ranch into the ground with all the legal bills. So I've been trying to keep the resort afloat and spending every spare minute praying, writing my representatives, the governor, every damned person I could think of, for all the good it did me."

"Yet you never gave up, did you? And just look at them," she said, gesturing toward the twins, now at the pavilion's edge, where Silvia and her brother were watching as a small swarm of hummingbirds jockeyed fiercely for position at a jewel-bright feeder hanging beneath the limb of a massive oak tree. "You have them back now, these two miracles."

"I have them back not because of anything I did, but because the old man—their grandfather—*happened* to have a massive heart attack and drop dead. Otherwise, no one would have ever dared defy the slandering bastard. And he got off scot-free. He never had to pay for what he stole from me—for what he accused me of doing to my Analisa. For the lies he and his wife told my own kids about me all these years."

Sara drew in a breath, realizing that bitterness had thrust its roots in deep, leaving deep scars on his heart that might never heal.

"It's a terrible thing, what happened to your family," she said as they resumed walking the short distance to the shade of the pavilion. "But you have a chance now to write a new chapter in that story, one where you finally get to be the kind of father these children really need."

He waited, gesturing for her to choose a picnic bench before they both sat down, on opposite sides.

Mac put his drink down on the tabletop and looked to Sara, the skin around his eyes crinkling with what appeared to be anxiety. "What if...what if it's already too late—if I've forgotten anything I ever might've known about how to be their father?"

Though he was older than she by perhaps eight years, and had clearly been through a great deal in his life, raw instinct had her reaching out a hand to gently touch the top of his. As the warmth flowed between them, his arm twitched, as if he had been startled by the contact.

Forging ahead, she told him, "The fact that you're asking, *wondering* if you're prepared to pick up the reins of fatherhood, strikes me as a *very* good sign, Mr. Walker—"

"Please. Call me Mac," he said, and in that simple invitation, she heard alarm bells ringing. Alarms that alerted her to the slippery slope that she'd set foot on with her innocent, supportive touch.

Feeling her face heat, she withdrew her hand from his, mentally kicking herself for forgetting that her professional obligations required her to assess this man's fitness, not to fret over his feelings, no matter how her stomach had swooped when he'd looked at her as if she might be the lifeline that he needed to keep from going under.

But she couldn't be that for him, she knew, not if he was ever going to learn to swim these treacherous waters on his own. And not if she was going to keep herself from slipping into fantasies of a life that she had long since forfeited any claim to.

"I—I, um…" She coughed to clear her throat, which had suddenly gone dust-dry, then took a tiny sip from her iced tea. "I think it's best that we maintain certain… certain formalities at this juncture, until I've completed my report for the court, just to keep everything professional and unbiased."

"All right, then, Ms. Wakefield—or do you prefer Ms. Chavez-Wakefield?"

"Miss Wakefield will do," Sara said.

By late Thursday morning, Sara and the children finally left the motel in town, once more traveling in the direction of Mac Hale-Walker's river camp. About halfway to the tiny community of Rio Frio, however, the directions to the rental where they would be staying prompted Sara to turn left, toward Colt's Head Mountain. As she did, she was forced to stop short by a pair of large jackrabbits who were standing on their hind legs, boxing in the middle of the dusty road.

"¡Mira, niños!" Sara said, pointing out the sight of

the two animals, who were apparently too involved in their battle to pay the car that could easily crush them any heed.

To her surprise, both twins squealed with laughter, the first she had heard from them since they'd let their guards down so briefly with their father over lunch two days before. Since then, within the cramped confines of their motel room, they had grown bored and listless, lapsing into troublesome silences despite her best efforts to engage them with basic lessons on their new home and the English language.

"Are those *maras*?" Silvia asked, from the back seat, where she sat with her brother. "But their ears are so *long*!"

As one of the floppy-eared pugilists chased the other into the brush, they continued driving.

"I don't know what *maras* look like," Sara said, assuming Silvia was referring to some South American creature, "but these are called 'jackrabbits.'" She used the English word since she didn't know the term for them in Spanish.

"¿Conejos?" Cristo supplied, giving her the word for rabbits, which Sara decided was close enough if not technically correct.

For the next ten minutes or so, she found herself doubting her directions as she passed up a variety of homes and cabins before turning off onto first one unpaved road and then another. She next proceeded uphill to an area where the property entrance gates were widely spaced and any buildings were mostly hidden behind shrouds of live oak and scrubby cedar trees.

After a long period of silence, Silvia finally gave voice to the question that had been plaguing Sara. "Are we lost?"

"Not lost," Sara assured her, though she was beginning to wonder if she should go back to the highway turnoff to retrace her steps. "I'm sure it's not much farther—*There*. That's the place. The real estate agent said she'd meet us up at the house with the keys."

With that, she turned into a driveway, careful to steer around the largest of the rocks before stopping to unchain the metal gate that blocked their path, one hung with two signs, the first reading *Welcome to Coyote Crossing!* and the second, the contradictory *Private Property: Keep Out!*

Though Sara craned her neck to look uphill, she couldn't spot the house above them. Out of the corner of her eye, however, she glimpsed a set of scales disappearing into the shadows between two rocks. Praying it had been a lizard and not its legless cousin, she hurried back to the car, her thumping heart in her throat.

Coaxing her Honda slowly up the uneven drive, she continued uphill, where the track turned to the right and opened up to a small clearing containing a one-story log cabin with a large wraparound porch and a trio of white-painted rocking chairs. Though Sara had been a little nervous when she'd been told they would be staying at a vacation cabin—since most of the rental market in this area was geared to tourists—it looked snug and well-maintained.

"Look, by the pond," Cristo said, directing her attention to a small pond not far downslope from the structure.

"It's the mama deer again," cried Silvia, her excitement unmistakable, "the one with the twin babies!"

Though Sara doubted they were the same animals, since they were miles from the river camp, sure enough, she spotted a white-flecked golden doe with a pair of fawns at her side.

"Can we go and see?" asked Cristo.

Mindful of the possibility of more snakes, Sara said, "Help me carry some of our things up to the porch first. Then we can peek inside the windows while we're waiting."

Once they climbed the porch steps, looking inside was the last thing on any of their minds.

"Look at this!" she said, trying the English phrase she'd taught them this time as she pointed out the broad green-and-gold expanse of the valley spreading out below them. Filling her lungs with the fresh, warm Hill Country air, she looked out over an open-range, wooded acreage and pastureland, all pockmarked with the occasional homestead or cabin and the highway and ridges of other mountains in the distance. Here and there, the shadows of the fluffy, building clouds darkened the tableau in patches.

"*¡Que bonita!*" Silvia exclaimed, as above them wind chimes jingled.

"*Home* was beautiful," Cristo stubbornly asserted, sticking to Spanish as he referred to the walled family compound where he and his sister had reportedly grown up amid luxurious surroundings. "But at least this is better than being stuck at that motel. It kind of reminds me of the national park where Abuelo took us to see the waterfall."

"I remember that place." Silvia's brown eyes filled with tears. "I miss Grandfather. And Abuelita must be so sad all alone without us."

"She will find us and bring us back," Cristo told his sister. "You'll see."

Sara laid a hand on Silvia's shoulder and told them both, "I know you miss your grandparents. Now let's go grab the rest of our things."

As they headed back downhill, a dust-covered white SUV pulled in with a magnetized sign on its side reading *Frio Canyon Classics Real Estate*. Moments later, a tall, lithe woman of about thirty emerged from behind the wheel. Dressed in a turquoise top over slim tan pants, she wore a pair of hiking boots that made a lot more sense than Sara's thin-soled flats in this rocky and uneven terrain, though the heavy lugs contrasted with the stylish purse she carried.

"I see you found the place." Flipping long and shiny, straight black hair over her shoulder, she smiled at them, her striking gray eyes sparkling. "Isn't it lovely? Coyote Crossing's normally one of our most popular vacation rentals. You were lucky there happened to be a cancellation. I'm Amanda Greenville. We've spoken on the phone."

She held out a hand, which Sara accepted for a friendly shake before introducing herself and then waving toward the twins. "The children here are Silvia and Cristo. I'll be translating for them."

"Hi, kids," Amanda told them without missing a beat. "It's been such a long time. I can't believe how much they've grown."

"You—you *know* them?" Sara asked.

"*Everybody* in town knew the twins on sight and all of the Hale-Walkers. They took those little ones everywhere, from the time that they were tiny." Though the children clearly didn't recognize her, it didn't diminish the warmth of her smile.

"Señorita Greenville remembers you," Sara explained to the children in Spanish, "from when you lived here before."

The twins spared her a second, shy look but said nothing, which wasn't surprising since they claimed to recall nothing from their early years here.

Appearing to notice their anxiety, Amanda changed the subject, suggesting, "Shall we go on up and have a look inside your new home?"

Nodding, Sara told the twins, *"Ándale,"* as she gestured toward the cabin.

While the children ran ahead, lugging the remaining tote and cooler of food they had picked up back in town, Sara told Amanda, "This property is certainly scenic, and the view's breathtaking. But didn't you have anything less...*isolated* for us?"

"City girl, huh?" Amanda smiled. "I *was* told you're from Austin."

"Guilty as charged, but I hope you won't hold that too much against me," Sara said, already having gotten the message from others in town that the seat of state government was decidedly unpopular with many of the rural area's locals.

"I have nothing against city people," Amanda assured her, "except for the occasional snob who assumes everyone who lives around here is some ignorant redneck."

"Please don't think I don't appreciate what you've done for us," Sara said, though she couldn't help feeling a twinge of guilt remembering how she'd testily referred to local law enforcement as the *hayseed brigade* on her first meeting with Mac Hale-Walker. Making a mental note to do better, she said, "It's just— I'm not used to quite so much *nature* in my nature. Like whatever it was I saw slithering down by the gate, for example."

Amanda raised sleek, dark brows. "Don't tell me you've met one of the resident snakes already?"

Sara shrugged before admitting, "It *might've* been a lizard."

Amanda stopped walking to regard her with what might have been concern. "We definitely have both, most of them harmless, but there *are* a few rattlesnakes here and there, so I'd recommend taking a stick along and poking any brush piles you might encounter when you walk the property to scare them off. And boots are never a bad idea."

Sara shook her head. "I don't have any here with me, but maybe we'll just stay on the porch, at least until my friend drives out to drop off some things from my apartment. And an emergency stash of coffee."

Nodding in approval, Amanda resumed walking. "That's a good friend, right there."

"The best," Sara agreed. "But getting back to this place, I couldn't help but notice the name…"

"Coyote Crossing?"

"Right. We won't really be *seeing* any of those, will we?"

Amanda's eyes crinkled with unmistakable amusement. "It's not likely, but don't be surprised if you hear them at night—the coyotes and the frogs from the pond. It's quite lovely, really," she said kindly. "People pay a lot to come here from the city, to unplug and be a part of nature."

"That might've been nice if I'd come for a vacation," Sara told her, "and not brought two heartbroken, homesick kids to the middle of Snake Central."

"Well, let's have a look inside, shall we?"

"Sure," Sara said, "and I'm sorry if I'm being… It's just, this whole situation wasn't something I was expecting."

Gray eyes softening, Amanda's fingers twisted at what Sara realized was a wedding set, the solitaire diamond in the engagement ring quite large.

"Now, that's something I can relate to, and I'm sorry. But let me show you what you have here…" After inserting the key, she fiddled a bit with the front door, saying, "These old doors are a little warped, so you might have to put a bit of muscle into— There we go." Once it came unstuck, she ushered them inside a large, open area bounded by warm golden-planked walls. To the right stood a good-sized kitchen, somewhat dated but functional.

"It—it's actually quite nice," Sara said, looking to the left, where a heavy oak farmhouse table was surrounded by a half dozen wooden chairs. Further in, a comfortable-looking array of seating—a navy sofa and a couple of reclining chairs—surrounded a large, oval, braid rug and freestanding woodstove. "Very homey feeling, like one of those old-fashioned, Norman Rockwell-looking jigsaw puzzles."

"Don't sound so surprised you like it." Amanda smiled as the twins rushed past the stove to check out the other doorways. Pointing after them, the agent added, "Those will be the two bedrooms and two baths, one off of the master."

"So the twins will have to share a room as well as a bath?"

"I'm afraid so, but I'm betting they'll love the stair-step bunk beds."

Sara thought about it a moment before nodding. "They probably need each other anyway right now. Everything else is so new to them." Looking around, she said, "Am I missing something, or is there really no TV here?"

"You *did* say old-fashioned, but I do think this works," she said, pointing out a radio on a wall shelf, "though I can't say we have a lot of choice in the way of stations out here."

Laughing nervously at the thought of a month of long, dark evenings, Sara said, "Nature sounds it is, then."

"And the stars. Wait'll you see the night sky, away from all the city lights."

"Sounds…relaxing," Sara said, momentarily distracted as she peeked into one of the bedrooms, where the twins were checking out the kid-friendly furnishings.

Amanda handed her a business card. "Here's my number, if you need anything at all and can't reach your foster care case manager or the children's father."

"Thank you."

"As you may've noticed, it's a *very* small community," Amanda said before shaking her head and gesturing toward the bedroom. "Small enough that we take care of our own."

"But I'm not—"

"Maybe not, but these are *our* kids," she insisted, her smile warm, "and as long as you're their caretaker, you're one of us, too, by extension."

Sara drew in a deep breath. "You don't know how good it is to hear that. At the grocery store and in the restaurants, some of the people—" She thought of the ugly looks and whispered comments, loud enough for her to overhear. *Who does she think she is, to judge him? What gives her the right?* "They've given me the impression that my presence here is not exactly welcome."

If they'd known about her personal history, they'd be demanding to know what gave her the right to judge anyone at all.

Amanda rolled her eyes and sighed. "I guess you really *have* met the resident snakes then. But I've found the best way to deal with ugly gossip is to keep holding your head high and going on about your business. Once they realize that their petty judgment can't touch you, they'll eventually move on to someone else they *can* hurt."

Both concerned and curious, Sara said, "You sound as if you're speaking from experience."

Twisting at her rings again, the agent frowned, pain sparking in her gray eyes. "It's not important right now. What matters is to keep moving forward, staying focused on what you're here to do—" she sounded a little as if she were giving herself a pep talk "—which in your case means getting these children back on track and the Hale-Walker family reunited."

"That's what everyone is hoping for," Sara told her, praying it would be the way things worked out. But knowing in her heart that it would take patience, tolerance and plenty of hard work from everyone involved to reach that goal.

Once Amanda took her leave, Sara went to check out the master, an attractive space featuring a rustic-style queen-sized bedroom set and attached bath, where she was delighted to find an old-fashioned claw-footed tub with a shower assembly. In the children's room, the twins were excited to show her the two colorfully made-up bunk beds, each making the case for why the one he or she had staked out was the superior choice. They'd also been excited to uncover a veritable treasure trove in the closet: a box containing several board games, a collection of colorful plastic dinosaurs and, to both children's delight, a decent soccer ball.

"No kicking it around indoors, though, okay?" Sara warned them as she headed out to the kitchen to wash up and make them lunch. "After that, it'll be time for another English lesson at the table—and then we'll—"

"But we want to go outside and play," Cristo protested, "or at least look around and see what's out there."

"We were stuck inside that stupid room at the motel *forever*." Silvia joined in.

Realizing that they had a point, Sara relented, despite her lack of appropriate footwear—and her worries over snakes—telling them they could do some exploring after they ate.

Much to her relief, their time outdoors turned out to be a welcome release valve from the pressures of the past week. Accompanying them, she taught them the English names for "pond," "mountain" and "cabin," and then had them compete to find small items like a "straight, long walking stick for poking brush to scare off any reptiles" and "a stone that fits in your palm." They also jotted down new birds and animals they spotted in English, a list she'd have them illustrate using colored markers once they went back inside.

When, a couple of hours into their adventure, Cristo, kicking the soccer ball into a slick patch near the pond, slipped in the mud and then threw a clot of it at Silvia for laughing at him too hard, Sara said, "All right, you two. It's time to come inside now and get cleaned up. But before we go in, we're going to have to hose off some of that muck."

"*¡Tan frío!*" they cried, protesting the cold minutes later when she used water from the hose to sluice off the heavy clods.

"Sorry," she said, before handing each of them one of the old but clean towels she'd found to wrap up with and sending Cristo to the hall bath and Silvia to the master to make use of the showers. "That'll warm you up."

Within minutes, both of them were calling to her, asking for her help because they couldn't get hot water. She had no more luck than they had, so after instructing each to clean up as best they could for now using washcloths, she tried calling Amanda, but the phone rolled over to the agent's voice mail.

After calling the office number on her business card, Sara reached a recording—an older woman explaining that due to a family emergency, the real estate office was closing for a few days. "If you need to," the voice continued, "feel free to leave a message, or reach out to us via e-mail through our web site."

Sara decided there was no need to trouble Amanda over what might turn out to be an extremely minor issue. But after finding the cabin's water heater inside the same alcove that housed the washer and dryer and discovering that it was cool to the touch, she had no idea of what to do to fix it.

What she did know was that the "rustic" aspect of cabin life would lose its charm in a big hurry if they had to go days without showers or the ability to properly wash their clothes or dishes. Feeling slightly self-conscious but reminding herself it was for the children's sake, she pulled up the number Mac Hale-Walker had given her, inviting her to call him any time they needed him.

He picked up almost immediately. "Hello there, Miss Wakefield. Are you all settled in?"

"We are—at a cabin called Coyote Crossing, in the Colt's Head neighborhood."

"The Parker rental place. I know it," he said. "I'll bet the kids're loving it up there."

"They are—or would be, anyway, if we only had hot water." She felt her face heat. "I hate to admit it, but I'm totally clueless about water heaters, except I know it's not a good sign when they're room temperature."

"Definitely not."

"I tried calling the real estate agent first, but it seems

Amanda Greenville's out of touch—some family emergency—"

"Hope they haven't had bad news." Mac sighed. "Everyone in town's aware her husband went missing back in February. I pitched in myself with a couple of the search parties around the areas where he was known to hunt, bunch of folks looking on foot, ATVs and horseback."

Sara frowned, thinking back to her father and his brothers and their annual hunting trips. "Isn't February past the end of hunting season?"

"It is, but Pete—well, Pete Greenville was known to have a relaxed view when it came to pretty much any kind of government rules and regulations," Mac said, his tone hinting that he hadn't been one of the missing man's biggest fans. "But no one ever found a trace of him. Even as isolated as I am out at my place, I haven't been able to miss hearing people's theories on whether something really happened to him or he just ran off."

"*Gossip*, don't you mean?" Sara asked, remembering Amanda's comment about the town's snakes.

"I won't deny there's been some loose talk, but my brother Hayden, the sheriff, says there's nothing to it, and as for me, I've been the target of too much gossip around this town to want to take part in it."

"I just hope she's okay," Sara said honestly.

"Same here."

"But about this water heater…"

Mac said, "Let me finish cleaning up after painting in the kids' rooms. Then how about if I swing by and have a look?"

"I'd really appreciate that," Sara told him. "And it doesn't have to be today, if it's not convenient."

"Are you kidding? Any excuse I have to lay eyes on

Silvia and Cristo again, maybe talk to them a little, is enough to bring me running."

She smiled at the warmth coming through his voice, a love that eight years, tragedy and a language barrier had been unable to extinguish. She thought of inviting him to stay for dinner, but since she couldn't be certain of how the children would react to his unexpected presence, she decided that a brief visit would be the safer option. The more often they saw him doing things like arriving with a friendly greeting, lending his help and then leaving without making uncomfortable demands or displaying the violent temper they'd been taught to expect, the more comfortable they would grow in his presence.

"Thanks so much, Mr. Walker."

"Remember, it's Mac, please," he requested, just as he had at their lunch.

Maybe it was her casual surroundings or the fact that she was dressed in a pair of shorts and a T-shirt she'd picked up in town, but Sara suddenly felt ridiculously stuffy for continuing to stick with formal titles. "Only if you'll call me Sara," she invited.

"I'll see you soon then, Sara."

As he ended the call, she stood still for a moment, stricken by how much she had liked it, hearing him address her by her given name. And reminding herself that she couldn't allow herself to do that, to respond as a woman to a man, her brain tricked into some sort of uncharacteristically domestic mode by the strange circumstances in which she found herself: isolated in the middle of nowhere for the better part of a month, caring for his children. She couldn't let herself start imagining he was anything to her except the subject whose progress and behavior the court had charged her to professionally evaluate.

Especially when, for all she knew, his cheerful offer of help and his seeming affability might be nothing but an attempt to con her into writing exactly what he wanted on her final report to the judge.

Mac hadn't intended to take Roxy with him to the rental cabin where Sara Wakefield was staying with the children, but the old girl had been feeling especially spry the past few days, since the vet had prescribed a new medication for her arthritis after pronouncing her otherwise fit. So when the gray-muzzled Lab hopped on her hind legs near the door of his pickup, wagging her thick tail hopefully, he didn't have the heart to make her go back inside.

"All right, girl, you can come," he told her, glad that neither of his brothers was around to harass him about coddling the dog. Where Hayden pronounced it "damned worrisome" that he'd walled himself off from other humans so long in preference for "the last flea-bitten relic of your old life," Ryan instead laughed at his oldest brother's fussing over Roxy's diet supplements and expensive memory foam dog bed—at least until Mac reminded the part-time rodeo reprobate that he was every bit as obsessed with the big buckskin roping horse he was currently training.

Fortunately, he and his brothers had finished their work on the children's rooms a couple of hours earlier, sprucing them up with a fresh coat of paint and new flooring after making way for the new furnishings due to be delivered. Since both had refused his offer to grill some steaks and have a couple of beers afterward, he'd instead shaken their hands and thanked them for their help again, accepting that, in spite of what they were doing for their niece and nephew, they were highly unlikely to ever darken his doors in the future.

And Mac, for his part, couldn't blame them one damned bit. He hadn't forgiven himself for losing the ranch that was to have been their collective legacy, either, and probably never would, but at the present moment, that didn't matter. The only thing he cared about was getting over to take care of the water heater issue at the cabin and maybe show his kids that he didn't have two horns and a tail.

In spite of the aging Lab's improvement, he refused to let her jump up into the rear seat, lifting her instead to spare her hips the wear and tear. Even so, she was ecstatic, happily panting over his shoulder at her good fortune in scoring a ride.

"Your breath," Mac complained, "could make a buzzard hand out tinned mints. What on earth have you been into?"

Roxy's only response was to slobber on his arm. Fortunately, the drive was short. Just long enough for Mac to transform into a bundle of nerves as he worried over what to say to Cristo and Silvia. Though their lunch meeting had seemed to go all right, he was all too aware of what an unnatural setting it had been, with the four of them all trapped at one table. At the cabin, their conversation—such as it was with the language barrier—would be even more difficult, since they would be able to escape him, running into another room if he made one false move or said anything they didn't like.

After stopping to open the gate and then returning to the truck, he said to Roxy, "Maybe you could help me out with that." From what he'd heard, on the day of their arrival at the river resort, the twins had never left the car, so they wouldn't have met the big dog that day, and surely, they still liked canines...didn't they?

Memories spilled through his brain, of Analisa's anger

when he'd brought home the wriggling, black puppy, a fat and fuzzy bundle of energy that had her declaring, "The last thing we need to be tripping over, with two babies underfoot. Take it back before it does something on the rugs!"

She had only relented after Mac had promised to do all the puppy wrangling and cleanup—and she'd seen how irresistibly the twins and the pup had been drawn to each other, laughing, cuddling and playing until they fell asleep together in a happy tangle. And so it was the three had grown together, with Roxy gradually transforming from a trash-can-toppling, slipper-devouring menace to the most loyal and lovable of family companions—whose heart had broken right along with Mac's when Analisa and the children the Lab had lived for had suddenly vanished from their lives.

Surely, they wouldn't remember each other, Mac thought, and he supposed it was possible, as well, that despite the early foundation laid down here in Texas, the twins no longer even liked dogs. But as Mac pulled up beside Sara's light blue Civic, now coated with a layer of orangey-gray dust, he thought of all the scores—or likely hundreds—of kids and adults Roxy had won over at the resort, and told her, "I'm seriously counting on you, girl, to lay on the total charm offensive."

After lifting her down from the back, he grabbed a flashlight and small tool kit.

Sara met him before he knocked, an apology in her eyes—which the setting sun's rays lit up in the moment before she raised her hand to shade her vision to better see him.

"Beautiful," he blurted, caught off guard—and, apparently, with his brain in neutral.

"Excuse me?" Confused, she shook her head.

"I'm sorry," he said, face going red-hot. *What the hell is wrong with you? Have you never met a human woman?* "It's only, when the sunlight caught your eyes like that, they looked as green as a glass bottle for a moment. It— it's striking."

Smiling, she snorted and flipped the ponytail she'd pulled her blond-streaked hair back into behind her shoulder, a complement to the casual red top and navy shorts that she was wearing. "I guess I should take some selfies in the sunset then, because, usually, they're more of a pond-scum color."

"Maybe our Hill Country sunsets just agree with you, then."

"Or maybe you're just thinking a little flattery never hurts a man's chances on his next report to the judge," she said, looking mildly amused.

"To tell you the truth, I'm a lot more competent in the handyman department," he said, raising the toolbox.

Nodding, she stepped back, a pleasant smile warming her face. "Please come in, and thanks so much for this. I feel so foolish for not knowing how to do this, but I've always had a maintenance crew at my apartments, so I've never had to fix anything like—"

"No need to apologize," he said, "not when you're doing *me* a favor, giving me a chance to say hello to Silvia and Cristo—or at least I hope so."

"Of course. But who's this?" she asked when the dog finally finished with whatever she'd stopped to sniff and walked up to poke her blocky head out from behind his leg.

"Remember, back at the resort, I mentioned my sidekick, Roxy? It wasn't my idea for her to come along," he said, lying shamelessly to advance his cause, "but I'm afraid the old girl jumped up in the truck before I could stop her and absolutely would not be budged."

Sara hesitated, and he could almost hear the rule-bound government employee imagining such scenarios as pet allergies and dog bites.

"She's up to date on all her shots, and she's the official greeter and hospitality officer over at the resort when we're up and running. Plus, you see…she was—she was—back when we were all a family…"

And that was when it hit him, just as it sometimes still did, his throat cinching closed at the enormity of what he'd lost—what had been stolen from him…by fate, by death and by the lies and deceit of Analisa's parents, the in-laws who had never wanted their daughter marrying some "damned cowboy" she had met while she'd been studying abroad in Texas. Thanks to the football scholarship he'd received to the same prestigious university, the two had met while he had still been flying high—a freshman quarterback whose debut had created such a stir that there were already rumblings among the alumni about letting him start if the team's star QB didn't improve his performance.

That had been before it all went to hell, of course, but even after the shoulder injury to his throwing arm that had ended both his future in the sport and set him scrounging for tuition, the beautiful and vibrant Analisa, the girl who'd captured him, heart and soul, almost from the moment the two of them were introduced at an on-campus party, had vowed he was the man for her. She'd sworn it made no difference whether he ended up the promising young football star with the backup of a business degree or—as it had turned out in depressingly short order—the dropout son of ranchers whose "wealth" was all measured in land and cattle rather than what filled his bank accounts and pockets. She'd wanted him and only him, and he'd been all too happy to oblige.

"Please, it's fine," Sara blurted, reaching forward, as if her first instinct was to take his hands. Stopping herself, she said, "Go ahead and bring the dog in. She's lovely, by the way. My neighbors had a Lab like her back when we were growing up. And he was always so...well, hello there, you."

At Sara's welcoming tone, Roxy approached, wagging, pushing her head into outstretched hands.

"She could probably use a bath," he apologized in advance, "and her breath's more than slightly—"

"Don't listen to the critics, Roxy. You're absolutely perfect, aren't you?" Sara was stroking the broad head as the dog smiled up adoringly. Turning, Sara called in the direction of what Mac knew to be the bedroom area, *"Venid, niños. Mira al perro y saluda a tu padre."*

Looking back toward him, she explained, "I asked them to come meet the dog and say hello to you."

"Smart to lead with the more attractive option." He smiled, mainly to cover the sick dread building when the children didn't immediately appear.

A few moments later, Sara's shoulders heaved. "I was afraid they might do this. I mentioned to them you were coming because I was afraid that catching them off guard might be an issue. It's possible they put their heads together and decided not to cooperate."

He dropped his gaze, unable to meet her eyes as his disappointment sank in. Reflexively, he reached out to stroke his dog's ears, and for a moment, their hands bumped.

A split second after her withdrawal, she laid hers overtop of his. "I'm sorry, Mac. It's going to take time. You have to understand, they're grieving the death of a grandfather they loved and their separation from their *abuelita.*

Every step they take toward you is likely to feel like a betrayal to them."

He jerked back his hand, anger spewing like hot bile. "Because they've been damned well lied to, *poisoned*— as if it wasn't enough that they literally *stole* my children from me."

Sara stepped back, her expression hardening, and Mac realized he'd just failed in his mission utterly, doing the one thing—or two, if he counted the cursing—that he'd sworn never to again in her presence. If he didn't get a handle on his resentment, he was never going to get to be a proper father to his children.

And worse yet, he would have no one else to blame for his failure but himself.

Chapter 4

The look of absolute horror on Mac's face told Sara that he feared he'd blown everything completely in that moment of frustration.

He shook his head, the lines across his forehead settling into deep grooves. "That's going straight in your report to the judge, isn't it? *Father has a temper. Uses profanity. Seems bitter.*"

She narrowed her eyes in annoyance. "You talk about me like I'm some grade-school snitch who runs tattling to the teacher over every tiny slipup. It's not like that. *I'm* not like that."

"But you *are* here to judge me."

She couldn't stop the scoffing sound before it was out. "I'm here to assess what's best for these children in the long run. And I have to tell you, I'm *always* hopeful that will be a reunification of the biological family. As long as it's a safe and healthy situation, I'll bend over backward to—"

"You have to understand," he said, clearly too wound up to hear her out, "I *am* trying, but this—this is hard."

"It's *impossible*." With an effort, she kept her voice steady and even. "And yet you're still here, trying for your children's sake. Just as you'll keep trying tomorrow and the next day and the one after that, the same way you did every day you fought to get them back into this country. Because *that's* what a good parent does. He doesn't quit when things get tough."

"I'm never giving up on them, not until my dying breath."

She nodded. "You have no idea how much weight that carries with me. You see, in my regular job as a social worker in Austin, I spend so much time fighting to get people to simply *care* about one other: preoccupied adult children to step up for their aging parents, family members to quit freeloading off a disabled relative's benefits long enough to see that they receive the basic care they need not to develop stage-three bedsores. It's absolutely heartbreaking, the indifference."

He studied her thoughtfully. "I don't know how the hell you do it. I'd probably end up in prison for beating some negligent jackass with a hammer."

She laughed softly. "Don't think I don't fantasize about it from time to time, but only as a stress reliever."

When he smiled at her, she responded in kind, their gazes catching—and lingering—for a moment too long before self-consciousness made her look away. "Um, let me show you to that water heater," she suggested.

Fortunately, he found the issue quickly after squatting down to remove a small cover, where he discovered the gas pilot light had blown out. "Here," he said, "let me show you how to relight this just in case it ever goes out again."

"Do they do this very often?" she asked once he'd used

a small gas lighter and made sure the tiny blue flame came on and stayed lit.

"Not usually," he said, offering a strong, work-calloused hand and carefully helping her back to her feet. "I doubt you'll have another issue with it."

"Well, thanks for fixing it. It'll be a relief to have a hot shower once the water heats up."

At the sound of barking near the door leading to the side porch, both of them turned their heads to look at Roxy, who was alerting them to a pair of squirrels running across the railing underneath the wind chimes.

"Hush, girl. That's enough," Mac said.

The Lab whined and pranced a little before giving one last woof of protest.

As she fell quiet, Sara heard the door open to the twins' bedroom just behind them. When she turned to look, she saw both children peeking out, Silvia's long waves hanging in the doorway below Cristo's curly head.

"Come see," she invited, switching to Spanish to speak to them. "It's all right."

For a moment, both heads withdrew and she could hear them arguing in whispered tones, something about what their *abuelita* said. But seconds later, the alliance— and their grandmother's admonitions—crumbled, with Silvia coming out.

Looking from the dog to her father, she asked timidly, *"¿Como se llama?"*

Sara began, "She's asking—"

But Mac held up his hand to stop her, his eyes glued to his daughter, who looked as timid as a fawn who might bolt at any moment. "Roxy's her name, Silvia. This is your dog, Roxy."

"Este es su perro, Roxy," Sara translated before elaborating in the same tongue, "from when you were little."

But Silvia paid her no heed as the dog approached, head lowered and tail wagging in a posture of unmistakable canine supplication.

"You are so sweet, Roxy," the girl said, sinking to her knees to stroke her again and again as the dog began to sniff her.

The tail-wagging picked up speed, the sniffing turning to a deep, enthusiastic snuffling. Then the Lab began crying—high-pitched, almost frantic whimpers of excitement. Breaking away from the girl, her dark body curved as she danced and then rolled onto her back and thrashed in a frenzy of pure canine excitement.

Drawn by the commotion, Cristo came out, and though Mac cried, "Roxy, no!" the dog leaped up and raced to the boy, nearly bowling him over in her exuberance as her happy yelps intensified.

"She *knows* them," Mac blurted, his eyes shining as he looked at Sara, who felt her throat tighten as she reached the same unmistakable conclusion. "After all these years, she still *remembers*! I never would've thought it possible, but—"

"Es Roxy," Silvia told Cristo, who looked utterly bewildered as he fended off slobbery kisses before she told her twin that the Lab had once been theirs.

By the time Mac was finally able to get Roxy settled, the children were brimming with questions about the dog they clearly didn't consciously remember but both seemed instinctively drawn to nonetheless. Or at least that was how it seemed to Sara as the children and the Lab sat on the living room rug, where she noticed the twins couldn't stop themselves from stroking the black fur or rubbing Roxy's belly.

Sara helped translate the rapid-fire conversation for Mac. "Were we all babies together?"

"Do we have the same birthday?"

"What games did we play then?"

"Where did she sleep?"

"Who did she like better?"

With both twins leaning forward, staring in breathless anticipation of his answers, Mac cut a look toward Sara before he burst out laughing.

"That would be your mama," he told them, so handsome in his happiness that years seemed to fall away from him. "No matter how many treats I sneaked her, your beautiful mama always had her heart."

But even before Sara translated, his use of the word *mama* had the twins' gazes coming together. She caught the lightning-swift change in their faces, the happy curiosity giving way to guilt, pain and suspicion in an instant.

"You hurt her!" Cristo accused his father, his Spanish raw and pained as he shot to his feet.

"Why?" Silvia rose, as well, her brown eyes full of tears and her small hands clenched with fury. "Why would you ruin everything and do that?"

Though Sara tried to calm them, they refused to listen to her, turning to race back to their bedroom. When Roxy tried to follow, they left her crying piteously outside of their closed door.

Gutted, Mac stared at the blank place where his children had been sitting, smiling and engaging with him so pleasantly, with the buffer of the dog between them, her tongue lolling as she rolled onto her side. For the short time it had lasted, the exchange had felt so very right, so sweetly natural, in spite of the language barrier that still lay between them. And then the pilot light of the hope he'd felt had been snuffed out by the memory of their grandparents' hateful slander.

Sara looked back over her shoulder, halfway to the children's room already. "I'm so sorry that this happened."

He could see she meant it, could feel the sympathy radiating from her. But he didn't want her pity; he only wanted, *needed* this endless nightmare, the nightmare of eight years, to finally be over so he could get to work repairing the wreckage of his life.

Eyes glistening, she added, "I'd better go see to them now."

His dog's whining cutting through his own misery, he nodded, his breath hitching at the sight of Roxy scratching at the twins' door. Still, it remained firmly closed to her love as well as his own—though he'd give his damned right arm for the chance to hug them once more.

"I guess I'd better—" He had to clear his throat, which was clotted with emotion. "Guess I'd better gather her up and get on down the road and leave you to it, then. Come on, Roxy."

The dog stopped her scratching but didn't budge, her gaze fixed on the doorknob.

"That would probably be best for now," Sara told him.

"If I could only talk to them *directly*, explain to them—"

"I'm not sure they're ready to listen, not in any language. Not yet," she said gently. "I'll call you with an update, though. Tomorrow, if that's okay?"

Nodding his agreement, he managed to get out a hoarse thanks, despite a lump in his throat the size of an unshelled pecan.

He gave a soft whistle. Reluctantly, Roxy came to him, though she kept looking back over her shoulder and whining.

"I know, girl. It's all right," he told her, grabbing his toolbox and flashlight before leading her back to the truck. Once he had them both in the cab and he had started up the engine, he pulled a biscuit from the stash he kept in a tin in the driver's side door panel. She snuffled half-heartedly before accepting the poor consolation.

"Or maybe it's not all right yet," he added, "but I swear to you it *will* be, if I have to turn myself inside out to do it."

But all the way home, he wondered what good even that would do against the insidious lies they'd been spoon-fed since they had been toddlers, stories in which he was the evil bogeyman, the monster whose own wife had supposedly claimed he'd violently assaulted her on numerous occasions.

Had they played the tapes for them, too? As he passed a slow-moving truck loaded with baled hay, his blood ran cold at the thought, his core turning icy at the horrific memory of the day his attorney at the time had called him to his office and sat him down, saying, "I'm afraid I have something here. Something that's going to be very hard for you to hear."

It had been an audiotape, its quality poor and its provenance uncertain, that had been mailed to him by a representative of the Rojas-Morales family in Buenos Aires, along with a note threatening to publicly release it if he refused to drop his legal efforts to have his custodial rights enforced. The recorded conversation had been in Spanish, but Mac had felt a sudden jolt when his attorney played it, thinking that he recognized the voice of the woman he had loved so deeply that her loss still felt like an amputation years after the fact.

But it was the transcript, translated into English, that the lawyer passed him that had tainted even his happy memories.

Heart pounding wildly, Mac had leaped from his seat,

slamming down his fist on the poor man's desk. "This is impossible! There's no way Analisa would've told such lies about me!"

And they had been lies, every single one of the awful allegations of his extreme mental cruelty, his physically battering. The woman on the tape had claimed he'd pushed her, punched and shaken—even *choked* her until she'd lost consciousness on more than one occasion.

Fortunately, his attorney hadn't believed the stomach-turning accusations, either, especially with the tape mysteriously appearing four years after Analisa's drowning. He'd subsequently sent the recording to an expert, who had—at great expense to Mac—compared it to a home video of Analisa Mac had provided for comparison. Though in the video—taken on the happy occasion of the twins' second birthday celebration—his late wife had been speaking English and the sound quality was less than ideal, their paid expert had stated she was willing to testify under oath that the voice profile didn't match the one from the audio recording.

Yet even now, Mac couldn't be completely sure whether the voice expert had been truly convinced it hadn't been Analisa on the muffled and in some places inaudible recording and not that of some actress. Could his wife, before her death, somehow have been coerced by her parents into saying such things? Or worse yet, had she maliciously chosen to lie about him for some reason he could not begin to fathom—a secret lover she had hoped to marry after ridding herself of him, or perhaps the realization, during her visit to her home country, that she couldn't bear to return home to him?

But no matter how many times Mac had re-litigated every detail of their marriage, or gone through each of the relics from the life lost far too young, he'd never found the first clue that Analisa had been unhappy. Even in casual photos, her beautiful dark gaze had been alive with warmth and vitality, her frequent smiles genuine. In several of the last pictures he had taken, she'd been caught with her mouth open, forever frozen mid-laugh over some mischief that the children or the then-rambunctious Roxy had gotten into.

Over the past few years, in his darkest and most doubt-soaked moments, he'd thought of setting fire to those photos, which he could no longer bear to look at. Somehow, though, he'd held on to just enough hope to keep them to someday show his children...

As he pulled in to the river resort road, that day still seemed as distant as the crescent moon that hung in an evening sky the color of a bruised plum. But Mac reminded himself he'd been down before, and if it had taught him nothing else, it was to shake himself off and stubbornly trudge forward.

So it was that, in spite of his exhaustion, he headed back inside with Roxy and, after feeding her, sat down and cracked a beer. After downing a few sips, he started the next lesson of the *Learn Spanish Pronto!* online video series he'd signed up for, because he was damned well going to find a way to reach his son and daughter.

No matter what it took.

Overwhelmed as she was by the challenges of managing the twins' care—along with the roller coaster of their emotions—Sara managed to completely forget about Rachel coming until the text came the next morning.

Inside your apartment right now. Anything in particular you want?

Excitement fizzing through her, Sara reminded the twins to be sure to brush their teeth after they finished breakfast. She then stepped out onto the porch to call the woman who'd become her closest friend after the two had been randomly assigned as roommates back in their freshman year of college.

"Hey, Sare. How're you holding up?" Rachel asked. "Kids doing any better?"

Sara's heart squeezed at the warmth and genuine concern in her voice. Over the years, the two of them had weathered a great many storms together. As harrowing as some of those times had been, the bond they'd forged left Sara trusting her friend, a pediatric nurse well enough acquainted with confidentiality requirements, not to share any of what she said any further. "Right now, they're pretending that yesterday's meltdown never happened. Probably hoping I'll ignore it instead of trying to talk to them about their feelings."

Rachel laughed. "Sounds like a pretty normal coping method to me. I do it all the time with Evan, the night after we've had a big dustup."

"You two, fight? I don't believe it for a second," Sara scoffed since the newlyweds were so cloyingly devoted to one another, it was sickening. Or would be, if Sara didn't adore Evan—a smart and funny geeky tech type they'd also met in college—and think of him as an honorary brother-in-law, just as she thought of Rachel as the sister of her heart.

But Sara wouldn't ever use the term, could barely think of the word *sister* without thinking of the family she had walked away from—and hadn't seen or spoken to in years.

If only she'd gone to a decent family like I wanted, came her mother's voice, floating across the dark chasm of years, *this never would have happened. She would've been alive still, and we would have never had to think of it again.*

Had she actually slapped her mother's face that awful day? Or had that cracking noise been the sound of her own heart breaking before she'd stuffed a single backpack with her things and left that house for the last time? Sara couldn't quite recall the details, remembered through the haze of her own tears.

"Usually, the argument's just some silly squabble over whose turn it is to empty the dishwasher," Rachel was saying, snapping Sara's mind back to the present.

"Oh, the horror," Sara said. "Just don't expect me to take sides. I told you two at the reception, when it comes to that, I'm a neutral country. I'll always love you both."

"Okay, Switzerland," Rachel joked. "Which boots did you want out of this closet?"

For the next few minutes, Rachel walked her through her choices, sometimes pausing to consult with Evan, who had taken off for the day, Rachel explained, so she wouldn't have to make the drive to the Hill Country on her own.

"I hope you don't mind that he sort of invited himself along," Rachel whispered, as if she didn't want him hearing.

"Absolutely not. It is a long trip, and you two are doing *me* the favor." Though Sara *had* been secretly looking forward to sitting on the porch or walking along the pond and confiding in her friend alone, in a way they hadn't been able to do nearly so often since the previous summer.

But part of life was accepting that situations changed, and she reminded herself that Rachel had been there for her even through periods when she'd been briefly obsessed with some new boyfriend or another. Though for the past year or so, she'd been taking a break from dating—still feeling burned after a couple of recent bad experiences.

After finishing with her requests, Sara insisted on giving Rachel directions to the cabin from town, assuring her, "You don't want to rely on GPS only to try finding an address around here, believe me."

"Where *is* this place, the end of the world?"

A smile tugging at one corner of her mouth, Sara said, "Let's put it this way. You'll need to be prepared to brake for wild hogs and boxing bunnies on the road."

When Rachel laughed, she interrupted. "You only *think* I'm kidding. Seriously. I'm standing on the porch right now looking out at a couple of jackrabbits and on the edge of the woods out past the pond, a deer with a great big rack of antlers."

"Listen to you, nature girl," her friend teased. "Okay, then. We'll see you in a few hours—though we may stop for lunch along the way, so don't hold us to an exact time."

"Take as long as you need. Enjoy the food and scenery. And thank you."

After they'd disconnected, Sara looked in to find that the twins had left the table, with one in the bathroom and the other in the bedroom, presumably dressing for the lessons she'd asked them to prepare for before they would be allowed to explore outdoors some more. Returning to the porch, she tried Mac's number, wondering as the call connected how much sleep, if any, he had managed last night and whether his stomach would clench with dread when he spotted her name on his caller ID.

He didn't pick up, however, which probably meant he was already hard at work, either on preparations for the twins' anticipated return home or on the post-flood repairs of his property. Unbidden, an image of his shirtless torso popped into her brain. She frowned, telling herself the last thing she should be thinking about was that killer six-pack—not when her only business with Mac Hale-Walker was assessing his suitability as a single caregiver to two children.

She left a voice mail for him, assuring him that the twins were doing well this morning and letting him know it would be fine for him to check in by text or phone later that afternoon. She was scarcely finished when Cristo called to her, asked if she'd seen the Argentina Soccer jersey-style shirt he practically lived in, since it was the same one he had been wearing when the twins were removed from their grandparents' home.

The remainder of their scant wardrobe, Sara had learned, had been hastily assembled by officials at the US consulate in Buenos Aires in the days before they were spirited out of the country. The fit wasn't the greatest, and Silvia, in particular, had definite opinions about the selections, as well as being forced to keep rewearing the same few outfits when she had an entire closet full of far nicer clothing back at home.

"Momentito," Sara told Cristo as she came inside to check the load she'd thrown into the dryer earlier. Finding the sacred soccer jersey, she peeled off a stray sock, which crackled with static as she removed it, before tossing it to him.

"Gracias," he said.

"Thank you," she corrected, since she'd been working on the children's English vocabulary—but his blank look had her wondering once more if she had made any headway at all, even with the simplest of terms. Certainly, she wasn't a trained teacher, but she felt competent enough to drill and make some flash cards. Yet no matter how

much time she put in with the twins each day or what techniques she tried to make the learning fun and interesting, they didn't seem to be retaining English vocabulary from one day to the next. They both seemed bright, alert and eager to please while they were working, but they grew red-faced—and Silvia teary-eyed—when Sara pressed them to recall vocabulary they'd reviewed just the day before.

Over time, she'd concluded that their systems were too overloaded by the shock they had experienced to truly absorb new information. They were grieving not only their grandfather's death, but the loss of their grandmother, their home and possessions and everything they thought they knew, as well. To make matters worse, they were undoubtedly deeply conflicted—at least on an unconscious basis—by the idea of relearning English, in the same way they were clearly having a rough time dealing with any softening in their feelings toward their father.

"Let's take a walk," she said in Spanish, deciding that exploring while discussing whatever subjects the children brought up would be a better use of her efforts than drilling lessons they'd be sure to have forgotten again by tomorrow.

With both twins happily on board with the idea, she grabbed the wide-brimmed hats she had purchased in town for everyone, along with their sunglasses, and ventured out, each of them carrying a water bottle. For the next two hours, they slowly made their way around the unpaved roads throughout the rural subdivision.

In no particular hurry, they stopped frequently to take photos with her phone of an interesting agave plant or a clump of blooming cactus, or when Cristo pointed out a bluebird on a fence post and later, Silvia spotted a small gray fox and her cubs before they darted into a grove of

live oaks. As their path took them uphill, Sara's feet—
and both of the twins'—started complaining, but they
were all rewarded when a vista opened up on the other
side of a wire fence to their right, with numerous ridges
visible across a span of verdant ranch land dotted with
multicolored wildflowers.

Gasping with pleasure, Silvia cried, "Look at all the
butterflies!" and it was true. Sara had never seen so many,
flitting from blossom to blossom, a wonder the graz-
ing cattle—thick-bodied black cows with calves at their
sides—ignored as they cropped the rain-lush grass.

It was magical—so stunning, Sara knew she had to
share it. After snapping a couple of shots that failed to
capture the grandeur, she asked the children, "Let me
take your picture, please. I'll have copies printed for you."

They eagerly agreed, and with their smiling faces in
the foreground, the shots were clear and beautiful—so
perfect that Sara showed them to the twins and said,
"These are wonderful—just look at you both here, look
at those smiles. Your father would just love to see it. Do
you think that maybe I could—"

Cristo's face immediately darkened, his expression
turning fierce. "No! I don't want him to think we're
happy here. We'll never be happy again, now that they've
taken us from our home!"

But Silvia took a different tone, her sensitive face
clouding. "What about Abuelita? She probably misses
us a lot and worries about us. Do you…do you think
maybe we could send that picture to *her*?"

Cristo's fists relaxed as his look of anger turned to one
of desperation. "We can give you her phone number. You
could text it to her—and then maybe we could call and
talk to her, too. *Please*."

Sara carefully measured her words before responding. She didn't want to either lie or give the children false hope. And she didn't like to upset them, either, but there were truths they had to understand.

"I'm sorry, but as I've explained before, we're not allowed to do that. You need to understand, your grandparents made a terrible mistake keeping you with them after your mother passed away."

The two went very quiet but said nothing, which she took as an indication to press forward, explaining, "But I'm sure that they were very sad, you see, because they had just lost your mother, whom they loved so much. So much, they couldn't bear to give you up—"

"But Abuelita must be sad now," Silvia said, "and scared about what's happened to us. She might even be crying, and looking for us everywhere!"

"It's understandable to be worried for her," Sara told them. "And I'm sure it is hard."

Cristo wiped his forearm across his eyes and looked out across the field, clearly not wanting her to see his face. "She'll find us, bring us home. I know it…"

"It was *never* really your home. They only told you that." Sara shook her head, not wanting to damage them by making them think ill of the grandparents they had loved but knowing that they needed more of the truth than they'd been given if they were to ever have any hope of accepting the man they would need to build a life with. "And I want you to imagine for a minute, how your father must have felt back here when he learned your mother had died and you were both stranded there, in Argentina."

"He didn't care. He didn't love her," Silvia said, only this time her voice sounded less certain than during their last conversation on the subject. Was she picturing her father rubbing Roxy's ears while calmly answering their questions last night? Was she struggling to reconcile his clear concern for them, the way he had come running to fix their hot water issue, with the terrifying creature they'd been warned would destroy them if given half a chance?

"Every family photo, every family friend here, tells a different story," Sara said, wondering how many other ways there were to say it, and which one it might be that finally sank in. "His heart was broken, but he packed his bags and jumped aboard the first plane he could catch to go to the funeral, to honor her memory and pay his respects and, most important, to come to comfort the two of you and bring you both back home with him."

Instead of shutting her down as he usually did at this point, this time Cristo frowned at her before asking, "So…why didn't he?"

Sara hesitated a moment before deciding that, even at eleven, they deserved to know more of the story. "Because on the way to the funeral, some very bad men, men with guns, intercepted his car and he was pulled out. Your father was beaten very badly—and told he would be killed if he didn't immediately leave the country."

"Why didn't he go to the police? The army?" Cristo demanded, looking outraged.

"He tried," Sara explained, leaving out the part about their grandfather's role in the operation, his influence in squelching a response, for them to put together on their own when they were old enough to process the betrayal—or when Mac decided, perhaps with the guidance of a therapist, to tell them. "But they wouldn't help a foreigner—and your grandparents refused to let you go back."

A long silence followed, broken only by the sound of a distant birdsong floating on the soft June breeze.

Finally, Silvia asked quietly, "What did our father do then?"

"He was badly hurt. He needed a hospital, so he had no choice but to return home to try to find help here," Sara told them. "He's been fighting for you ever since then—I can show you copies of some of the letters if you'd like—and missing you every single day. And all that time you were away, your grandparents never allowed a single phone call, returned all of his gifts and messages to you unopened—and never sent him so much as a photo of you. It's why he didn't know you that first afternoon when we drove up."

The girl looked at her brother, their gazes holding a conversation, before finally she turned back to Sara. "All right," Silvia said with a small nod, "you can send him our picture."

"But tell him," Cristo added, "this doesn't mean that we believe his story. Or that we aren't leaving this garbage dump and heading straight home as soon as Abuelita finds us."

Chapter 5

"Come on, Roxy. Look at this—I made your favorite," Mac coaxed the old Lab that afternoon, when for the second meal in a row, she ignored the pellets she normally couldn't get enough of and instead walked to scratch at the door.

He slid the egg he had finished frying several minutes earlier on top of the kibble and walked the bowl over to hold the warm, fragrant enticement—usually her favorite treat—directly underneath her nose.

"Please, girl. Just the egg, at least," he urged, irritated over her frequent whining to go out last night and then again this morning. It had been bad enough when she'd merely run straight to his truck's passenger door, where she'd sat and turned to look at him with sadly pleading brown eyes, but earlier, when he'd taken his attention off of her for a few minutes, she'd vanished, failing to respond to his shrill whistle as she normally would. His worry ramping up when he'd failed to find her in any of her usual spots, he'd jumped behind the wheel to go look for her—and finally caught her trotting along the shoulder of the highway, heading back in the direction of the Colt's Head subdivision and ignoring the vehicles that sped by.

Her message couldn't be clearer. If he wasn't going to go and get her children and bring them back home where they belonged, she damned well meant to take matters into her own four capable paws—even if she had to risk getting run over to do it.

"You're under house arrest, dog," he said, sticking the bowl beneath her nose again. "Now eat your dinner before I change my mind and put you on bread and water rations."

Whining her displeasure, she used her nose to flip over the entire bowl, sending egg and pellets flying across the kitchen.

As Mac was cleaning up the mess she'd made and wondering what the hell he was going to do to get the dog to settle down, a text came through on his phone. He opened it and his dark mood instantly lifted, a smile spreading over his face to see his son and daughter looking so happy, standing in front of cattle fencing overlooking a particularly scenic swath of range.

But a pang soon followed as it struck him that he knew that view, that pasture, that had once belonged to his family, part of the legacy that he'd been afforded the responsibility of safeguarding. Though his mother had, up until her death, fully supported his legal fight to reclaim his family, he couldn't help but wonder, had his single-minded obsession all those years twisted him into a man deserving of his brothers' and his children's hatred? And was it possible that he could ever break through the barricades erected around his son's and daughter's tender hearts…or find a way back to the brothers he had once counted as his closest friends?

Beneath the photo, he belatedly spotted Sara's message.

Progress! it read. They gave their consent for me to send this!

At the string of enthusiastic emojis that followed, he smiled, picturing her beautiful green eyes, so full of life as she had sent the message.

He replied, thanking her and adding, Please tell them both I said gracias—but make sure you do it in a crummy Texas accent so they'll know it's me.

When three dots appeared, indicating she was writing a reply, he felt his heart speed up with anticipation. His smile broadened when her message came through.

Why don't you tell them yourself?

Just name the time and I'll be there, he texted back. Roxy's been driving me wild demanding to come back ever since we got home.

While he waited for her reply, he caught the big dog, out of the corner of his eye, slurping up the egg from the pile of kibble he'd swept together for the dustpan. As he watched, holding his breath, she sniffed at her food before once more turning from the pellets to resume her post by the door.

Deciding that Sara must have gotten distracted, since she didn't immediately reply, he finished with his cleanup and then headed for the shower, since he'd been out working much of the day and hadn't bothered with a shave that morning. Afterward, he dressed again, donning a pair of shorts and a Don't Trash Where You Splash T-shirt from the last river cleanup volunteer day he'd attended.

When he checked his phone again, he felt the sting of disappointment to see that Sara still hadn't responded. On impulse, he decided to head over anyway, using the dog—and the twins' potential concern for her—as an excuse. To sweeten the deal, he went to the spare room and picked out three more of the T-shirts, because, as one of the volunteer organizers of the annual event, he happened to have a supply of leftovers, which were due to be donated since the logo was to be updated before next year.

As he decided on their sizes, his mind lingered as he pictured Sara, mapping out the feminine contours of her slender body.

Easy there, he admonished himself, his own body stirring in a way it had no business doing. She was his kids' temporary guardian and someone he needed to impress with his maturity, steadiness and patience as a father. But he doubted she'd be impressed at all if she had any idea that she was the first woman in an age who'd inspired a completely different sort of interest.

Even if she were not fulfilling her current role, she was surely too young for him, he told himself, clearly no older than her very early thirties. Though he wouldn't turn forty until next spring himself, he felt prematurely aged by everything he'd endured. It was a damned wonder his hair hadn't fallen out or turned snowy white yet.

Aside from that, he had little to offer any woman, strapped for cash as he was. And soon, he hoped to have two half-grown kids under his roof, as well, children who would require every scrap of his time and attention, as well as every dime he could scrape together. And even if, by some miracle, he ever found a woman crazy enough to sign on for the privilege of spending time with his cantankerous self, the mere thought of Analisa—of what part of him still believed he'd heard his wife tell her parents on that muffled tape—turned his guts to ice water.

Mac asked himself, if he could have been wrong about her, could have believed, with all his heart, in their love, how could he ever trust himself to judge another woman's loyalty again?

Rachel and Evan had only been at the cabin for a short time, but much to Sara's own surprise, she was already wishing they would climb back into Evan's cherry-red convertible, a luxury model so new it still had its paper tags, and head back to Austin. Maybe it was the fact that Cristo was so obviously impressed by the soft-top's gleaming paint job. Or perhaps it was the fact that in this setting, the couple's eye-catching, designer outfits and expensive jewelry struck Sara as wildly out of place. It was yet another reminder that Evan's financial status, as a programmer with an Austin tech firm that had recently gone public, had changed her friends in ways she wasn't quite sure that she liked.

No sooner had Sara greeted both of them with hugs, thanking them for coming and asking the children to stop kicking around the soccer ball to say hello, when Evan gave her a big grin and casually reached behind the front seat of the car. "On the way out of the city, I got to thinking it wouldn't be right to come all this way bearing gifts for you and forget about your young friends."

He then pulled out a box containing a drone that Sara knew had to have cost several hundred dollars. Or maybe more, knowing his love for cutting-edge electronics.

"Evan, you shouldn't have," she said, feeling slightly

queasy at the over-the-top extravagance of the gesture. "Seriously, you should have talked to me first."

The children, not surprisingly, had no such mixed feelings. When he handed them the box, after an explosion of *"¡Muchas gracias, señor!"* they ran to examine it on the porch.

Sara called after them, urging them in Spanish to be careful and to leave the box unopened. When she turned back to Evan, Rachel, looking almost like an exotic bird in the bright plumage of her fuchsia top, striped skirt and strappy sandals, said, "Don't blame Evan. I was the one who mentioned you were at your wit's end trying to think of some way to keep them entertained way out here."

"I know you were only being thoughtful," Sara admitted. "It's just that—I have no idea how to fly one of those things. What if I break it?"

"I'll show you before I leave," Evan told her. "It really couldn't be easier, and you'll all have lots of fun with it. I promise."

"Well, thank you, then," she said, though she doubted that Evan's idea of easy and her own would prove to be a match.

"Let's get your things inside, shall we?" Rachel suggested, her normally dark brown hair brightened with fresh highlights. "Before we lose my husband. I can see he's itching to help the kids get their new toy out of the box."

But once they carried her things inside, packed up in a suitcase and several tote bags, Sara realized that the surprises weren't yet over. "What's this?" she asked, her heart thumping at the sight of a box inside the largest of the bags. "Tell me that you didn't."

Rachel smiled sheepishly. "I know, I know. It's too much. *We're* too much, but what can I say? We love you, and we wanted to make your life this month a little easier—"

"Don't take that out!" Sara warned—perhaps a little more sharply than she meant to—as Rachel removed what even Sara recognized as the hot new gaming system of the year.

But it was her own tone that betrayed her, drawing the attention of both children, who gasped excitedly and ran across the room, the drone suddenly forgotten as they oohed and aahed at the console for a system that had clearly been as heavily advertised in Argentina as it had been here in recent months.

"This is really very generous, but it's *way* too much," Sara protested. It wasn't that her friends couldn't afford it—or that the children, who'd been through so much, didn't deserve a distraction. But she couldn't help thinking they should be learning that the life their loving father was prepared to give them wasn't going to be about expensive presents. And there were other considerations to think about, as well.

"Oh, don't fuss so much. Just let us spoil you, will you?" Rachel said before scanning the living room with a dubious expression. Frowning, she said, "I *do* hope you have a decent high-speed wireless connection. And where's the television, so we can get started on the setup?"

As the children gasped and pointed, chattering excitedly to each other, it was left to Sara to shake her head. "I'm afraid that there's no Wi-Fi," she said. "We don't even have a TV to use with it for the screen. That's why I didn't want them seeing."

"Oh, come on," Evan said, giving her a puzzled, impatient smile as if he were waiting for the punch line. Tall and slim, he had a leanly sculpted face crowned with dark hair gelled high on top and buzzed tight on the back and sides—a look Sara knew Rachel teased him about tending with the same meticulous precision that he did the details of his work and wardrobe.

"I'm *not* joking." Sara handed the bag back to Rachel. "Thank you both. I so appreciate the thought. I truly do. You're beyond generous, but I'm afraid you'd better take this back. In fact, take back both of them. It's really not appropriate for you to bring them such expensive gifts, and there's no way we can—"

Apparently catching on to her refusal, both children cried out, *"¡No! ¡Por favor, no! ¡Queremos nuestros regalos!"*

Of course, they wanted to keep their unexpected gifts. What children wouldn't? As grateful as she was to her friends for driving all the way out here with the clothes and other items she needed for her long stay, Sara was furious with them for putting her in this position.

"Please let them keep the gifts," Evan pleaded, his hazel eyes contrite. "Maybe they'll find another place to use it—or I'm happy to have a flat-screen TV delivered. Then you could hotspot off your phone to get them set up and—"

"I think you've bought and done enough already, Evan," Sara said firmly, though she knew she was about to break the children's hearts—and possibly upset her friends, as well. "It all has to go back. There are legal reasons they aren't allowed near any kind of system with messaging capability or GPS locators that might log in and report their whereabouts."

"Of course," he said, seeming to grasp that modern games allowed players to log in and speak with one another. "But maybe I can go in and disable that functionality in the settings if I rewrote the code for—"

"I'm sorry." When she shook her head, the children started crying before shouting that they hated her.

"Lo siento," she said, trying to apologize, to make them understand. But they were on the run already, heading back to their room in tears.

"Oh, Sara. We didn't mean to—" Rachel started, her eyes shining.

"If you'd only asked me first," Sara said, barely biting her tongue before adding *instead of using this as one more opportunity to throw your money around.*

"This is all my fault," Evan said, looking truly guilt-stricken as he tried to take the blame. "It's just— When I think about what these poor kids have been through, losing their mom so young the way they did, and all the mess with their grandparents."

"Rachel—*told* you?" Sara glanced in her friend's direction, unable to believe she would breach her confidentiality in such a matter.

"I promise you," Rachel swore, blanching. "I didn't give him any details. I would *never.*"

"She didn't have to," Evan said. "I knew you'd gone to Argentina to escort two children back home after a custodial situation, and when she told me you'd been asked to assume temporary guardianship because they'd forgotten their English, I put that together with that case that was all over the news some years back. I saw the father interviewed. Hale-Walker, I believe his name was, and recalled that he was from a big ranching family out here. He was trying to pressure state officials to get involved in the fight."

"He did put it together," Rachel said, "but it was all on his own."

"Evan, I need you to understand that this can't go any farther," Sara said, blaming herself for saying as much as she had to her friend, to tip him off. "The privacy and security of these children is a very serious matter. And I'd really like to keep my job, too."

"I understand all about nondisclosure agreements and that sort of thing," he said, immediately relating it to the tech world, "so, of course, I'd never mention it to anyone. And I'm sorry I've made such a mess of things with my dumb idea about surprising the kids like some kind of out-of-season Santa."

"You kind of did," Sara told him before her stern look melted into a smile. "But I love you both for caring so much. Come here, you big goof—both of you."

She first hugged Evan, still remembering the awkwardly insecure young geek he'd been when they'd all three attended the university together, and then gasped a little when Rachel's hard little belly pushed against her.

"What the—" Pulling back, Sara looked down, her mouth rounding in surprise. "When were you going to *tell* me?"

Rachel looked to Evan before both of them erupted with the biggest smiles she'd ever seen.

"Right now, apparently," Rachel said. "We decided early on to keep things on the down-low through the first trimester."

"How could you—from *me*?" Sara couldn't be more shocked since, if anything, her best friend tended toward oversharing personal information.

Rachel's smile faltered, her brown eyes filling, and Evan put an arm around her.

"It's okay, baby," he said. "The doc says we're out of the woods now."

"Out of the woods?" Sara shook her head. "I'm so sorry, Rach. Was there…was there some issue with the—"

"You know I've taken a little time off work," Rachel said.

"I thought you had some vacation time stacked up you needed to use," Sara said. "You told me you were working on the new house."

"Actually, I was having some tests and resting with my feet up. There was quite a bit of bleeding. The obstetrician wasn't sure for a while… It was all very stressful."

"I wish you'd let me help you through it."

"I—I only wanted Evan," she admitted, "and I was afraid if I talked about things too much, wanted it too badly, I was going to somehow— I know it's ridiculous, but I felt like I might jinx things."

Sara hugged her, telling herself it was perfectly understandable. There *was* no other reason. "I'm sorry you had to go through that scary time. But everything's okay now?"

"The doctor feels it will be," Rachel said.

"And I *know* it will." Evan slipped a hand behind the small of her back. "I promise you, babe, in about four months, we'll be a family of three. A perfect family."

"I don't know about that. He's going to spoil that kid rotten, you know," Sara warned.

Smiling, Rachel said, "There'll be no stopping him, I know, but all I care about is holding my baby girl in my arms."

"A girl?" Sara's heart stumbled as their gazes caught.

"We—we just found out," her friend said, her voice stiff and awkward. Because she knew about the tragedy that had changed the course of Sara's life forever, the loss that cost her not only her family but the desire to ever have another.

Can you confirm for me that you're the child's mother? The officer's voice rang in her head as she'd struggled to see past him to the poolside gate.

To see it standing open.

She'd thought of all the heated bottles, the 2:00 a.m. feedings and the seemingly endless string of diaper changes, and yet she'd answered honestly, shaking her head no. Though in her heart she would always know she was the closest thing that Promise had ever had, the one whom she had first called "Mama" in her sweet babble, because "Aunt Sara" was too hard to say and the divorce had turned her grandmother into someone so cold and hard she'd forgotten how to love even a tiny child.

"I see," Sara said to Rachel, rubbing the gooseflesh that had erupted on her arms, though the cabin's air-conditioning was struggling to keep up with the afternoon's heat. Because she understood that her history was the real reason why her best friend hadn't broken the news to her earlier. Sara supposed it had been out of love.

But it didn't stop the pain from sinking in, deep as a set of fangs in tender flesh.

"I'm *very* happy for the two of you. You should know that, *trust* that, Rachel." As hard as she tried to keep it steady, her voice was shaking as she spoke. "You'll make incredible parents, both of you."

"Oh, Sara." Rachel's eyes misted in the moments before she threw her arms around her and squeezed. "I just can't bear to lose you. Please tell me this won't change things. Tell me you'll still be there for me. For *us*."

From somewhere, Sara dredged up a smile. "You won't get rid of me that easy, girlfriend."

But she already knew that things would never be the same between them. Rachel had crossed into a territory that she—for all the pseudo parental duties she was fulfilling in her temporary role as guardian and translator for the children—could never follow on her own. Because she had already learned there were tasks she wasn't equal to—and pain she could never survive a second time.

"Thank you again for bringing my things," she added, a wave of fatigue rolling over her. "I really do appreciate it. But I'd better go try to talk to the twins now, and see if there's anything I can do to smooth things over."

As Mac pulled into the cabin's driveway, he was forced to stop his pickup short and back out to allow an expensive-looking—and brand-new—red Mercedes to exit the property through the narrow gate. For a moment, he tensed, but the couple inside the vehicle waved their thanks. He nodded in reply, wondering who these people might be and what they'd been doing around his children.

After making a mental note of their license plate number, he chided himself, thinking they scarcely looked like the type who could handle changing their own flat tire, much less undertake a kidnapping. For one thing, their two-seater's trunk wasn't big enough to fit two gangly eleven-year-olds inside it. For another, he couldn't imagine the children's grandmother sending someone here to take them.

It wasn't that he didn't believe that Elena Rojas Morales—the woman who, along with her husband, had so callously destroyed his happiness—lacked the will to have the two of them snatched back. He was stone-cold certain there was nothing, including his own murder, she would balk at if she thought it would return life to what it had been for her a few short weeks before.

But even if she dared to risk the children's abduction in this country and had some master plan for safely getting them back home, she would surely face harsh legal repercussions. The kind of repercussions that even someone with her resources would be unable to avoid, especially now that Don Roberto was no longer around to bribe or intimidate any who might question his actions.

Despite the absolute hell she'd helped to put him through for all these years, Mac reminded himself she was a woman of over seventy, who'd had the children she had loved dearly—Mac had no doubt of the truth of that—torn from her arms within days of losing her husband of nearly fifty years. After decades spent tending their home and raising children, the new widow was surely reeling with grief—and most likely struggling to keep her husband's shipping empire from falling prey to the competitors who were undoubtedly clamoring to wrest it from her.

Mac could almost bring himself to pity her, until he thought of his own mother, crippled after a stroke but trusting him to use the family legacy, the ranch that had been in her family for four generations, to fight the evil his in-laws had done. He thought of his own failings, in the way he'd used that trust without first talking to his brothers, for fear they might refuse or even sue to stop him from doing what he'd had to.

"Whatever you're suffering right now, you damned well deserve," he muttered to himself, thinking it was about time karma paid the mother-in-law from hell a visit.

From the back seat, Roxy whined and gave a little half growl before erupting into an excited bark. When he heard the thumping of her wagging tail against the door, he knew she somehow sensed that they'd returned to the last place she'd seen the children.

"That's right. We're almost there," he told her as he pulled up next to Sara's Civic. "You'll get to see your kiddos in a minute."

Or at least he hoped that Sara would allow it, since he'd come without warning. Grabbing the extra T-shirts, he jumped out of the truck and hurried to let the dog out before she clawed the door's interior to pieces.

He tried to lift her down again, but Roxy leaped over his shoulder and bounded past him, barking joyfully as she raced for the porch, sprier than she'd been in years. As he strode after her, Silvia emerged from the front door, her eyes red and swollen and her hair mussed, as if she had been weeping.

But the moment she saw Roxy, she cried out with what sounded like relief and dropped down to her knees to open her arms. As Roxy pranced and licked, tail wagging, the girl buried her face in the thick fur. Cristo came running, as well, curls flopping and a huge grin brightening his sullen face when he saw his sister hugging the dog.

"She missed you," Mac explained to them, wishing that his rudimentary Spanish would gift him with the right words.

Though they undoubtedly didn't understand, both of them looked up, smiling at him. More likely it was because they were excited to see the dog again, but Mac would happily take what he could get.

"Buenas tardes," he said, remembering how to wish them a good afternoon at least.

"Hola," Cristo told him, his manners kicking in as he knelt down to join his sister.

When Sara appeared a minute later, he noticed that her nose was a bit red and her eyelashes clumped with moisture. She'd been crying, as well, he realized with a jolt, but before he could ask her what was wrong or if there was anything he could do to help, she said, "Mac,

I didn't realize you intended to stop by just now," her smile a bit cooler than it had been on previous occasions.

"I hope it's all right," he said. "You see, it's Roxy. The old girl's been crying, pacing, refusing her food. I was worried she'd make herself sick if she didn't get to see the kids again."

Expression softening, Sara moved toward the excited trio and reached to stroke the Lab's back. "Of course, we couldn't let that happen. You're always welcome, Roxy." She looked up, meeting his eyes before adding pointedly, "Though I do hope that next time, you'll take a moment to at least text before you head on over."

"Text first?" he asked, irritation flashing through him at the thought of having to ask permission to visit his own children, as if he were the stranger and *she*, a bureaucratic busybody who'd barged in and taken over, their natural parent. But he reminded himself that neither anger nor impatience was going to solve their court-mandated issue. "Sure, I can absolutely do that, and I'm sorry I didn't think about it this time. Did I catch you at a bad moment? As I drove in, I saw that you'd had visitors…" *Were they the cause of your tears?*

"It's fine," she said, glancing at the twins, who were rubbing Roxy's exposed belly, before heading for the rocking chairs. Once there, she kicked a soccer ball out of the way and waved an invitation to him to sit.

"Can I get you something to drink? Earlier, I made a pitcher of iced tea."

"I'd love a glass," he said, mostly because he thought it might give him an excuse to linger.

"Sweetened or—"

"Unsweetened's good for me, thanks."

Shifting to Spanish, she then asked the children something—perhaps offering them a drink, as well.

Both stiffened at her question and curtly told her no, their sharp responses and hostile expressions drawing what sounded like a rebuke from Sara.

The children went back to petting Roxy, neither continuing whatever the conflict was nor apologizing for it.

When Sara sighed, Mac's curiosity got the better of him.

"Everything all right here? The three of you seem a little…"

"They're pretty upset with me at the moment," she confessed. "When my friends dropped off my clothes and things from Austin, they thought it would be nice to surprise them with some gifts to help keep them entertained out here."

"That sounds awfully thoughtful of them. So why does everyone look so thoroughly unhappy?" Including her friends from Austin, he thought, recalling their expressions in the car when he'd initially spotted them.

"Because they didn't ask me about it first. Not only did they show up with inappropriately expensive presents, they were electronics that required an internet or cellular log-in."

"I see the problem," he said grimly. "So I take it, you had to be the bad cop and spoil everybody's fun?"

"Including mine, I can assure you. Of course, the children don't understand safety and security measures."

"I read those after I got a copy of the paperwork from the court," he said, recalling how grateful he'd felt that others had thought through sensible precautions to prevent the twins from attempting to contact their grandmother during this transitional period. "No wonder you looked so upset when I showed up—I'm sorry."

"Don't be. You couldn't have known."

"I could have, though, if I'd given you fair warning,"

he said before sighing. "To tell you the truth, though, I was kind of afraid you might say no."

"Well, you're here now," she said, her smile indulgent, "and, honestly, I'm grateful. Roxy's just the distraction the kids need right now, and it sounds as if she needs them, too. Let me go get that tea."

"Thanks, Sara."

When she returned a couple of minutes later, he was practicing a bit more of his Spanish on the children, asking how they were. He decided he owed Roxy some extra biscuits for their cooperation because they answered haltingly, their smiles polite enough as they continued stroking the thoroughly contented dog.

"Here," he added, switching to English as his supply of memorized phrases fell short. He thrust the two smaller T-shirts he'd brought toward them. "For you."

Though they seemed reluctant, they accepted his offering. Cristo wrinkled his nose at the design, but Silvia murmured, "*Gracias*—thank you," smiling shyly with her heavily accented effort—a smile that sent warmth blooming inside him before her brother glared at her and her gaze dropped, her delicate face flushing.

"The shirts are perfect," Sara enthused, passing him a cold glass of amber-brown liquid topped with a slice of lemon. "They don't have much from Argentina—and only what was on their backs from home."

"If there's anything they need, let me know," he offered. "And I've brought you a T-shirt, too—if you're interested."

"Thanks. I'd love one," she said, her obvious surprise to be included making him glad he'd thought of her, too.

"Let me put all of these inside, though, before theirs, at least, end up covered in dog hair," she said, handing him her drink, as well, so she would have two free hands.

While she was inside, he set the glasses on the porch railing and then pulled a brand-new tennis ball out of his pocket. "Hey, Roxy. Look what I've got."

The Lab's eyes lit up with pure joy and she rolled to her feet to prance near his. After making sure the children were both watching, he gently tossed it down the porch.

With two bounds, Roxy snatched it up before returning to push it back into his hand.

"Now you," Mac said to Cristo, since it was crystal clear that winning his son over would be the greater challenge. Offering him the now slightly soggy ball, he held his breath, watching Cristo's hesitation. "See how much she wants it?"

Though he knew Cristo wouldn't understand his words, Roxy provided the translation as she whined, tail wagging, before giving an impatient woof.

Smiling, Cristo said something to her in a soothing tone before he took the ball—careful not to touch Mac—and tossed it as his father had.

When Roxy almost immediately returned it, Silvia was right there, insisting, *"¡Mi turno ahora!"*

"Take turns, you two, but don't throw it too hard," Mac instructed as Sara came back outside. "She's not a young pup anymore, and I don't want her to get sore."

Sara translated what he'd said, but Silvia's first throw bounced between two porch rails, plopping down onto the grass below.

As the children, trailed by Roxy, went down the steps to get it, Sara called something after them.

"I've been doing some online Spanish lessons," he said, "but I'm afraid I'll never be able to untangle rapid-fire sentences like that one."

"It means a lot that you're making the effort, though,"

she said. "And I just told them it'd be all right for them to play right there on the grass, as long as they stay in sight—unless you'd rather they come back up?"

"Let 'em run around. It'll be good for all three of them. With any luck, Roxy'll work up enough of an appetite to eat her dinner tonight."

"I just hope they watch where they're stepping," Sara said nervously. "Amanda told me there could be snakes."

"Poisonous ones are fairly rare, and usually you'd only find them around rocks or brushy areas near the water, not mown sections like where they're playing. And if she does spot one, Roxy'll bark up a storm. That dog would never let anything she perceived as a threat near her kids."

"What an amazing animal," Sara said. "But that does make me feel better. And the twins are obviously smitten with her. I have to wonder if, on some level, they might remember her, too."

"I'd sure as hell love to believe that…" Mac said as they looked out to where the twins were tossing the ball back and forth, playing keep-away with Roxy, who was clearly thrilled with this new variation of their game.

"Because that might mean they remember you, too," she said gently, the look in her green eyes so perceptive, it sliced through layers of scar tissue like a surgeon's scalpel.

"Crazy, isn't it?" he said, his voice thickening. "To imagine they might remember just because *I* recall so clearly what it felt like to play with them and read them stories when they were little. They used to laugh so hard when I did the funny voices. And I swear sometimes I can still feel them in my arms, the way we'd cuddle up if one or both of them got sick or scared or just needed a Dad snuggle after I came and cleaned up from working cattle."

"That's right. You were a rancher back then."

"My family ranched for generations," he said, an ache in his chest at the reminder of the way of life that had been lost. "It makes me sick, thinking that all those memories were stolen from them, only to be replaced with hatred and suspicion."

Reaching over, she touched his hand. "For what it's worth, I think it's still there—maybe not the specific, detailed memories, but at least the remnants of the emotion they once felt for you, for home, lying dormant the way their feelings were for their dog. But they have so much to work through, Mac, and you can expect the road forward to be bumpy."

Reflexively, he turned over his calloused hand, wrapping it around her slim fingers. He saw her surprise, her beautiful green eyes flaring. But whether it was out of pity or loneliness or simple human compassion, she didn't pull away from him, didn't make a sound.

For the next few minutes, they sat that way, neither daring to say a word or move a muscle as they listened to the children laughing and Roxy occasionally barking for another toss of the ball. And Mac could scarcely breathe, he was so overcome with a contentment he hadn't known in more than eight years.

But even that filled him with terror, for he knew now how fleeting, how fragile and rare such perfect moments were. And how quickly they could be snatched from him, whether by indifferent fate or cruel intention.

Finally, however, Sara came to her senses and shifted, taking a drink from her iced tea, and Mac remembered something else he probably ought to mention to her.

"Earlier today, I dropped by the hardware store in town," he said, "and I heard that surveyors discovered what they figure to be Pete Greenville's body in a remote area in the mountains outside of town. There'll be a full investigation and autopsy, but word was it looked like he might've taken a tumble while illegally poaching on private land."

"Oh, my gosh. You're talking about Amanda Greenville's missing husband?" asked Sara, looking both shocked and concerned on behalf of the real estate agent who had helped her.

He nodded. "According to the ID on him."

"How horrible for her."

"I'm not so sure it *is* such bad news, exactly." Mac shrugged. "I know people don't like to speak ill of the dead, but old Pete not only had money to spare, he also had himself a temper. Always did, even back in school. And ever since he disappeared, people can't help but notice that Amanda hasn't had to wear any long sleeves or turtlenecks out of season. And she's really blossomed in her business, without him calling every twenty minutes or spying on her whenever she's showing properties to male clients."

Frowning, Sara shook her head. "The man sounds like a nightmare, but I got the impression that all the loose talk since his disappearance might be hurting her even more. I'm glad you let me know, though. I'll try not to bother her while she's dealing with this."

"If you have any issues here at the cabin, you can call me anytime," he offered. "Thanks to the resort, I've got a lot of experience with on-the-spot home repairs."

"I really appreciate it."

He shook his head. "Not half as much as I appreciate

the chance to get my face in front of my kids as often as it takes to convince them that I'm not the monster they've been warned will hurt them the first chance that I get."

Chapter 6

Three evenings later, as Sara was toweling off after her shower a little after ten, she heard ringing from the bedroom. She shoved her feet into her pajama bottoms and raced across the room, eager to grab the phone before the noise woke the children—or alerted them to a time of day she'd left the forbidden fruit of the cell unguarded.

Though she'd taken the precaution of blocking outgoing international calls from her carrier, she didn't want to tempt the twins into trying to find some messaging app or other work-around that could result in who knew what sorts of headaches with the children's grandmother.

She stifled a groan when she saw the name on the screen but realized she couldn't avoid speaking to her friend forever. Better to get past whatever awkwardness still lay between them so they could get back to supporting each other as they had for so long.

"Hey, Rachel," she said cautiously.

"I—I'm so relieved you actually answered."

"Why? Is something wrong?" Sara asked, her stomach tightening when she heard how strained Rachel's voice sounded. "You're not having any more issues with the pregnancy, are you?"

"Nothing like that, thank God. It's just that every time I've replayed our last conversation in my mind, I cringe, thinking about how we must have come off like a couple of rich, clueless show-offs, turning up without warning with those expensive gifts."

"It's okay, Rach, really." Sara felt her heart squeeze, thinking so what if her bighearted friend was occasionally awkward in handling her and Evan's huge upgrade in financial status? Both of their families had struggled to make ends meet when they were growing up—much more so than Sara's—so it wasn't as if they'd had experience or role models to teach them how to deal with money. "There's no need to be embarrassed about trying to do something kind for someone. But you were already doing me the biggest favor just by being so generous with your time, both of you."

"Do you really mean that?" Rachel asked through sniffles.

"Of course, I do. And if I were there with you, I'd give you a huge hug to remind you that *you're* the sister of my heart and always will be." As well as the only functioning family Sara had left now, with her biological sister long ago lost to her addiction and the survivors' relationships in hopeless shambles.

And try as she might, Sara knew there was nothing she could ever say or do to fix it, no matter how many children she helped, how many broken lives she mended in her professional career.

She'd lost the one that mattered, and nothing would ever be the same.

"N-now you've gone and done it. You've really got me crying." Rachel's sniffles were followed by the sound of laughter. "Darned insufferable hormones. You'd think, as a nurse, I'd have *some* idea of what I'd be in for."

"You're fine," Sara assured her, her vision blurring as she pulled on her pajama top.

"No, I'm not. I'm a hot mess. Evan's gone to Seattle to lead the staff through training at the company's new satellite office. I should be used to it by now, as often as he has to travel."

"But you're all right there alone?" Sara asked, thinking of Rachel's recent issues with her pregnancy.

"He's been calling me at least three times a day, promising he'll be on the first plane if I have the slightest issue—and he's sworn no more trips out of the country. Plus, he's pausing all the travel for the first six months after the baby's born."

"Well, that'll be a godsend, but for now—"

"I have my obstetrician's office and Evan's sisters— including the one who's a general practitioner—all on speed dial."

Sara breathed a sighed of relief. "Sounds like you're well covered, then. And you know I'm always here to talk to, even if I've been a bit…preoccupied of late."

"I can certainly see why."

"What's *that* supposed to mean?" Sara asked, catching her friend's suggestive tone.

"It *means* that on our way out, we encountered a guy in a pickup driving up to see you. And from what I could see of him, he was *quite* good-looking. As in, if I hadn't already been pregnant, I might've actually ovulated then and there."

"I'm telling Evan!" Sara said, breaking into laughter. "But before you go getting too excited, he wasn't coming to see me at all. That was the twins' father."

"I suspected as much," Rachel told her. "But you never mentioned he was *smoking* hot. You've been holding out on me, girl."

"That's because I hadn't noticed," Sara blurted. "In case it hasn't come to your attention, I've been too busy trying to keep these kids from falling apart while shoe-horning at least a little English into their heads so they'll be able to function in their new home."

"I know I should've checked your pulse while I was out there."

"What? *Why?*"

Rachel snorted. "Because unless you're stone-cold dead or having some kind of serious eye issue, you're flat-out lying to me right now. Which means you've *definitely* noticed and are feeling a bit conflicted about that. Maybe...because *he's* noticed you, as well?"

"You have a very vivid imagination," Sara scoffed, hoping her friend couldn't detect the way her stomach had just flipped at the laser-like assessment. "He's only working to make a connection with his children, that's all, under very trying circumstances."

So trying that Sara had found herself offering to supplement his online Spanish instruction by helping him practice his conversational skills for an hour on each of the last few evenings. It gave him an excuse to drop by after dinner. Since he brought along Roxy for the ride, as well, the children were eager to see him coming—enough that Sara had been able to entice them to participate in helping their father a bit each time he visited.

But she decided not to mention any of that to Rachel, knowing her friend would only tease her about having

"ulterior motives." And maybe Sara *did* find herself looking forward to the adult company each evening…and
thinking about him more and more as she lay alone beneath her covers during the quiet nights that followed.

"Sara, are you listening to me? I asked if you'd heard
the news from Austin."

"Oh, sorry," Sara said. "I'm afraid I've been kind of
enjoying a break from the real world out here."

"I just wondered if anybody from your office had told
you that that governor's aide you mentioned to me, the
one who sent you to Buenos Aires, had passed away in
the hospital?"

Sara's heart bumped, her eyes filling. "Paul Barkley
died? I hadn't heard that."

"I'm so sorry."

Sara shook her head, a lump forming in her throat.
"It's not as if I knew him well, not personally. It's just—
we'd spoken so many times about the children's return,
and I know he'd worked so hard to make it happen. It's
so unfair that he was hit just as they were finally on their
way home…"

As her words trailed off, she wondered, What if the
timing was more than coincidental? She quickly dismissed
the notion, reminding herself of the unfortunate fact of
life that traffic deaths, including hit and runs, happened
every day on Texas highways.

"Do you know if the driver who hit him was ever arrested?" she asked Rachel.

"Apparently not. They asked again for anyone having
information to call the number on the screen. But since
there were no cameras in the area, I'm not sure they'll
ever find the person."

"I don't know how anyone could live with it…hitting
someone and just driving off," Sara said with a sigh.

"I know I'd never manage to keep my mouth shut," Rachel told her. "Sorry to be the bearer of such awful news."

"Don't be. You were right that I'd want to know," Sara said, part of her brain still stuck on the sad irony of the accident's timing.

"Well, on a cheerier note," Rachel said, clearly eager to move on from the depressing topic, "I was wondering how you liked the chocolates."

"Wait, what?" Sara racked her brain, but came up blank. "I'm sorry?"

"Those amazing Belgian chocolates I slipped inside the suitcase with the clothes I brought you. Don't tell me you haven't unpacked it yet, as gung ho as you are about organization."

"Of course, I did. It's just— Let me look again." Sara pulled open dresser drawers and looked through the things she'd put away. "I'm so sorry. I don't see them. I don't know how I could've missed something like that."

"Neither do I," Rachel said. "It was a good-sized box wrapped in gold paper with a beautiful bow."

"You don't think—" Sara lowered her voice "—the children?"

"Well, they *are* kids," Rachel pointed out, "and it *was* candy." She sighed. "Quite *expensive* candy, but candy nonetheless."

"But they've always been so respectful of my space, and their manners are usually very good."

"As I remember, their manners slipped quite a bit after you denied the two of them *their* presents," Rachel said dryly. "So perhaps it's not overly surprising that they decided to deny you yours."

She was right, Sara knew. Still, she remained troubled, though her friend hastened to assure her that, considering all they'd gone through, it was only natural that the children act out in some way.

"I wouldn't be too hard on them about it," Rachel advised.

"I don't intend to be," Sara said, "but I do mean to have a serious talk with them about it."

Once they'd ended the call, however, she decided to postpone that discussion until morning. For one thing, she didn't want to wake the twins if they were sleeping. For another, she wasn't about to level an accusation—of theft, of all things—while she was upset about their intrusion into her room. Better she should get a good night's sleep, too, first, allowing her emotions to settle before dealing with the problem in the morning.

First, though, she needed to wind down, which meant some time spent curled up with the e-reader she'd brought with her on her trip abroad. Looking forward to losing herself once more in the light romantic story, she went to the nightstand where she'd left the e-reader and looked beneath the magazine she'd also left there.

Her heart sagged when she saw that the e-reader was missing, too. "Oh, no," she murmured to herself. "Don't tell me that they—"

Not allowing herself to finish the awful thought, she looked methodically through the rest of the room, searching the dresser and its drawers and behind and underneath the furniture. But the small tablet, which she normally kept inside a bright red leather cover, was nowhere in evidence.

She decided that she must have taken it elsewhere and forgotten, so she ventured out to the living room, where she searched every surface and between and behind the sofa and seat cushions. After checking the kitchen and dining area with no better luck, she grabbed a flashlight.

She then headed outside to look on the porch, since the night before last she had been out there reading, until some annoyingly persistent gnats had finally chased her back inside.

As she looked down and around the rocking chair where she'd been seated, a sound—like the clatter of small rocks kicked by rapid movement—made her look up sharply. Pulse bumping in her throat, she turned her flashlight toward the pond, where she reminded herself she and the children had seen several deer drinking earlier.

Braced to see some wild animal by the water, she instead was surprised when a large moth fluttered into her beam, followed by a bat whose wings hurtled toward her face. Shrieking, she jumped backward as the bat pulled up and flew harmlessly away. But Sara's right foot came down on something unexpected that rolled and spurted out from underneath it—the children's soccer ball, she realized. Overbalancing to compensate, she crashed down hard on her opposite side, despite her attempt to break her fall with her left hand. With a splintering sound, the flashlight landed on the deck beside her.

For a few moments, she lay there groaning, rattled by the fall and aching in a half dozen places from what she decided had to be the most ridiculous accident of all time. But it was all right, she told herself. All she had to do was breathe through her pain and panic—and thank her lucky stars that no one had happened to have a camera handy and a way to immortalize her gracelessness on the internet forever.

"See there. You're all right," she told herself as her heart's hammering subsided.

Feeling a little steadier, she moved to push herself into a sitting position. But the moment she put her left hand to the deck, pain shot through her, so bright and fierce that she nearly passed out with it.

Mac had just drifted off to sleep when he heard the cell phone across the room ring on its charger. His first impulse was to ignore the damned thing, since he was in no mood to deal with whatever scammer or robocaller was phoning after eleven. But he rolled out of bed anyway, his body remembering that he'd given his phone number to Sara in case of any issue with the cabin or the twins.

Sure enough, it was her name on the caller ID window. He jolted completely awake. "Hello, Sara. Everything all right over there?"

"I—I'm afraid not," she said breathlessly. "There's been an accident of sorts."

His stomach dropped, his brain automatically shifting into Worst Case Mode. "The kids? Are they hurt—or has she come to take them?" Since he'd learned of their return, he'd been plagued by nightmares of black-clad commandos arriving to drag the children back to Buenos Aires, some of the same sort who'd nearly killed him when he'd attempted to collect his twins in Argentina after Analisa's death.

"They're fine," Sara assured him, "still fast asleep. I just looked in on them."

He gulped a breath, struggling to control his shaking. So the worst hadn't happened, at least, but he heard in her voice that something was still very wrong. "So what is it, then? You sound—"

"I'm really sorry to bother you at this hour," she said, her voice shaky, "but I'm pretty sure I've just broken my wrist, and I don't think it's going to wait 'til morning."

"What the hell?" he asked. "What happened?"

"I fell out on the deck just a bit ago, and I have no idea

what to do about it. I'm not sure I could drive the way I am right now, even if there *were* somewhere to go nearby this time of night around here."

"Where are you right now? Are you safe?"

"I'm back inside, on the sofa, with my arm elevated on some pillows. I have some ice wrapped up in hand towels to help keep down the swelling."

"Okay. That's a good start. I'm getting dressed right now," he said, rising from the bed and groping in the darkness for a pair of jeans. "So, this injury of yours—is there bone sticking through the skin? Blood?" he asked, recalling compound fractures he'd seen on the gridiron.

"No, thank goodness," she said, "but I absolutely *know* my wrist is not supposed to be the shape it's in now."

As he stepped into the pant leg, he asked, "Have you taken anything for pain yet?"

"I think I might have some over-the-counter headache pills in my room," she said, "but, honestly, every time I move, I want to throw up."

"Better just sit tight, then. I'll be over quick as I can to see what we can do to stabilize you and then get you to the nearest medical facility," he said, knowing that would involve something of a drive.

"I'm so sorry," she said again. "I feel like such a klutz."

"First off, quit apologizing, or I'll be forced to show you all the scars from my previous misadventures. And trust me, *nobody* wants to see that."

"Please," she said, in a voice dripping with unfamiliar sarcasm. "You could probably sell tickets to the ladies around these parts."

He snorted. "That only goes to show you're underestimating country women's savvy. They're plenty smart enough to know a cranky, broke man when they see one.

Now, take care of that arm, and I'll see you in just a little bit."

After dressing, Mac took Roxy out, but instead of taking her with him, he left her behind with fresh water and a couple of biscuits, along with the admonition, "Keep an eye on things around here for me."

In truth, the Lab was sleeping so heavily these days, she didn't make much of a watchdog, so he could only hope that the signs he'd posted warning of security cameras, prosecution of trespassers, and armed deterrence would be enough to safeguard the building materials he'd had delivered yesterday. But with his mind on Sara's situation, he put aside the worry and set his home alarm before heading out into a moonless night so dark the bright band of the Milky Way cut a faintly glowing path across the ink-black firmament.

After reaching the cabin without incident, he hopped out of his truck and hurried to the porch. As he passed a window that looked in on the living area, he spotted Sara inside on the sofa, looking pale and small, with her knees curled up but her arm elevated on a pillow and covered with a towel. He thought at first that she might be sleeping, but when he tapped lightly at the door—half-afraid that he might startle her—she looked at him with pained eyes before waving an invitation to enter.

"Thanks for coming," she said, her voice as thin as starlight.

"How are you holding up?" he asked.

"Wishing I'd never set foot on the porch tonight."

"I hear you. And I'm sure you're hurting pretty badly, too. I didn't know what you'd have, so I brought along some over-the-counter ibuprofen," he told her, pulling a bottle from his pocket. "How about if we get you started with a couple of tablets and some water before we make our plan of attack?"

She nodded. "Please."

Once he brought her water, she drank down the pills before handing him back the remainder of the glass. "That's good, thanks."

"Do you need some fresh ice for the arm yet?"

"I'm okay for now. I still can't believe this happened."

"Exactly how did you fall?" he asked, realizing she hadn't told him.

"It's pretty stupid, actually. I was out on the porch looking for my e-reader when something startled me and I ended up tripping over the kids' soccer ball. I reached out to catch myself and—" Gritting her teeth, she shook her head.

Frowning, he said, "That's not so stupid, Sara. But what scared you?"

"A noise." She shook her head. "Probably some animal walking on the rocks down by the water. When I turned to look with my flashlight, there was this bat, coming right at my face and—"

"They're pretty thick around here this time of year." He'd seen more than one of his city-dwelling visitors shriek and run inside after one of the harmless creatures flew too close while diving for their dinner. "The wildlife around here can get especially wild after dark."

"As far as I'm concerned, you can keep your wildlife," she grumbled. "I'd trade all of them for decent security lighting, paved sidewalks and good broadband."

Allowing that she had plenty of reason for her bad mood, he changed the subject. "Mind if I take a peek at that wrist now, see what we're dealing with here?"

She sighed. "It's probably time I took the ice off to give the skin a break now anyway."

"Good thinking," he said as she gingerly shifted her weight, putting her feet down on the floor again before lifting away the towel with the ice pack wrapped inside it.

Wincing, she said, "I can't stand to look at it," and turned her head.

He could see why, since the bump distorting her now crooked, swollen and discolored wrist offered instant evidence that she hadn't been exaggerating the injury.

"Looks like you're going to the hospital tonight," he said with forced cheer. "You were right that that can't wait 'til morning. We've got about a forty-five-minute drive ahead, to the nearest emergency room, in Uvalde."

"I hate that I'll be costing you so much sleep."

"I'm awake now, and remember what I said before. No more apologizing."

"All right," she agreed, "but I think I'd better check with my insurance."

"Maybe you ought to wake the kids first. I'm afraid that if I try to do it at this hour, I'll scare them half to death."

"Okay," she said, though he noticed her hesitation. "I'm just a little afraid of shifting all this."

"I can certainly understand that. Let me help you up here. I'll support this pillow for you until you're on your feet."

Carefully, he assisted her in the maneuvering, stepping behind her as she rose until she was steady within the sheltering framework of his arms.

"There you go," he said, his throat thickening as it hit him how many years it had been since he'd stood like this with a woman. Despite what he'd told Sara, it wasn't for want of opportunity. But he hadn't been able to let his guard down and trust another woman after what he feared that Analisa may have done to him—or focus on anything other than nurturing his anger and the dim hope that he would ever again see his children.

With Sara now, however, he felt something unfamiliar: a tenderness that he'd almost forgotten, a concern for her well-being that went beyond her role as temporary caretaker to his children and evaluator of his so-called progress as a parent. And even more than that, an awareness of the beautiful, kindhearted woman he'd come to look forward to spending time with every evening as she helped him with his still rudimentary Spanish. A woman he found himself wondering about, contemplating after going home alone nights, on a far more personal level than he had any business doing.

"I'll take it from here," she said, shifting her good hand to support the pillow. As she turned, her shoulder brushed his chest and her beautiful green eyes locked with his, both of them going still as an awareness of the hour and the blood rushing through their veins struck them.

"Sara," he said quietly, "I want you to know, getting to know you these past few days… I've enjoyed it. Very much. And I—I'm glad you thought to call me when this happened."

"Thank you, but I should…" she started, the discomfort in her voice hitting him like a spray of ice water.

"Of course." He stepped back out of her way, mentally kicking himself for opening his mouth and making things awkward. Had she imagined he was about to make some move—maybe even try to kiss her—with the image of her clearly broken wrist still firmly in his mind?

Moving carefully, she went into the children's room, where he soon heard a quiet conversation that went on longer than he might have expected.

When she finally came out, she told him, "I thought

I'd never wake them. Cristo, especially, sleeps like the dead once he's finally out."

"But they're both up now?"

She nodded. "When I told them we were going to have to go to the hospital, that finally woke them up. Silvia's in the bathroom and Cristo's dressing in their room."

"They'll probably fall asleep again on the way."

"I'm not so sure about that. They're feeling pretty upset right now because I mentioned that I'd fallen on the soccer ball they'd forgotten on the porch. Not that I was blaming them but—"

"Then why would they be upset?"

She gave him a troubled look. "I gather they had very strict rules at their grandparents' about putting their things away... Cristo immediately assumed I'd be taking the ball away, maybe even destroying it."

"Destroying it?"

"There were tears in his eyes, Mac. And both of them were shaking. It seems...they've witnessed things they've loved destroyed in front of them before."

"That son of a bitch—it had to be their grandfather," he said, anger throbbing at his temples. "Analisa told me— She told me how he used to be with her, back when she was just a kid herself." During all the years he'd fought to get his children back, he'd prayed that his twins were at least being well cared for. That the years and the loss of his only daughter had softened their grandfather, enough that he'd raise them to know love unshadowed by cold fear. "Yet he had the balls to accuse *me* of—"

When the children emerged, he stopped himself, glimpsing the terror in their eyes at his voice before softening his tone to greet them. *"Buenas noches, Cristo, Silvia."*

Worried glances passed between them before they mumbled greetings.

Understanding that was the best he could expect for now, he told Sara, "I've been thinking it might be best if I drive us in your car. I'm afraid that right now, my back seat's piled up with more tools, building supplies and dog hair than any of us want to contend with."

Sara agreed, and after suggesting that the twins each bring along a blanket for the journey, they loaded the children in the back of the Civic and Sara in the front passenger seat—along with a pillow and a fresh ice pack for her wrist—and started off.

They left the subdivision, passing only one vehicle on their way to their next turn. Approaching the river, Mac tapped the brakes, automatically checking a roadside depth gauge before proceeding across a low spot where the still swollen waters flowed gently across the paved surface of the road.

As the small sedan splashed to the other side—only half a foot or so deep now—Sara said, "These river crossings scared me when I first got here. I'm used to bridges spanning every trickle in the city."

"Too expensive to build so many out here, where there are so many river crossings and so few people," he said. "All you have to do is pay close attention to the signs and gauges."

"I'll keep that in mind," she told him.

"You have to, and never let your guard down if you want to stay alive."

"What?"

"I'm serious," he said. "Around here, you might've noticed, we don't do streetlights, guardrails, and they don't call the mountain highways around the area the Twisted Sisters for nothing. Accidents are a major cause of death in the Hill Country—and all too often it's the tourists getting too distracted by the beauty to watch out for the dangers."

"Thanks for the warning," she said. "But maybe you should've given me this particular TED Talk *before* I decided to go one-on-one with a bat and soccer ball tonight."

He chuckled, surprised that she could still joke despite her pain. And vowing that, whatever it took, he would find a way, despite this injury, to convince her to stick around at least for the remainder of the month she had agreed to.

Fortunately, the emergency department at the hospital was having a slow night, so Sara was quickly taken back for a preliminary exam and X-rays while Mac and the children were relegated to the waiting area. Sensing their worry, he did his best to put their minds to ease, but if his Spanish was weak, he realized that Sara hadn't been exaggerating about their lack of progress with their English lessons. She'd assured him that their inability to retain her lessons had to be emotionally based, since she'd found both not only cooperative but bright and at least a couple of years ahead of where she'd expect them to be in terms of their math and Spanish-language reading skills.

"You have to expect some temporary setbacks," she had told him, her gentle smile reassuring, "but with time and patience, I've seen children heal and thrive even after far worse trauma."

After refusing his offer of a snack or drink from one of the vending machines, they sat in silence, wrapped in their blankets with the TVs overhead droning mindless home improvement program reruns.

Eventually, the twins nodded off again, but Mac found himself unable to get comfortable in the hard plastic chairs—and far too worried about Sara's condition to get any rest himself. So instead, he split his time between checking news and weather on his phone and taking long looks at his sleeping children, now that he was finally allowed the luxury of studying them without making them nervous or conflicted.

He smiled, noticing how the shape of Silvia's nose resembled his late mother's and how the warm golden brown of Cristo's curls had lighter streaks the same shade Mac had inherited from his long-dead father. In other ways, however, the twins were living memorials to the only woman he had ever loved. He saw it in the warm, light tan of their unblemished skin, their slim build, too, and in the way Silvia gestured with her hands while awake and speaking, so much as her mother once had. He realized that he couldn't wait to see how the tapestry of influences came together as they grew into adulthood. *If I can only keep us all together.*

A door opened from the exam room area and a petite younger woman, with short black hair and dark eyes, came out and looked around the waiting area before making a beeline for him. "Mr. Walker, is it?" she asked.

Rising to speak to her, he glanced down at the name badge that identified her as *Cara Navarro, RN.* "How's Sara? Can I go back?"

"She asked me to fill you in on her status," she said, keeping her voice low and her expression sympathetic. "She was concerned about the children in particular and thought you might need my help translating after you and I are finished speaking."

His pulse picking up speed, he asked, "Why? What's going on? Is she going to be all right?"

"Why don't we step over here to talk?" She gestured

toward the counter near the triage area, which was currently unoccupied.

He quickly crossed the room, turning to keep the
sleeping children in his line of sight, though none of the
few others in the waiting area had given them a second
glance.

"First off," Nurse Navarro told him, "Ms. Wakefield
wanted me to assure you her commitment to caring for
the children hasn't wavered."

"That's great, but how is Sara? That's what I need to
know now."

"She's going to be fine. It's a distal radial fracture—
the most common wrist fracture people get from falling
onto an outstretched hand. The orthopedic surgeon who
consulted remotely has advised she'll need a closed reduc-
tion. Basically, that's when they pull the bones to realign
them so they'll heal correctly."

He made a face. "That doesn't sound fun."

"It wouldn't be, if she were awake to feel it," the nurse
said. "That's why, first thing in the morning, she'll be
put under general anesthesia. By the time she wakes up
again, her wrist will be in a cast."

"Why wait until morning?" he asked, hating to think
of her spending all night in pain.

"The staff won't arrive until first thing in the morning, but this isn't an emergency situation, and she's being
kept very comfortable for the time being, with the arm
iced and elevated and good medication."

"How long before she'll be ready to go home?"

"I'd think she'll be out of recovery and finished with
her casting by 10:00 or 11:00 a.m. at the latest. Too long
for you to wait here with the children, she insisted."

He grimaced. "I hate leaving her here alone."

The nurse smiled. "We'll take good care of her, I promise."

He attempted to return the smile, though he was still uncertain.

"Would it make you feel any better if I told you she's sound asleep right now, zoned out on the good stuff?" the nurse asked. "She suggested you should take the children back to let them sleep in their beds at the cabin, where they'll be most comfortable. You can stay there overnight and return to pick her up tomorrow."

She handed him the key to the cabin door.

"I suppose I can camp out on the sofa there easily enough," he conceded. "But I'm definitely glad you're here to explain things to the twins. It's important that they both feel safe and understand what's happening."

Nurse Navarro nodded, her dark eyes sympathetic. "After Ms. Wakefield goes home," she said, "she'll most likely need a little extra help, especially for the first few days."

"I can promise you," Mac told her, "I'll do whatever it takes to get her through this—and I mean to see that my son and daughter pitch in, too."

When Mac and the children arrived to pick her up from the hospital late the following morning, Sara couldn't help but smile. They looked like a real family, walking together into the recovery area where she waited, her left arm feeling odd and awkward in a cast that reached nearly to her elbow and the sling she would wear for the next week. With help from the nurse earlier, she'd managed to dress and get her things together, and any discomfort she felt seemed far more distant than the smiles on all three of the Walkers' faces.

"*¡Mira, Sara!*" Silvia said excitedly, running toward

her with a bouquet of colorful flowers and a sweet, but blessedly careful, embrace.

"*Muchas gracias.* How nice," Sara said, hugging both her and Cristo, who presented his get-well balloons with a shy smile as he nervously tugged at the curls that made up his forelock.

"How are you feeling?" Mac asked, his blue-gray eyes concerned.

"A whole lot better than the last time you saw me," she said. "How did you all make out overnight?"

Though neither of the twins responded to her question, asked in English, a look of relief swept over Mac's handsome face. "Better than I could've imagined. Having that nurse explain the situation to them really helped, I think. Thanks. And we stopped at my house on the way back and picked up Roxy, too. I let her stay in the room with them, and I think that made them feel safer."

"*Great* idea," she said, though she felt a pang, thinking how unfair it was that he should keep having to turn himself inside out to keep his own children—the children she was certain he'd give his life for if necessary—from panicking at the thought of being left alone with him overnight. For a moment, she tasted the bitter anger she'd heard flare in him toward his late wife's parents, for poisoning the twins' innocent minds against him as they had. "Honestly, I'm impressed you thought of it, especially in the wee hours of the morning."

He smiled but didn't answer as this morning's nurse, a fortyish woman who wore her blond hair clipped up, came in then to review her instructions for discharge. Looking at Mac, she said, "She'll definitely need another adult on hand today, until the anesthesia's all out of her system."

"I've got her covered," Mac said. Looking at Sara, he added, "If you're okay with my company, that is."

Sara thought about it, knowing that in a normal foster situation, what he was suggesting would be unthinkable, with the two of them being at the cabin together—especially with her in her vulnerable state. "It's very kind of you to make yourself available. But I'm going to have to make a call to my case manager to run this by her...under the circumstances."

The nurse's curious gaze flicked from one to the other and then to the two children, but she was too much of a professional to say more than, "As long as there's *some* responsible party with her today."

"You have my word, there will be," Mac vowed, his gaze never leaving Sara's.

"All right, then," the nurse said before asking Mac to go and pull the car around to the front, where she would wheel out Sara in accordance with hospital regulations.

A short time later, they were all in the car and on their way back to Real County. Now seated in the rear, the children, who'd mostly been quiet inside the hospital, came out of their shells while Mac focused on their drive through the small town's outskirts.

"Does it hurt much?" Silvia asked worriedly in Spanish.

"Not so much at all now," Sara told her, her arm propped on a pillow as she sat in the front passenger seat, wearing sunglasses against the bright June day. "And over the next few days, it should start to feel a whole lot better. In six weeks, if it heals well, I should get the cast off."

"Six whole weeks!" Silvia sounded stricken.

But Cristo interrupted, blurting an apology. "*Lo siento, Señorita Sara.* It's all my fault the soccer ball was out on the porch last night." Taking a deep breath, he bravely added, "Please don't punish Silvia for what I did."

"That's very grown-up of you to take responsibility," Sara told him. "But my tripping was an accident, and no one's getting punished."

He hesitated before asking in a small voice, "Really?"

"Absolutely." She turned to look over her shoulder, needing to see their reaction. "But I *was* out there looking for my electronic reader in the red case. Has either of you seen it?"

What she thought she detected was confusion followed by a quick check-in as their gazes found each other's before both shook their heads and claimed that no, they hadn't seen anything like that.

"I hope you'll help me look for it around the cabin, then," she suggested before adding, "and there was a wrapped gold box, too. It was in the suitcase my friends brought for me—before I…misplaced it somehow, I suppose."

If she hadn't been watching carefully, she would have missed it—the way both twins stiffened slightly before turning their heads to look out the window as if they were suddenly fascinated by the flat and featureless soybean field they were passing.

"So you'll look for the box, too?" Sara pressed. "My chocolates, I mean. They were a special gift, but I thought we might all share them."

"We…we'll try to find them," Cristo said, his voice sounding somewhat strangled.

Silvia only nodded, her small face flushing a deep pink as her fascination with the farmland intensified.

Now certain they were hiding something, Sara blew out a long breath. Inclined as she was to show the twins compassion because of their recent trauma, she knew that if she didn't set some boundaries, they would think they could get by with such behavior in the future. "I appreciate that. But you won't need to check my bedroom. I'll take care of looking in there, alone. Do you understand?"

When they dared to glance at her, she held eye contact long enough to watch both of them nod without speaking, practically squirming with what she read as guilt before she slowly turned back around.

"I didn't catch most of that," admitted Mac, glancing over at her, "but if I was reading the tone right, it sounded kind of intense."

"I'm not sure that's the right word for it," she said, "but I'd like to speak to you about it later. As their father, I could use your input on the situation."

"Sure thing."

Worried over whether she was handling the situation correctly, she rubbed her eyes, overcome by a wave of fatigue that had settled over her. Closing her eyes against the road glare, she soon found herself nodding off.

The next thing she was aware of, her head was jerking as they bumped up the unpaved driveway to the cabin. As the car bobbed in a pothole, she grunted, coming fully awake.

"Sorry for the rude awakening," Mac said. "It's easier said than done, steering around all the ruts on this drive."

"I'm surprised you made it this far before you hit one," she said, straightening to readjust the pillow under her arm.

"Hope you're not hurting too much."

"I'll be fine," she said, bracing herself for the next hole she saw ahead.

He managed to steer around it and soon had them parked. As they left the car, from inside the house, she heard muffled barking.

"That'll be Roxy," Mac explained. "I hope you don't mind that I left her here."

"I'm sure she's fine," Sara said. As Mac took the bag with her instructions and pain medication from the car and walked beside her toward the door, the twins both ran ahead. Glancing at him, she said, "Before we head on in and I make that call, I want to tell you how very much I appreciate everything you've done so far—coming to my rescue last night, driving back and forth from here to the hospital twice."

He shrugged a pair of shoulders whose breadth she couldn't help admiring. "You needed help. I helped. You would've done the same for me."

"Maybe," she said.

"You would have," he insisted, sounding confident as they started uphill toward the cabin. "If you'd known I didn't have other family or friends around to help out, because you're the kind of woman who can be relied on to always do the right thing."

"So you think you know me that well?"

"Well, you *are* a professional do-gooder, aren't you?"

She smiled at him, an expression that soon changed as the barking from the house increased in volume and the old Lab appeared from nowhere, running out to greet the children.

Shaking her head, Sara looked at Mac. "Didn't you say you'd left her inside?"

Looking equally confused, he said, "I did—and I could've sworn the doors were all locked, too." He frowned toward the children up ahead. "Cristo, Silvia!"

When they turned their heads to look back his way, he beckoned them to him with a wave. "Come back. Now."

Turning to Sara, he ordered, "Ask them to wait here with you and Roxy while I check out the house to make sure everything's okay inside."

"Those old doors are a little warped," Sara said, re-

Get ready to relax and indulge with your **FREE BOOKS** and more!

**Claim up to FOUR NEW BOOKS & TWO MYSTERY GIFTS –
absolutely FREE!**

Dear Reader,

We both know life can be difficult at times. That's why it's important to treat yourself so you can relax and recharge once in a while.

And I'd like to help you do this by sending you this amazing offer of up to FOUR brand new full length FREE BOOKS that WE pay for.

This is everything I have ready to send to you right now:

Try **Harlequin® Romantic Suspense** books featuring heart-racing page-turners with unexpected plot twists and irresistible chemistry that will keep you guessing to the very end.

Try **Harlequin Intrigue® Larger-Print** books featuring action-packed stories that will keep you on the edge of your seat. Solve the crime and deliver justice at all costs.
Or **TRY BOTH!**

All we ask in return is that you answer 4 simple questions on the attached Treat Yourself survey. You'll get **Two Free Books** and **Two Mystery Gifts** from each series you try, *altogether worth over $20*! Who could pass up a deal like that?

Sincerely,

Pam Powers

Harlequin Reader Service

Treat Yourself to Free Books and Free Gifts.

Answer 4 fun questions and get rewarded.

We love to connect with our readers!
Please tell us a little about you...

DETACH AND MAIL CARD TODAY! ▶

	YES	NO
1. I LOVE reading a good book.		
2. I indulge and "treat" myself often.		
3. I love getting FREE things.		
4. Reading is one of my favorite activities.		

TREAT YOURSELF • Pick your 2 Free Books...

Yes! Please send me my Free Books from each series I select and Free Mystery Gifts. I understand that I am under no obligation to buy anything, as explained on the back of this card.

Which do you prefer?

❑ **Harlequin® Romantic Suspense** 240/340 HDL GRCZ
❑ **Harlequin Intrigue® Larger-Print** 199/399 HDL GRCZ
❑ **Try Both** 240/340 & 199/399 HDL GRDD

FIRST NAME   LAST NAME

ADDRESS

APT.#   CITY

STATE/PROV.   ZIP/POSTAL CODE

EMAIL ❑ Please check this box if you would like to receive newsletters and promotional emails from Harlequin Enterprises ULC and its affiliates. You can unsubscribe anytime.

membered the way they stuck at times. "Maybe one of
them didn't get closed right and popped open?"

"That's probably it," Mac agreed. "It was Silvia who
shut the side door. I came behind her and checked to see
that it was locked, but she might not've had it pulled
quite tight enough. Still, humor me a minute, will you?"

It was on the tip of Sara's tongue to tell him that it
wasn't necessary, that surely no one was going to bother
them all the way up here. But she couldn't help but think
back to Cristo's references to the children's grandmother
finding them to take them home.

Telling herself not to get worked up over the boy's fantasy, Sara switched to Spanish to tell the children, "We
need to wait here for a minute while your *papá* sees how
the dog got outside."

The twins looked after their father for a moment before turning as one toward the pond and the trees and
brush beyond it...

Sara felt a prickling behind her neck, remembering the
clattering she'd heard along the bank last night, the noise
she'd taken for the movement of some animal. *What if
it had been human?* "What are you looking at? Do you
see something out there?" *Or someone?*

Turning her graying muzzle in the same direction,
Roxy gave a low growl, the hackles on her back rising.

"Grab her collar," Sara urged.

"Don't you hear that?" Cristo asked as he complied.
"It sounds like something digging. Look!"

Sara spotted something—several dark shapes, long
and low and moving in the shadows beneath the trees.
Her mind conjured black-clad, armed men, crawling beneath the branches with their weapons, like the men the
children's grandfather had once sent to keep Mac from
his children.

Had their grandmother dared to send such commandos here, too, hoping to abduct them and spirit them away?

Sara drew a deep breath, about to shout a warning to Mac, who was disappearing around the corner of the cabin's wraparound porch.

"What kinds of *animals* are those?" Cristo asked her.

Pounding heart wedged in her throat, Sara blinked— and the jet-black shapes resolved themselves into more familiar, four-legged forms.

"Are those *cerdos*?" Silvia asked her.

"*Pigs*, yes," Sara said, supplying them with the English word as four of the animals broke for another clump of thick brush, with a line of a half dozen tiny, dusky piglets trailing in their wake.

"Piggies." Silvia giggled as she used the English word, but her laughter ceased abruptly at her brother's sharp look.

"*Cristo,*" Sara challenged, "why would you be angry at your sister for using English?"

"Because 'piggies' sounds so stupid. English is a stupid language. And we don't need to learn it anyway because we're going home soon."

"You already *are* home, here in Texas," Sara said, frustrated, "so you might as well learn to talk to people, because I won't be around to translate for you forever."

"Abuelita will send someone for us, you'll see," he insisted, his small face flushed with anger. "Just you wait and see if our grandmother doesn't."

"What makes you believe that?" Sara challenged. "Since she hasn't done so up until now?"

"She's just— She's just waiting for them to find—" He glanced toward Silvia, who was shaking her head, her lips pressed together and her eyes practically begging her brother to shut his mouth.

"Waiting for who to…?" Sara pressed. "Silvia, do you know something? Something that you need to tell me? Something about your *abuela*?"

Her brown eyes rounding with panic, Silvia quickly shook her head.

Before Sara could say any more, Mac's voice floated toward them from the porch. "Everything looks fine inside. It's just like you thought—the side door popped back open. It was still locked and everything, but it's safe to come on in."

"All right," Sara called back. "We'll be right there."

But as they headed for the cabin, she felt more uneasy than ever…and worried that the children's hopes for a reunion with their grandmother might be rooted in something far more sinister than she had ever dreamed.

Chapter 7

While Sara updated her foster care case manager on the situation from the bedroom, Mac decided to make himself useful. Checking both the fridge and pantry, he discovered a large can of tomato soup and the makings for grilled-cheese sandwiches. He decided to make lunch, since it was already early afternoon and he suspected that Sara and the children were all getting hungry just as he was.

Though he'd hoped to get the twins involved, they'd already retreated to their room with Roxy. He thought of calling them, perhaps to try to get through to them his expectation that they start taking on some chores around the cabin. But his lack of vocabulary to get his point across had him deciding he was going to need Sara's help.

It was a reality that left him both frustrated and worried since no amount of study would make him miraculously fluent in Spanish over the next few weeks and Cristo and Silvia's progress in English had been even slower. How the hell were they ever going to manage on their own? He thought about asking around town to see if he might find a bilingual housekeeper or nanny to help out. But even if he found the right person, he worried about the added expense.

After washing up, he poured the soup into a pan and started it on low before taking out a skillet. A short time later, as he was grilling the first of the buttered cheese sandwiches he'd put together, Sara came out to the kitchen, smiling when she saw him.

"Mmm. Grilled cheese and tomato soup. We always used to have the same thing whenever one of us stayed home sick from school. I can picture my mom making it…"

"Mine, too," he said before noticing the sadness in Sara's green eyes. "Is…is your mother gone, too? We lost mine about six years back, to cancer."

"I'm so sorry to hear that," she said before shaking her head. "But no, my mom's still living. At least, as far as I know."

"You're not— Not close?" he asked carefully.

She shook her head, her mouth tightening. "Not with any of my family, but if you don't mind, I'd rather not get into the gory details."

"Believe me, I understand estrangement," he said.

"So I've heard…" She gave him a look steeped in sympathy. "But I saw that your brothers were with you in court."

"They've made it clear that they stand by their niece and nephew," he corrected. Pausing to move the finished sandwich, now golden brown and oozy, to a plate, he started another before stirring the heating soup. "I'm not sure if they'll ever forgive me, though, for the way things went with the ranch."

"They actually showed up, though. It's a start." She grimaced. "If I had as much… But enough about all that."

"Sure thing," he said, nodding to acknowledge her pained look before changing the subject. "How are you feeling?"

"Kind of groggy," she admitted. "If you don't mind, I'd like to lie down for a little while after lunch."

"That's why I'm here," he reminded her. "So should I assume you got hold of your foster care person and she was okay with my presence?"

"Actually, I think she might have been a little scandalized. But since she doesn't have anyone else to send out here and Judge Cartwright asked her to give me some extra leeway because I'm an experienced social worker, she said she was willing to trust my professional judgment."

"In other words, she'll let you take the blame if anything goes wrong."

"Let's just see that it doesn't, all right?" Sara pointed toward the skillet. "And I think you'd better flip that. Smells like it's about to burn."

After taking her advice, he said, "I'll do my best. That's all I can promise."

"I have to tell you, I very much appreciate everything, including the lunch. I missed breakfast this morning, while they were casting my arm."

"Here, then," he said, cutting the first sandwich on the diagonal and passing her half of it. "Start eating while I finish cooking."

"I can wait for everyone to sit down."

"But you don't have to," he said, tearing off and passing her a paper towel from the roll. "Consider it a perk of the broken wing."

"Well, now that you put it that way…" She bit into the sandwich, murmuring with gratitude. "Oh, yum."

His libido took definite notice of her purr of pleasure before he ruthlessly pushed back his desire. Sure, he found her attractive—beautiful even, despite her rough night—as well as kind and caring. But he reminded himself she was there to do a job, and what he'd begun feeling for her was as inappropriate as it was one-sided.

"Later on, while you're resting, I'm going to have a look at the door that popped open earlier and see what I can do to make sure it's closing good and tight."

"There's really no need for you to go through the trouble."

"The place needs to be secure," he insisted, "and there's no point bothering Amanda Greenville over it when I have nothing else to do around here anyway."

"All right, then," she agreed, "and thanks."

Laying the next sandwich in the skillet, he said, "Earlier, in the car, you said there was something you wanted to talk to me about, some issue with the kids?"

Swallowing, she wiped her hands. "I'm afraid there is, yes." Forgetting the sandwich for the moment, she filled him in on her reasons—convincing reasons, he had to admit—to believe that Cristo and Silvia had taken a wrapped gift that her friends had brought her.

"It pains me having to tell you this," she said, regret lining her forehead, "and I hate even more to think about accusing them directly, especially considering everything they've been through."

"I won't have them using what's happened to justify taking things that aren't theirs," Mac insisted. "Or using their anger as an excuse for poor behavior. Let's all talk after we eat. But let me take the lead on this."

"You— You're sure about this? They may be pretty upset," she said.

"If they are, so be it," he said as he plated the last sandwich. "But if I'm going to truly be their father, I have to learn to set limits and consequences as well as offer them love. And maybe it's better that they see I can discipline them calmly instead of turning into some kind of raving lunatic, the way they've been taught to expect."

Once he'd turned off the stove, Sara touched his elbow. "I know you were worried before, that you might've forgotten how to be a father. But it's sounding to me like it's all coming back to you quite nicely."

He smiled at the approval in her voice. "Fortunately, I have a professional around here to remind me exactly how such things are done."

"I'm just a social worker," she said, "definitely not anybody's parent. But I like to think I know a good one when I see one."

A lump formed in his throat. "I'm not so sure how good I am. They're still half terrified that I'll turn into the madman from their grandparents' stories the first time they turn their backs on me. To tell you the truth, it scares me, too—not that I would ever hurt them. I would literally *die* before I'd do that."

"Then what?" she asked.

"That I might scare them with my grumpy tone or even forget myself and yell at them when I get frustrated." His own father, who had been a champion shouter, had often threatened to snap him and his brothers like matchsticks if they didn't quit their bickering. But Mac didn't like to think of his own kids hiding from him, trembling until the storm passed, the way the three of them once had.

"I'm sure you will slip up from time to time," Sara

told him. "That is, unless you're superhuman. Nobody's expecting you to be the perfect parent every minute, any more than they're going to be the perfect kids."

He slanted a look her way. "Wait a minute. Are you seriously telling me that my kids aren't perfect?"

"I think you know that I adore your children, absolutely," she said, "but honestly, they *can* be perfectly aggravating at times."

Catching the twinkle in her eyes, he said, "Well, in that case, I can stop wondering."

"Wondering about what?" she asked.

"If they returned the *right* set of twins from Buenos Aires." A grin spread over his face. "Because now I know for certain they're definitely my children. There's never been a Hale-Walker born who couldn't test the patience of a saint."

The children ate with gusto, especially enjoying their sandwiches. As they were finishing up their soup, Sara said to them in Spanish, "Your father wanted us to all talk for a few minutes, about what happened last night... and our conversation in the car."

At the mention of that conversation, both children grew instantly alert, stiffening in their seats. Cristo's face reddened, and Sara's heart constricted as he reached for his sister's hand and squeezed it, as if to reassure her— or himself.

As hard as it was to see them so anxious, she knew Mac had been right. They had to learn that difficult conversations needn't be an occasion for terror. Forcing herself to do her job, she translated what she'd said into English for him.

He nodded in appreciation and laid his napkin down beside his empty plate. "Sara says she's had a couple

of things go missing," he said, his gaze thoughtful as
he studied both children's faces. "I want you to tell me
truthfully everything you know about that—but before
you do, there are some things I need you to understand."

He paused, giving Sara an opportunity to convey his
words to the twins. Once she'd finished, he explained,
"When you were both very small, your mother and I
talked about the way we wanted to guide you as you
grew up when you chose the wrong path, as every child
does from time to time. We both agreed that if you mis-
behaved, there would be consequences, things like a loss
of privileges, but never hitting or destroying things. That
was especially important to your mother."

As Sara conveyed his words to the twins, he saw them
watching his face intently, as if they were surprised to
hear him speaking of the mother neither of them remembered, except from stories their grandparents had told
them. But Mac pulled out his wallet now and passed the
two of them a photo, worn at its edges as if it had been
much handled over the years.

Sara caught a glimpse of what appeared to have been
a candid shot of the young family, with the beautiful,
dark-haired woman who had been his wife laughing as
a younger-looking Mac bent to blow a stream of bubbles
from a wand toward the chubby-legged toddlers reaching for them, with an openmouthed puppy leaping by
their side.

"Roxy!" Silvia pointed out to her brother, causing the
old dog to rise from her spot on the rug nearby, tail wagging at the mention of her name.

"Nuestra mamá," Cristo said, his voice cracking as
he focused on their mother.

"I have and will always honor the promise I made
to her," Mac continued, "never to lay a hand on you in

anger, but I *do* expect you both to live up to the Walker name, to be honest and admit your mistakes, even when it's very hard."

As Sara translated, Cristo pushed back his chair, springing to his feet with an intense expression. Shaking visibly, his face darkened.

Sara caught her breath, fully expecting an explosion of emotion to erupt at any moment, and Silvia whispered, *"No, Cristo. Por favor, no—"*

But instead of shouting, the boy turned and bolted for his bedroom. "Cristo!" Mac called. "Please come back here."

As the door slammed behind him, Silvia rose, clearly feeling compelled to follow.

But her father said, "Silvia, please," his eyes imploring as he gestured toward her chair.

Eyes welling, the girl sat, her hands clenched and lips trembling as she visibly battled her emotions.

"Cristo will be all right," Sara told her. "And so will you. We understand it's been difficult, coming to a new place, learning to know and trust your *papá* all over again. But you loved and trusted him once. Can't you see it in the picture?"

As Silvia's gaze went to the photo, still lying on the table, Roxy came up beside her and nudged her hand with her nose. Relaxing a fist, she stroked the dog's head and looked at Sara. *"Lo siento,"* she said in a soft voice.

"What are you sorry for?" Sara asked, while Mac looked on, probably only catching a few words here and there.

"Your— Your present. The candy," Silvia said, head hanging.

"Did you take it, or did Cristo?"

Cheeks coloring, Silvia looked up sharply. "It wasn't

fair, not letting us have those things your friends brought us! It was like you didn't trust us when we hadn't done anything wrong!"

Sara thought for a moment before turning toward Mac and telling him in English, "She's apologizing for the candy, though she isn't saying which one of them took it."

Nodding, he rose from his seat. "Let me go and see if I can talk to Cristo—not that it'll be much of a conversation but—"

"The effort is what matters," she said, nodding in agreement. "Here's hoping he'll see that."

As Mac headed for the children's bedroom door, she once more switched to Spanish, telling Silvia, "I understand why you two were upset. I hope you know that if my friends had followed the rules set up for your safety, I would have been glad for you to have those gifts. Because you and Cristo are good children, and you've had a difficult time lately. You deserve something nice."

"So...so did you," Silvia said. "But we were too mad, so we— Cristo stomped on your box and I threw it in the pond. I'm sorry." Tears streamed freely down her face now.

"I see," Sara said. "And my e-reader?"

Mac knocked at Cristo's door, calling his name softly.

Silvia shook her head. "I promise you, I have not seen it. I would not take anything valuable like that."

Sara thought about the e-reader's limited ability to pair with her cell phone, allowing her to download another book from an online store. "Not even if you thought you might be able to use it to contact your grandmother?"

Sara had never thought of it before this moment, but the idea occurred to her—on a blazing streak of raw fear—that it was at least theoretically possible that the device might be used in some manner to send an online message. It had never occurred to her to attempt such a thing before, since her phone and laptop were both better suited for that purpose, but what if the children were both desperate and tech savvy enough to figure such a thing out?

At the bedroom door, Mac knocked again, repeating Cristo's name with greater urgency.

"I told you, I never saw it," Silvia said in answer to her question.

"What about your brother? Does Cristo have my e-reader? Has he been using it to talk to—"

Sara cut herself off, distracted when Mac rattled the doorknob.

"It's locked," he said, turning to look her way. "Can you ask him to at least let us know he's all right in there? I think he'd be more inclined to answer you, and I need to know he's safe."

Dread squeezing her lungs, Sara rose and joined him, calling through the door in Spanish, "Cristo, are you all right in there?"

Then she held her breath, fully expecting him to angrily shout at both of them to go away and leave him alone—since he had clearly been upset and was too proud to want them to hear him crying.

When there was no answer, Silvia, too, came from the table, looking up at Sara as if for permission before saying, "Cristo, let me in, please. Only me, I promise."

Sara nodded her approval, thinking that perhaps right now what the twins really needed was some time to decompress together. But Cristo didn't respond to her, either, and Mac shook his head, his expression grim.

"It's way too quiet in there," he said. "You know, the last thing I want to do is scare him, but..."

When he looked down at the doorknob, she realized his intention.

Deeply worried about Cristo, she told Mac, "Do whatever you need to."

Silvia moved back as Sara took her by the arm. The girl squeaked in fear as Mac smacked his shoulder and upper arm against the door above the knob.

"Todo saldrá bien," Sara said, praying she was speaking the truth and everything was going to be all right.

But when the door swung open, Mac cursed as he charged inside the empty room.

A moment later, Sara's gaze landed on the open window—the same one that Cristo had evidently climbed out of before running away.

Chapter 8

"I don't see any sign of him. Do you?" Sara's face had gone dead pale and her eyes huge with alarm as she stood on the porch with a pair of binoculars Mac had brought from his truck. She'd already called for Cristo several times, her voice echoing across the clearing.

After having retreated to the bathroom for a few minutes, Silvia returned to stand beside her, looking especially forlorn as she clutched a fluffy, buff-colored teddy bear to her chest as if she were a much younger child.

On the grass below, with Roxy at his heels, Mac shook his head. "You stay there and keep watch." It wouldn't do Sara any good jostling her arm, for one thing, and she'd have a better vantage from her more elevated perch. Besides, he wanted her where she could keep an eye on Silvia so his daughter wouldn't attempt to slip away, too, to join her brother. "I don't see anything yet, either, but I'm going to check all the way around the house, and then down by the pond, to look for any footprints."

"Check there first." Sara was trembling, her eyes expressing the fear she wouldn't voice, the one he shared, as well, since she had translated for him the conversation she had had with Silvia. *Could Cristo have gone into the pond to try to retrieve the ruined box of candy?*

As he hurried for the water, he heard Sara say, as if to herself, "Where on earth did *that* come from?" before asking Silvia something in Spanish. But he put it out of his mind as he studied the grass along the pond's bank between the cabin and the muddy water.

His heart hammered when he saw that some of the stalks were flattened, but he couldn't tell how recently. But he breathed more easily, seeing that the only fresh tracks around belonged to feral hogs, deer and possibly raccoons, and Roxy's half-hearted sniffs told him the activity wasn't recent and hadn't included Cristo. After jogging most of the way around the pond's edge, he satisfied himself that wherever his son had run off to, it hadn't been the water—that he hadn't slipped underneath it as Mac had feared.

Next, Mac made his way back to the house, circling all the way around it before he stopped to talk to Sara, who had the binoculars pointed up the hillside. "Anything?"

"I thought I might've seen some movement in the trees about fifty yards up the slope." She shook her head. "But it could've been an animal…or maybe wishful thinking. I don't see how Cristo could've gotten way up there already."

He stopped walking the porch perimeter to look up at her. "Which direction are you talking?"

She pointed toward the rocky outcrop on the mountain known locally as the Colt's Ear for its teardrop shape. "Below where that rock is jutting upward. But maybe—maybe you shouldn't go up that way alone."

"It'll be fine. If it's Cristo, I won't scare him."

She shook her head, her forehead creasing. "Right this minute, I'm not worried about him so much as I am you."

"What are you talking about, Sara? I've been running around these hills since I was a kid. It's Cristo who could be hurt or—"

"Hold on just a second," she said as she made her way down the step to join him. Reaching out to touch his arm, she lowered her voice. "I'm scared, Mac—terrified the children might've been in contact with somebody. You see, I've just realized that the e-reader that's gone missing had a live link to my cell phone, so I could download books. But that might've allowed anyone who had it to get online if they were in range."

"You don't think the twins somehow figured out how to reach their grandmother?" He looked up on the porch toward Silvia, who was sitting in one of the rocking chairs, cradling the teddy bear as if it were a baby as she stared into its stuffed face.

"She *didn't* have that bear before," Sara whispered. "I *know* she didn't because I personally packed her bag…"

The hair on the back of his neck rose as he watched his daughter rock the plush toy. "Could she have found it here somewhere? I know there were a few toys around the cabin, like that soccer ball."

"That's what she's claiming—that she came across it way back in the bedroom closet. But just look at her with it, Mac," Sara whispered. "I don't—"

"If she was homeschooled with her brother, they've probably only rarely been separated in the past," he suggested. "She may just be afraid now, maybe even in shock, imagining he's abandoned her. So let me go and find him, and everything will be all right."

"I think you should call your brother," Sara urged him. "The sheriff, I mean. Get Hayden out here right now."

Mac's gut clenched at the thought of what she was suggesting. What if she was wrong about the toy, the e-reader—this whole crazy notion that someone other than themselves might be up on this quiet hillside? Would his brother think he was incapable of handling a simple family matter without law enforcement backup?

"There's no point in bothering the sheriff right now," he said. "Not when Cristo's more than likely hiding somewhere nearby, sulking."

"I didn't put this together before," Sara said, her voice sounding more strained by the second, "but the governor had an aide spearheading this whole operation, a man named Paul Barkley who recruited me to go to Buenos Aires."

"Paul Barkley, sure. He's been my point of contact with the state for the past few years," Mac said. "I've reached out to him at least half a dozen times trying to get various Argentinian officials to act on my behalf. I had no idea, though, that he'd been working so hard behind the scenes."

"The children never would've made it home without his work," she insisted. "But did you hear that within days of them being removed from the compound, he was struck and gravely injured in an unwitnessed hit and run while bicycling outside of Austin?"

Alarm blazed through him. "What? I had no idea! Is he—"

"I should have realized you would know him. I'm sorry to have to tell you he was killed, Mac—just as you could be if you happen to walk alone into an ambush."

His blood rushed in his ears, his gut turning to ice water. "Are you telling me you think my son's up there, all alone, with some kind of hired *assassins*?" If they'd be brazen enough to take revenge on a state official, who knew what else they might have been paid to do?

From the trees beyond the pond's edge, what sounded like a crow cawed, its harsh voice echoing beneath a nearly cloudless sky.

"I know it sounds far-fetched," she said, "like something from a movie. And for all I know, I'm way off base, imagining Paul's hit and run was more than an accident, but just imagine for a moment it's related—and the children's grandmother's somehow behind—"

From somewhere nearby—around the corner of the house, Mac thought—he heard the creak of wood. Or had that been a child's muffled cry of pain? Whatever it was, Roxy raised her head and rushed off after it with a low growl—a noise that rose to loud, determined barking as Mac made the corner.

There he found the Lab frantically attempting to dig her way through a loose sheet of wooden skirting at the bottom of the wraparound porch. As he stood watching, a small hand emerged, attempting to hold the skirting down.

A moment later, Cristo whispered harshly, "No, Roxy! *¡Cállate!*" A shushing clearly meant to get her to stop her noise and go away.

But the big dog wasn't giving up. And Mac, for his part, was equally determined, moving Roxy aside and crouching to rip away the loose skirting to expose Cristo, who was kneeling, filthy and tearstained, in the gritty soil.

Instead of grabbing the boy and physically dragging him out to hug him as he so desperately wanted to, Mac, seeing the way his son was cringing as if expecting to be hit, merely offered him a hand up to help him out.

Cristo studied him, clearly weighing his decision before raising his forearm—not to take Mac's hand as he'd hoped, but to show him a large, swollen and reddened bump on the skin. *"Duele mucho,"* he said, a tear breaking loose from his eye. *"Me mordió."*

"Did something *bite* you under there, Cristo? What was it?" he asked before turning to shout, "Sara, I need you, quick! But grab a flashlight first, please!"

Silvia was first to reach them, throwing her arms around her brother and hugging him hard as she scolded him in rapid-fire Spanish. Or at least it sounded to Mac as if she were lighting into him for scaring her—or perhaps for leaving her alone with him. Whatever she was saying, she was clearly so upset that Cristo couldn't get a word in edgewise, but Mac saw that the poor kid was pale and sweating.

As soon as he spotted Sara coming with the flashlight, however, Cristo spoke over his sister, showing her his swollen forearm and telling her about it.

While Sara was distracted by their conversation, Mac took the flashlight from her. Tucking it beneath his arm for a moment, he first pulled out and opened the pocket-knife he always carried, hoping the four-inch blade would be enough to deal with whatever it was under there that had bitten his son.

"Did he see what got him?" he asked Sara as he switched on the bright beam. "It wasn't a snake, was it?" He hadn't gotten a close enough look at the swollen spot to make out any fang wounds but prayed that wouldn't be what they were dealing with here.

"He says it was too dark. He felt something move against his arm, and then it started stinging."

Mac pulled away more of the skirting from beneath the porch. "I'd put my money on a scorpion," he said. "If there's anything those damned things love, it's holing up in dry, dark shelters— Hold that thought."

Bending lower, he scrambled carefully forward and stabbed his knife down into the ground, impaling what he believed to be the writhing, wriggling culprit on the end of his blade.

"Got it!" he called out to Sara and the children before emerging half a minute later with the now dead many-legged creature—all seven inches of it—skewered on his knife to show them.

"What on earth is *that*? *Eew!*" Sara shrank back, looking horrified while Silvia hid behind her. Cristo merely gaped in disbelief at its size.

"Redheaded centipede," Mac told them, "sometimes known as the giant centipede. This isn't the biggest one I've ever seen, but he's definitely on up there."

"Are they…are they poisonous?" Sara asked him. "Should we get Cristo to the hospital?"

"For most people, they're no worse than, say, a wasp sting. They definitely hurt like the devil at first—I was stung myself as a kid once—and might swell and itch some, but unless he happens to be allergic, they're usually no big deal. Can you tell him all that, for me?"

She nodded, and he could see the effort she made to pull herself together, taking a deep breath before she explained what he had said to Cristo.

Once he had responded, she switched to English, telling Mac, "He wants to know if you cried when it happened."

Mac looked at him and nodded. "I'm not ashamed to say I did a bit. Those damn things *hurt*. You want to chop his head off? Make sure he never pinches anybody else again?"

Sara raised an eyebrow, though Mac wasn't sure whether she was disapproving of his language or the macho remedy he had suggested as he carefully removed the blade from the centipede's now still body and gestured to the spot where Cristo ought to make the cut. But after listening to Sara's translation and watching Mac carefully for guidance, Cristo smiled a little as he figuratively slew his dragon—especially when Mac nodded in approval, clapping an approving hand on his son's shoulder as he told the boy in Spanish, "Well done."

Since he could see Sara fading by the minute—undoubtedly drained by the emotional turmoil as well as the aftermath of her injury—Mac insisted she rest on the sofa and elevate her arm once they went inside.

"But I need to make sure that wound's clean and put some antiseptic spray on it," she tried to argue.

"Just tell me where to find the spray, and I'll help him," Mac said. "It won't do you any good if you end up getting that cast wet."

Chastened by his ordeal, Cristo was more cooperative than Mac might have expected. After dressing the wound and giving him an ibuprofen to help with the discomfort, Mac decided that the localizing swelling and redness weren't serious enough to indicate a serious allergic issue. But the emotional upheaval had clearly taken its toll to the point where, as soon as he'd cleaned up, he trudged into his room, where he lay down with an ice pack Mac had made him to hold against his forearm.

When Silvia came in to see him, the bear clutched tightly to her chest, Mac, sensing her distress over what had taken place, lifted his hand toward her, offering her the solace that he ached to give. Dark eyes going liquid, she took his breath away, ducking beneath his arm and giving him a swift, hard—and all too fleeting—hug. The first he'd had from either of his children in more than eight years, it sent a jolt of sweet-hot pain lancing through him.

"Los amo tanto a los dos," he told them, a phrase he had looked up and practiced many times. *I love you both so much.* And then he smiled as he left the two of them, not wishing to spoil this moment—or tempt fate—by awaiting a reply.

As he softly closed the door behind them, Mac could hear them speaking in low voices.

"Is everyone all right?" asked Sara, opening her eyes to yawn when he walked back into the room where she was.

"I think maybe they will be," he said. "Cristo let me help him, and Silvia—she hugged me. Just for a second, mind you, but it…it gave me the chance to tell them how I feel."

"Oh, Mac. I'm so glad for you. For all of you."

"Thanks. It's been quite a day." Gesturing toward the children's room, he said, "I can't help wondering what they're discussing in there."

Sara sat up a little straighter. "From what I've gathered, Silvia's pretty angry with him right now, but that's only because he scared her so badly when he took off like that."

Mac thought about how furious his mother used to get at him and his brothers when one or the other of them frightened her with one of what she'd referred to as *their fool stunts*, but all of them had understood it was because she couldn't bear the thought of losing any of them. "They really do love each other, don't they?"

"They've had to depend on each other a lot, I think," Sara said, "but they don't always see eye to eye."

"In what way?"

"Silvia's naturally more adaptable, more prone to accepting new realities, including the fact that you're not what they've been told. She's an openhearted and affectionate child by nature. But Cristo keeps reminding her of what he sees as their true loyalties and trying to hold both of them back."

"I see it, too," he agreed. "Kid inherited my stubborn streak for sure, I see. But what can I do to change it?"

"Keep working to win him over, and you'll have both their hearts. But it's not going to be easy."

"I'm doing everything I can think of," he said.

"That was a good move, trusting him with the knife out there. I wondered for a moment," she admitted.

He chuckled. "You know, I wasn't entirely sure he wasn't going to stick *me* with it when I passed it to him."

"You really do have good instincts." Smiling, she reached out to lay her uninjured hand atop his, gently caressing his fingers lightly with hers. "Better than mine, with all that crazy talk about assassins earlier. Please forget I said any of that. I'm sure Paul Barkley's death, tragic as it was, had nothing to do with your kids or this situation."

"Are you?" he asked, wondering if she was even aware what she was doing with her hand now, or if, in her groggy state, she'd unconsciously let her guard down with him. Either way, he sure as hell wasn't complaining.

She nodded. "When you first went in to help Cristo, I got to thinking about it and looked up the most recent article from the newspaper in Austin. It mentioned that a number of people had died along that particular roadside where he was struck over the past decade. Area residents are petitioning to have something done about the narrow shoulders and the blind curves."

"So now you're convinced it was an accident?"

"It had to've been," she said. "Buenos Aires is half a

world away, and the children's grandmother is by all accounts a frail and bereaved woman. She's probably still reeling from what's happened."

Frowning, Mac removed his hand. "You sound almost as if you feel sorry for her."

"Don't get me wrong. I absolutely *hate* what she and her husband did to you," Sara said. "But according to the children, she was always very caring with them."

"You know, back when I still ran the ranch, we used to have this old boss Angus cow who'd steal calves from the first-time heifers when they had theirs. She'd take every one of 'em if she had her way."

Sara smiled, clearly picturing some sort of fairy-tale-like version of his story where the Pied Piper pranced as she led her many fat and happy calves around the pasture.

"Trouble was, she left all those poor young mamas bawling for their babies with their udders swollen, and of course, Old Dry Mama couldn't begin to feed all those hungry calves. But she'd charge any man who showed up to sort things all out, would gladly do him serious harm if he was foolish enough to turn his back at the wrong moment."

"So what'd you do about it?"

"Let the girls figure out a new boss cow to fill the vacancy that suddenly came up in the herd."

"You mean you— *Oh*," she said as one of the harsher realities of cattle ranching sank in.

Squeezing her hand, he said, "I'm going to step out on the porch and make a call. But before I do, is there anything I can get you?"

"Maybe just that blanket throw, off the foot of my bed," she said sleepily. "I'm so comfortable right here, I hate to move a muscle…"

He smiled, rising. "Don't worry. I've got you."

When he returned, her eyes had closed again already, and her breathing had smoothed and lengthened. He spread the cover over her, leaning close to tuck it carefully behind her shoulder. And pausing, before he could stop himself, to gently touch his lips to her temple before slipping away.

Outside on the porch, he stood for a few moments, wondering whether he'd done what he had only because he didn't yet dare to kiss his children. But in his heart, he knew this was nothing like that, just as he knew he was playing with fire by giving in to his need for her approval, his desire for her touch...

You have no business wanting any woman right now, he reminded himself sharply, *and this one least of all.* Instead, he needed to stay focused on his duties as a father, the first of which was making certain his kids were well and truly safe.

With that in mind, he opened his cell phone and then hit connect on the contact he had pulled up before he could change his mind about the call.

Though he more than half expected Hayden to let it go to voice mail, as was his brother's custom, on this occasion he answered right away, saying, "What's going on, Mac?"

"I'm wondering, you got a couple of minutes? I could really use your professional opinion."

"Unless I lose the signal, I do. I'm driving out to interview the landowner who reported the human remains discovered just the other—"

"Pete Greenville's body?" Mac asked bluntly. "I heard about the ID found with it."

"We're still waiting on an official confirmation on that from the ME, but, off the record, I can tell you, that's the assumption we're working with."

"Sorry to hear it, for the family's sake," Mac said, thinking of Pete's aging parents, who had put up a reward for information on his whereabouts and organized multiple searches, aided by Pete's sisters and their families. But part of him wondered whether this discovery was making life easier or harder for Amanda Greenville as the locals commented on the authenticity of her grief. Too little, Mac knew, and they'd condemn her as heartless—or possibly involved in her late husband's demise. Too much, and they'd just as surely suspect she was making a show of mourning a man that any fool could see she was better off without. "Any idea what happened to him?"

"Tell me, Mac, what is it I can do for you?" Hayden asked, his shift in tone indicating that he had said as much about the ongoing investigation as he was going to.

"I'd like to run a situation by you related to the kids. It absolutely may be nothing, but I'd feel better if I got your take on it before I chalked it up to paranoia and blew off the whole idea."

"Hold on a second. I'm pulling over so I don't have my signal drop out on you heading over this next hill."

"Thanks, Hayden. I'll keep it quick as I can." Mac went on to recount how Cristo had briefly disappeared this afternoon, along with Sara's fears that the children may have been in contact with their grandmother via an e-reader that had gone missing. "She thought for a minute she might've seen someone moving in the brush up near the Colt's Ear, too, but she said herself that it could've been an animal."

"The Colt's Ear? Don't you remember the year we tried to get up there by ATV— Oh, I guess that was Ryan and me. Anyway, it's steep as hell, and the rock's so loose, you'd have to be half mountain goat not to send it tumbling."

"Well, it definitely wasn't Cristo," Mac said. "We found him not long after that, holed up underneath the porch. But there was something else, too." He mentioned Silvia's teddy bear, as well, her seeming fixation with a toy he might expect a far younger child to play with—along with the excuse that she had recently come across it inside the cabin.

"So what do you think?" he continued. "Given the history, and the fact that those two are always whispering to each other in Spanish, do I have any real reason to be worried?"

"I think it's only natural," Hayden said carefully, "that anybody who's been put through the absolute hell you have wouldn't want to let those kids out of his sight even for a single second. But this scenario with the reader device, and the whole idea of two scared, sad, eleven-year-olds pulling off secret international communication and being able to keep quiet about it seems mighty far-fetched. Isn't it easier to figure that your little girl might've come across something soft and fluffy at a rough moment and then latched onto it for dear life?"

"When you put it that way, sure," Mac agreed, realizing the idea truly had been far-fetched. "I probably should've bought 'em both something like that straight off, but I didn't really know what kids their age would like—or whether they would toss whatever I gave them in the trash can just to spite me."

"I'm sure it's a tough situation," Hayden said. "And you wouldn't want 'em thinking you're trying to buy them off with cheap bribes, either, to change their minds about you."

Mac laughed weakly. "Only because I can't afford the quality, high-dollar ones right now. Otherwise, they would've totally gotten a matched set of pinto ponies and whatever else I could've come up with that I thought would've helped."

Hayden made a huffing sound that probably had less to do with humor than impatience to get back to his work. "Well, listen, man. I'm gonna have to get on down the road now. Was that all that you needed?"

Mac thought about mentioning Paul Barkley, but he couldn't bring himself to bring up a hit-and-run accident that had taken place hours away in Travis County after his ridiculous suspicions about a stupid fuzzy stuffed bear. So instead he let it drop, thanking his brother for setting his mind at ease and promising the two of them would catch up soon...

Even though both men knew it would never happen.

By the following morning, Cristo's arm was looking and feeling considerably better. Sara, too, found herself much improved, following a full night's sleep and the breakfast tacos Mac had brought back for each of them for breakfast after his early grocery store run.

So it was that when Mac received a call from a contractor he'd hired to remove the remaining debris from the river resort, she raised her coffee cup and said cheerfully, "Go ahead and do your thing, please. We're good here now—and I know you need to get everything cleaned up so you're one step closer to getting the place back up and running."

"You're sure you can get along without me?" Mac asked as he stood from the table where the two of them had lingered talking long after the children had finished eating and asked to go kick around the soccer ball outside with Roxy. "I don't want you straining yourself if you're still hurting."

"Really, I'll be fine," she assured him. "My arm's feeling a lot better, and Silvia and Cristo have both promised they'll be extra attentive to their lessons and help out around here, too, even with the sweeping and the dishes."

She smiled, realizing that, whether or not the twins would admit it, they had been influenced by their father's good example. Initially, she'd noticed them watching with surprise, if not suspicion, when he'd taken on tasks their traditionally minded grandfather never would have deigned perform, taking care of their meals and clean up without comment or complaint. Soon, however, they'd begun pitching in, clearly wanting his approval—at least on an unconscious level.

Mac nodded. "Glad to hear it, but I'll check to see they're following through as promised."

"I'll let them know," she said, standing from the table, "but I can't imagine it's going to be a problem. Thanks for staying over again last night—I hope the sofa hasn't been too uncomfortable to sleep on."

A teasing smile lit up his face. "You should know it's not, considering all the hours you put on it napping yesterday afternoon yourself."

She snorted. "I was pretty out of it from those meds they gave me, wasn't I? Too tired to move a muscle…"

She went still as it came back to her how safe she'd felt, lying there as he'd carefully placed the blanket over her and how he'd—

"What is it?" he asked. "You have the oddest look on your face."

"Yesterday, when you covered me up on the sofa…" She felt the warmth of his lips skimming the warm flesh of her temple, a memory that sent up a flutter beneath her stomach even now. Or had she imagined—or even daydreamed—it?

"When I covered you up, *what*?" he asked, blue-gray eyes searching hers.

That was when she knew. She *hadn't* imagined it at all. "You *kissed* me, didn't you?" The question came out half a whisper.

"I'm not sure I could even call that a proper kiss," he said, looking both troubled and guilty nonetheless. "But it still didn't give me any right. It was just...you looked so worn out, and you'd been through so much, with your broken wrist and Cristo disappearing, and I felt responsible, with you here, caring for my children..."

"And you thought *kissing me* would somehow make it better?"

"It was just an innocent kiss, Sara, as if I were tucking one of the twins into bed at night."

Crossing her uninjured arm over the right one, she channeled one of her late grandmother's no-nonsense looks. "So now you're trying to tell me you think of me as another one of your kids."

He sighed, scrubbing a hand over his unshaven jaw. "I *know* you're not a child. Far from it. Maybe I thought it'd make *me* feel better somehow, but of course, I had no right to—to be so familiar with you. And if you can see your way clear to leaving it out of that report of yours, I promise you, I won't touch you again."

Thinking of how kind he'd been with her, how gentle and how caring, and what he'd suffered all these years himself, she answered before she could stop herself, heart pounding with her daring. "Maybe you shouldn't make that promise, Mac. Maybe you should only give me your word that next time... I'll be fully awake to give permission."

His brows rose, one corner of his mouth curving upward. "So will you? Give permission, that is?"

She shook her head. "Probably not. I don't know. I'm sure it's unprofessional to even think about it."

He took a step nearer, taking her good hand in his and lifting it to his mouth. "I have a solution, then. Don't think about it, lovely Sara."

"What if you're just trying to—" She closed her eyes as he pressed a kiss to her hand, the whiskers scraping the tender flesh close to the knuckles just inside her palm. There may have even been a flick of tongue, weakening her knees. "To seduce me to get a positive report to the judge."

"You think I would do that?"

"For your children's sake?" she scoffed. "Seriously, Mac, I think you'd try to seduce a sixty-year-old with a face like a mule and the disposition to go with it if you figured it would make a difference."

He laughed at that. "Guess I won the lottery, then, ending up with someone who's as young and gorgeous as she is kind and caring. So what about it, Sara?"

Tingling all over by then, she glanced at the door to the porch and then nodded quickly, before she could change her mind.

He wasted no time, lowering his head and angling in to press his lips to hers in a kiss that tasted of raw need and longing—and a bond that blazed to life between them. Feeling the heat of the flame that she sensed could only grow if fed on trust, she leaned into his strong arms, allowing her lips to part as their connection deepened. As it blazed through her blood, the attraction she felt burned away all rational thought of her role here and her duty to stay neutral—or even of the children playing just outside…

At least until she heard the dog's bark out on the porch and the children's footsteps on the wooden boards.

When Mac abruptly pulled back, the look of guilt and panic on his face was enough to break the spell—though the footsteps quickly receded as the twins and Roxy both ran back into the yard.

"You're right to look horrified," she said, her heart still pounding. "We both should be. If they had seen that—they're already dealing with so much right now, and I wouldn't want them upset or confused about the situation."

"It doesn't change the way I'm beginning to feel about you, Sara—or the fact that you're the first woman since..." He sighed. "The first woman in forever who's been able to make me feel anything at all. But that doesn't change the situation, does it?"

She shook her head. "They need to be able to trust me, as an unbiased advocate. And I can't do that if we're... personally involved."

"And I have to put their needs first, too, so I believe that settles it. But I *am* sorry to have put us both in such an awkward position."

"Let's just— Let's try pretending that this whole conversation never happened, shall we?" she suggested, though she knew she never would forget it. "Now don't you have somewhere to be?"

He nodded. "I do. And I'll probably be working pretty long hours for the next couple of days, while I have the crew around to help out, so I'm afraid I won't be stopping by, unless there's something pressing you need."

"I'm sure we'll be fine," she said, feeling both bereft and relieved at this opportunity to let things cool down between them.

"I'll call and check in when I can, though, and please don't hesitate to let me know if there's anything at all you need."

"Thanks. I'll be sure to do that." And then she watched as what she didn't need but definitely wanted in the worst way headed out the door.

Chapter 9

"When do you think our *papá* might be back again?" asked Silvia about thirty minutes into their English lesson the following morning.

"I wish he had left Roxy here," Cristo complained. "She would have been happier staying with us."

"You heard what he told you," Sara reminded them. "She needs the medicine he has for her at home and a good rest so she'll be ready the next time you see each other." She suspected, too, that Mac was using the beloved Lab as insurance that the twins would also look forward to his own return. Looking at them expectantly, she said, "Now, when you see him, tell me how you'll greet him if he comes for breakfast tomorrow, *Cody* and *Emma*."

The children grinned, clearly delighted that she was using the names they'd chosen yesterday, when she'd gotten the idea of letting them pick their own role-playing names as they'd acted out scenarios forcing them to practice English greetings. To Sara's surprise, the element of fantasy seemed to distance them from their anxiety over the lessons, and this morning they readily—and correctly—responded to each one of her questions.

"*¡Padrísimo!* That's great!" She grinned, so happy, she stood from the table and did a little dance that got them laughing.

"Ouch," she said, wincing as her forearm reminded her she wasn't quite ready to go wild. Returning to her seat, she instead turned her optimism to encouraging the twins to practice another scenario in English. At first, they stumbled through asking after each other's health, but with a little repetition, they soon had this down perfectly, as well.

"Well done. That's it for today," she said at length, dismissing them in Spanish while things were still going well. She wanted to leave them with a taste of success and the hope that when they did see their father, they would prove willing to show off a little of their newfound knowledge.

That evening, after the children went to bed, she was putting away some laundry left stacked on her dresser when her cell rang. Seeing Mac's name pop up, she grabbed it and connected.

"I'm surprised to hear from you at this hour," she said.

"I hope I'm not too late," he said. "I meant to call earlier, but by the time I got cleaned up and grabbed a couple of sandwiches—"

"You're fine," she said. "I was just picking up a bit around here before bedtime."

"Arm still feeling all right?" he asked, the concern in his voice a reminder of what had happened between them in the kitchen.

"I'm doing fine," she assured him, craning her neck to peek behind the dresser as she spoke. Because somewhere in that stack, surely she should've had several more pairs of panties.

"Good to hear. And what about Cristo and Silvia? No more big flare-ups, I hope?"

"They had something of a breakthrough with their lessons. I was very pleased," she told him. "But what about you? Is everything on track with the cleanup?"

"It's coming along well. Made quite a dent in it already. We're supposed to get a little rain this evening, but by tomorrow, we expect to get the last of the debris hauled off."

"That must be a relief." She pulled open a drawer to check for the missing items and frowned when she didn't see them. Could static cling have left them stuck to one of her T-shirts or some other garment? Putting aside the search for now, she decided to take a harder look once she'd finished her phone conversation.

"It feels great, seeing the place look less like a war zone and more like the resort that's been written up as one of the most scenic getaways on the Frio River," he said. "There's still about a month's worth of work to be done on the guest cabins—"

"But not inside your home, right?"

"No, my house is on higher ground. And thanks to my brothers' help, it's all ready and waiting for the kids to move in. I think it's high time they come see it—so they can start picturing themselves in those new rooms of theirs, in the home I mean for them to grow up in."

"That's a very big step," she said. "I'm not sure I would mention anything about *forever* to them quite yet."

"Well, how about we start with lunch then?" he suggested. "I'll pick you all up at noon the day after tomorrow, at the cabin, and bring you over to show you around and grill some burgers? From there on in, we'll play things by ear and follow their lead to see how the day goes."

"That sounds like a great plan," she said.

"Speaking of plans," Mac added. "I know I agreed, for the children's sakes, that any feelings I might have for you were—"

Her heartbeat sped up. "You're not the only one with feelings," she said. "I like you, too, Mac, a great deal. But my first duty's to your children."

"Just as mine is," he agreed, "but that doesn't mean that once all of this is over, we couldn't take some time to get to know each other better, to see if maybe…"

"I don't know about that. It'll be hard, once I go back to my work in Austin, my life and my apartment there."

"Over the next few weeks, I want you to ask yourself a question. What if you didn't have to go back? What if…if you could find a way to make a life out here…with us?"

Hearing him ask the question, she blinked hard as it hit her what he truly saw in her. Not so much a woman or even an individual at all, but a desperate lifeline—a means of communication as well as a stand-in mother to the children he was going to have to learn to parent on his own.

Her heart shuddered with the blow, for she'd been telling the truth. She really was drawn to him—deeply. But she hadn't signed up and never would to be these children's— or anybody's—mother, because that was the one choice she could never again make.

All right, she could still hear her mother saying, her voice brittle as Sara had cuddled the infant her sister had abandoned, already head over heels in love with the tiny girl's beautiful brown eyes and delicate, dark curls, the soft skin that smelled of soap and baby powder. *We'll try it your way—at least for now, but you need to understand, this will mean your time as a normal fifteen-year-old is over. I won't completely give up my life for another of your sister's mistakes.*

"Listen to me, Mac," she said now, fear making her voice brittle, "and listen well because I'm only going to tell you this once. You might *think* you're being honest right now. For all I know, you've even convinced yourself that you're suddenly, conveniently, falling for a sympathetic ear, handy translator and free babysitting service all in one—"

"You're selling yourself short, Sara, if that's how you think I see you."

"Please, let me finish. You've been alone for eight years, desperately hoping, praying, fighting for a second chance to be a father to these children. But now that they've returned, there are unexpected complications. Complications you'd make any sacrifice to overcome."

He was quiet for several moments, apparently absorbing what she'd said before asking, "Is that how you view yourself? Some kind of *sacrifice* for a man?"

"Absolutely not," she insisted. "But the fact is, you don't know the real me well enough—you couldn't possibly, in such a short time—to see me as anything but as a means of making fatherhood a little easier for you. And I *can't* be that for you, not now and not ever."

Late the following morning, Sara was just finishing up a lesson with the children when she heard the crunch of tires on gravel. Predictably, Cristo—who always looked for an excuse to wriggle out of any assignment involving writing—sprang from his seat at the table to run to the window to check it out.

"It's that pretty lady with the long black hair," he told them, "the one who said she knew us back when we were babies."

Scarcely believing it, Sara rose and peeked outside, too. Sure enough, she recognized Amanda Greenville's white Ford Explorer pulling up beside her Civic. Moments later, the tall, slender woman left the SUV before moving to the tailgate.

"Now would be a great chance for you two to practice your English greetings with her," Sara told the children, while reminding herself to offer the real estate agent her condolences on her recent news about her missing husband as soon as possible.

But Silvia balked at Sara's request, her face reddening as she jerked her head from side to side and clutched the teddy bear on her lap—an item she seemed more deeply attached to than ever—more tightly.

Seeing his twin's attack of apparent shyness, Cristo said, "We'll stay inside and go over it together."

Exasperated with their sometimes maddening fits of stubbornness but deciding to choose her battles, Sara refrained from rolling her eyes at them. "All right then. You do that. And I'll expect each of you to finish writing that paragraph I asked for, too, before you do anything else. And no copying each other, either."

Heading outdoors, she met Amanda, who wore a sleeveless blouse over a flowy summer skirt with sandals and carried a large tote bag with its strap over one shoulder. The smile beneath her gray eyes was friendly, if a little worn, and her mascara provided a slightly smudged reminder of her personal situation. "I saw that I'd missed a call from you while I was out—and then I heard about your wrist, so I thought I'd personally stop by."

"You ran into Mac?" asked Sara, confused about how that might have come about.

She shook her head. "Mac? No. Donna Milburn, your CPS case manager, is a friend. She happened to mention it when she stopped over with her condolences after—"

"I heard about your…your husband," Sara blurted. "That has to have been a terrible shock. I'm sorry."

Pressing her lips together in an unreadable expression, Amanda nodded. "It's been— It's been so strange. His being missing—leaving me not knowing whether he'll come back angry or even if he'll come back at all—"

Sensing her distress, Sara said, "Your bag looks awfully heavy. Would you like to set it on the porch?"

"Actually, it's for you and the twins. People keep bringing food by my house. Casseroles and sandwiches, pies, even a whole ham," Amanda said, shaking her head. "I can't deal with all that, but I thought, since you'd been hurt, maybe I'd pack up several meals' worth and bring it by."

"That's so thoughtful. Thank you. We can use it," Sara told her. "Why don't you come up on the porch and sit a while? I'll take this inside and put it up. Then I'll bring you out some iced tea. It's awfully hot already, isn't it, and we'll visit for a bit."

"I—I shouldn't bother you," Amanda said.

Sara offered her a smile. "Are you kidding? I'm completely trapped here without entertainment since I can't drive for now, and you're adult company. I'd love to chat." Even more than that, she could see that the poor woman needed someone to talk to, someone who hadn't known her husband and wouldn't pass judgment on whatever emotions were right now threatening to overwhelm her.

"I'll take you up on the offer, but let me help you put

away the food. It'll go a lot more quickly if you're not struggling to do it all one-handed."

"Deal," said Sara, "if you can deal with two slightly grumpy children in the kitchen, where I left them to finish some practice writing in English."

"Really? How's that going?"

Sara managed a tight smile. "Are you looking for the *polite* answer or the unvarnished truth?"

Amanda's gray eyes sparkled. "I'm rather hoping that you and I can be 'unvarnished truth' friends, since I've grown pretty tired of people politely lying until they have a chance to start sticking in the knives behind my back."

Sara touched her arm. "I'm so sorry."

Amanda thanked her before sucking in a breath, as if she'd just remembered something. "I need to ask you. I brought along a little something for the twins. It's in the bag, too. Just a small toy set I ordered online, before everything else happened, since I got to thinking of them up here alone without other kids around. It's one of those plastic building kits children love snapping together. Would it be all right for them to have it?"

"I'm sure they'll be delighted," Sara said, beyond relieved it wasn't another electronic item she would be forced to refuse them. "That was so thoughtful of you. Thanks again!" She gave the taller woman a one-armed hug, which Amanda accepted somewhat stiffly.

They headed inside after that, where, to Sara's relief, the twins were reasonably well mannered, murmuring hellos and responding to Amanda's queries about how they were, both briefly and more or less correctly. When she presented them with the rectangular box, wrapped in brightly colored paper and tied beautifully with ribbon, instead of accepting, they looked nervously to Sara.

"It's all right. You can open it. And keep it, too, this time," she said in Spanish. "I promise."

The smiles spreading over their beautiful faces—faces that, for all her efforts to harden her heart, she was growing more attached to with each passing day—made her forget her earlier irritation with them. Her own smile broadened, watching their excitement as they noisily tore into what turned out to be a space-themed building kit, one that included male and female astronauts, a space shuttle with working cargo doors, and other tricks of the trade.

"¡Muchas gracias, señora!" Cristo told Amanda, beaming.

"Thank you very much," Silvia said in English. *"¡El espacio es nuestro favorito!"*

"She says they love space," Sara said. "How did you ever know?"

"Just a lucky guess. Whew," said Amanda, pretending to wipe her brow in relief.

But as Sara turned away to begin unloading the packed food from the tote bag, an instinctive tightening in her stomach had her wondering if her knowledge could have been more than coincidental…and if Amanda's visit here might have some darker purpose than a simple friendly gesture from a woman who seemed in desperate need of one herself.

Chapter 10

They had been loading wrecked material onto the dump truck for only about an hour after lunch when one of the younger guys—a skinny, tanned and blond-streaked white kid of maybe eighteen or nineteen who looked more like a lost surfer than a member of this hardworking, mostly Hispanic crew—approached Mac to ask if maybe he could use the bathroom in the house.

"I really hate to ask, man," he said, a hand over his flat stomach as he shifted uncomfortably from one foot to the other. "But that spicy burrito I had earlier was a huge mistake in this heat, and there are some things you just don't want to do behind the trees."

"Whoa, dude." Mac laughed, holding up his palms in protest. "That's more detail than I needed. You go ahead. There's a half bathroom just inside the back door. All I ask is that you treat it like your mom's place and not a dive bar men's room."

Flashing a set of straight, white teeth that looked like they should be starring in an ad for some dental practice, the kid said, "You'll never know I was there, I swear it."

But when Mac happened to think about it again twenty minutes later, he realized that the kid hadn't yet returned. Heading over to the supervisor, a heavyset bald man by the name of Gonzalez who was standing just outside the truck's cab doing something on his phone, he asked, "That young guy you've got working for you…how long's he been with the crew?"

"College kid, you mean? Name's Tommy. I just brought him on last week on the recommendation of another client. To tell you the truth, though, I haven't noticed that he's all that interested in actually *working*. Speaking of which, where the hell's he disappeared to now?" He looked around, as if trying to spot his newest hire.

"I gave him permission to use the bathroom inside. But that was a while back, so I'm heading in to check up on him."

"You catch him up to anything," Gonzalez said darkly, "you got my permission to break that *huevón* in half."

Mac wasn't familiar with the name but didn't waste time asking. Instead, he turned and jogged toward the highest of the bluffs overlooking the river, the one on which his two-story, cedar-and-native-stone home sat.

The moment he entered the back door, he could immediately see the half bathroom door standing open, the room dark and empty, and heard Roxy farther inside the house. As friendly as she normally was, her deep barks of alarm alerted him that there was something she perceived as wrong. Something like larceny, Mac figured, realizing the whole bathroom story must have been a ruse to cover a search for cash or easily pocketed valuables this Tommy could make off with. Possibly, College Kid had a drug habit, or maybe even a serious addiction, but Mac didn't really give a damn what his excuse was. He just wanted to drag his ass out before the kid could do any damage—or pry his way into the locked gun cabinet that contained a few weapons Mac had brought with him when he'd left the ranch.

The thought had him hesitating, wondering if risking interrupting the intruder was the best idea since he'd already been inside alone for more than twenty minutes. Unarmed himself, Mac didn't relish the idea of ending up shot with one of his own weapons.

But Roxy's barking, he soon realized, wasn't coming from the master bedroom downstairs, where the gun cabinet was tucked in the rear of his walk-in closet. Instead, he spotted the Lab at the bottom of the spiral staircase—which had a gate at its base to keep her from going upstairs and into the two recently repainted and refloored bedrooms. Mac had set up the twins' new furnishings inside, as well, before writing each of his children a simple but heartfelt personalized message of welcome on a notecard, which he'd left in a sealed envelope on the desk he'd bought each child.

It was at this desk in Silvia's room where he discovered the tall, blond Tommy standing. The younger man had torn open and discarded her notecard's envelope and was using his cell phone to, of all things, *photograph* the handwritten message. At the sight of the violation, in a space Mac had taken such pains to make special for his long missing daughter, Mac felt engulfed by a wave of red-hot fury—one that had him rushing up behind the intruder.

Distracted by the barking of the dog downstairs and focused on the note in his hand, the younger, more lightly built man never discerned the danger coming until Mac pounced on him and put him in a headlock, exerting pressure to cut off his air and drive him to his knees. His phone clattering to the floor, Tommy kicked and elbowed, flailing desperately as he fought to fill his lungs. But Mac was too angry to let up until the kid collapsed, going limp in his arms.

"Damn it. Go ahead and breathe now. Do it," Mac said, finally coming to his senses and lowering the teen to the floor. Kneeling, he shook Tommy's shoulders and slapped his reddened face—then breathed a prayer of gratitude to hear his sudden inhalation. Because as furious as Mac was, he damned well wanted answers, and he wouldn't get any of those from a dead body.

Nor would he get the chance to be a father to his children if he ended up locked in prison for choking this idiot to death with his bare hands.

By the time the kid came around several minutes later, Mac was sitting at Silvia's desk chair, scowling as he scrolled through the intruder's cell.

"Hey, that's mine," Tommy protested, his voice raspy as he attempted to get up, brown eyes filled with panic as he lunged for his phone.

"You can sit back down, or I can knock you down," Mac warned, pulling it out of reach. "I suggest that you choose wisely."

"Look, I'm sorry, man, for coming up here. I was just curious." Tommy sounded desperate—his gaze locked on the phone as if he were wondering just how much Mac had seen on it.

In truth, Mac hadn't gotten any farther than the photos, since those had been open. A password had been required to access messages or e-mail, and unfortunately, the kid hadn't had touch ID activated, so he'd been unable to open it by swiping Tommy's thumb.

"*Curious* I might go for, if I'd only caught you doing a little light snooping," Mac said, feeling his mouth twisting with disgust, "not taking pictures of the inside of my house. Especially my children's bedrooms and private messages I've written to them. So tell me now, who the hell was it that sent you?"

"Nobody sent me!" Tommy said, desperation ringing in his words. "If you want to know the truth, I was— I was just casing the joint, you know, with the idea that maybe me and a few buddies could come back and hit the place later. You've got a damned nice TV and—"

"Bullshit," Mac said, figuring whatever he had really been up to must be seriously bad news if he was willing to cop to planning a burglary. "Besides, there are no pictures of any so-called *valuables* on here. Yet you've got a half dozen photos of each of my kids' bedrooms, along with a close-up of the note that you tore into. I'm giving you one chance, right now, to tell me why."

"I was in too big of a hurry to really read it." Tommy tried again, splaying out his hands as he leaned forward. "But I figured it might have some clue about your schedules to help me figure when to come back."

Fed up with the lying, Mac slammed his bootheel down on Tommy's right hand, eliciting a scream that accompanied the sound of bone and cartilage cracking. Curling in a fetal position, the kid pulled the damaged hand to his chest, sobbing.

Mac stared down at him, feeling nothing but contempt, both for the young man's weakness and for himself, for allowing his rage—and his fear for his children's safety—to make him into the very monster he'd been so appalled to be accused of being. The kind of man willing to intimidate, injure and threaten a younger, weaker person in an effort to extract answers.

But as Tommy's sobbing rose in volume, an acrid taste filled Mac's mouth, and he knew damned well he could neither justify nor stomach further violence against a helpless man. A bluff, though, he could pull off. He told himself that, with his children's safety in the balance, he had no other choice.

Bending forward, he clamped down on one of the younger man's arms and jerked him to his feet, a move that surprised the kid so much that he abruptly forgot his injury and stared, cringing and trembling, at this new threat.

"Please don't— No more—" he whimpered, shrinking into himself.

"You want that nice smile of yours to stay in one piece?" Mac asked, channeling the biggest, baddest tough guy he could think of as he got right in Tommy's face. "Then give me the name of your employer—or I promise you, you're gonna be spitting pieces of those nice teeth for the next week. Your soon-to-be ex-boss, Gonzalez, has already given me permission to do whatever I want to you since you're a crap employee anyway."

"I don't know, I don't know, I don't *know* who sent the message!" the kid cried out, jerking free of Mac's grip and backpedaling several steps. "The offer came through this freelancing app I get work off of, you know, for photography? That's kind of my thing."

"Explain," Mac ordered.

"In place of a name, though, the person offering the work was just a random string of characters—but on these apps, that's not all that unusual. The customers just make deposits directly to your accounts. It's the new gig economy." Tommy shrugged, as if this explained everything. "Lots of people pick up extra cash that way."

"I know what it is," Mac said. "But how many of these *gigs* of yours have involved breaking into people's houses?"

"I didn't— I didn't *break* in, exactly."

"Okay, so you conned your way in. Did you really imagine that's any better? Or in the least legal?"

"You knocked me out and smashed my hand, man." Tommy angrily displayed a swelling right hand, which was already beginning to go a mottled purple. "You should be talking!"

"This is my children's safety we're talking, so count yourself damned lucky it was your hand and not your skull—or I don't toss you through that window." He gestured toward the rock-studded river far below the bluff's edge, an undoubtedly fatal drop. "And tell me more about this so-called *job* of yours."

Tommy gusted out a sigh. "I should've known it was a bad deal when whoever it was conned me into communication outside of the app. That's just how they made the initial contact. But the money they were offering—it was crazy good, and it wasn't like I was doing any real harm, just taking a few photos, kind of like a real reporter."

"That's what you think, is it? Do you have any damned idea…? The last time my kids were kidnapped, I didn't see them for *eight years*. Eight years of pure hell, that cost my family nearly everything we'd ever owned, not to mention each other."

Color draining from his face, Tommy shook his head. "K-kidnapped? I swear I didn't know anything about that! If I had, I'd've never in a million years—"

"Where the hell are you from? Don't you read the papers? Watch the news or—"

"My family only moved to Texas a couple years back, I swear! I was just trying to get some money together to get back to school next semester." Shaking his head in denial, he started crying again.

"Oh, pull yourself together," Mac said, pulling out his cell phone. "Let me get you a bag of ice for that hand, and then I'm going to call the sheriff."

"The sheriff? So you're having me arrested?"

"Whether I press charges depends on how helpful you decide to be—because it's not you, but whoever's hired you that I'm after."

Sara soon came to the conclusion that she was being ridiculously paranoid, suspecting that Amanda Greenville had anything more in mind than a kind gesture toward two children she remembered fondly from years before. With her own personal life in crisis, there was no way the poor woman could possibly have anything in mind in giving them a simple gift. The only wonder of it was that she could manage to think of anyone or anything at all outside of her own difficult situation.

"So tell me," Sara said as the two of them stood with their iced tea at the railing overlooking the pond, watching white cumulus clouds begin to build behind Colt's Head Mountain, "how have you been holding up since getting the news about…about your husband?"

As soon as the question was out of her mouth, she wondered if she'd gone too far, since as far as she'd heard, there hadn't yet been an official identification of the body. But judging from Amanda's sigh, she held out no hope that the remains found with her missing husband's ID and clothing could be any other person.

Shaking her head, she said, "To be perfectly honest, I've been— Can I trust that you won't share this?"

"Of course," Sara said, the wind chimes hanging nearby tinkling faintly in the light breeze.

"I've been bouncing all over the place emotionally," Amanda admitted, her gray eyes deeply troubled. "I *am* sorry he's dead. I truly am, at least for the sake of the family that loved him. But there's also this enormous sense of relief that I can finally stop looking over my shoulder and flinching at every tiny noise—and maybe learn to sleep at night without keeping one hand on the pistol tucked underneath my pillow…"

So there *had* been abuse in the household, as Mac had believed. Sara felt honored that, for whatever reason—possibly because she thought of her as a safe person, as a social worker, or maybe just due to the fact that she had no ties to the town, with all its interconnections and long history of judgment—Amanda had trusted her with such an admission. "I'm so sorry you've had to live like that. Is there anyone…anyone you can talk to?"

Amanda shook her head. "Heavens no. I can't possibly— People around here…half of them believe I was a fool to stay with Pete. The other half think I might have…"

Did she mean to imply that people actually believed she could have *killed* her husband? To Sara, Amanda's behavior seemed far more consistent with that of the victim of violence than a perpetrator. "What about your family?"

Another shake of the head. "Not everybody has that."

Sara winced. "Believe me, I'm well aware of that. And I imagine he didn't like you having friends, either? Your husband, I mean." Many domestic abusers, she knew, went out of their way to intentionally separate their victims from all means of emotional support.

Staring out across the valley, Amanda said bitterly, "He said I didn't need them, didn't need anyone except him. He could barely stand to let me work, except he liked the money I was bringing in. Though he reminded me all the time it was nothing compared to what he was worth just by virtue of being born a Greenville."

"I can help you find a professional," Sara offered. "A counselor who works with those who've experienced—"

"I don't want or need any *counselor*," Amanda insisted, a brittle edge to her voice. "But I can't tell you how grateful I would be to have your friendship if you'd have me."

Realizing what it must be costing her to make herself so vulnerable to ask, Sara offered her a smile. "You know I don't expect to be in the area for long," she said honestly, "but I'd be honored if you'd consider me your friend, whether I'm here or back in Austin."

"Thank you, Sara. Thank you," Amanda said, clasping her in a brief hug before quickly checking her watch. "But I'd better get moving if I'm going to finish my other errands before this front blows through."

"Mac said something about us getting rain this evening."

Amanda nodded. "There could be some pretty heavy thunderstorms, I understand."

"They aren't expecting any more flooding, are they?" Sara asked, her thoughts turning to the resort cleanup that was underway.

Amanda shook her head. "No, thank goodness. The line's supposed to pass through fairly quickly. But don't be surprised if there's some wind, thunder and lightning. When those squalls come ripping over the mountains this time of year, they can be quite the noisemakers."

"Good to know," Sara said before thanking her again for the food and her gift to the children.

"I really wish you hadn't gone and stomped his hand like that," Hayden said, giving Mac a look as dark as the clouds huddled on the horizon as they stood outside his department SUV, where Tommy sat slumped and sullen in the back seat. At least he'd finally quit his sniveling and was just sitting there, probably feeling fortunate that he'd been allowed to keep the ice bag, his wrists cuffed in the front to keep it in place.

"A damn shame how it just so happened to get in the way where I was stepping," Mac said mildly, though he knew full well his brother hadn't bought that version of events the first time. But Hayden had been outraged enough after seeing the photos on Tommy's phone and hearing Mac's account of what had happened that he'd shown no inclination to listen to the suspect's complaints about assault.

"It really *is* a shame," Hayden griped, "because otherwise, I could've just tossed this jackass in a holding cell for a few hours to stew on his life choices before I questioned him. Soft as he looks, I would've had him coughing up full access to his phone and anything else he might know in no time flat. But now, instead, we have to coddle the sorry little snot-smear, and I have to waste a deputy's entire evening making sure the kid receives 'timely medical treatment' so I don't have to hear about it from some damned defense attorneys later."

"I'll remind you, *he's* the criminal here," Mac argued.

"I get what you're saying, but you saw those straight white teeth on him, right? And that fancy, practically brand-new phone? You mark my words. That kid's from the kind of family who makes trouble. You'll be lucky if they don't want to sue you for his injuries."

Mac rolled his eyes. "I'd like to see 'em try. And whose side are you on, anyway? He was inside my house, spying in your niece's bedroom. For all I know, he was planning on sending those photos to whoever my ex-mother-in-law has working on getting past my security precautions and snatching back the kids."

"Don't worry about those photos. I'll make sure all copies are deleted. But speaking of precautions, what the hell is that dog good for?" Hayden gestured irritably at Roxy, who lolled her tongue and wagged her tail.

"Mostly, hospitality," Mac said with an offhand shrug. "I'm counting myself lucky that she barked."

"And what's the use of you having a high-dollar alarm system we helped you get rigged to all the doors and windows if you don't bother turning it on?"

"I'd been coming and going out of the house all morning, between dealing with the contractors and some paperwork for my insurance—and anyway, I'd really gotten the alarm more for when the kids came to live here."

There was a brief lull in the conversation as one of Gonzalez's crew used a forklift to dump a final load of debris to be hauled away near the cabins located along the lower bluff. Horrified when he'd been told of his employee's misdeeds, Abe Gonzalez had already informed Mac there would be no bill sent for any of his crew's work on this job, insisting over Mac's objections, *It's the least I can do. I should've known that gold-brickin' slacker was up to something.*

"So someone saw this as a window of opportunity," Hayden told Mac once the echoes died, "but I have a few other ideas who that might be. Since the children's return, has anyone attempted to contact you? From the media, I mean? After all, your story was big news for a long time, and people do talk—even out here in the country."

"*Especially* out here in the country, it sometimes seems," Mac said, grimacing to think of how the news coverage of his children's custody case had made him into something of a local celebrity—and a major target of gossip—in the area over the past eight years. "And to answer your question, yes. I've had a few messages from reporters requesting my comment on rumors that the twins have been repatriated. I responded with one of those generic messages stating that the family requests privacy during this time, without confirming or denying any details."

Hayden gave him a skeptical look. "And you really think they're going to let it go at that?"

"Why wouldn't they, at least if they hope to get some kind of comment from me later—or maybe score an interview or photos of the children. Not that I'd ever allow my kids' images to get out like that—"

"You're talking about *respectable* news media, but in this day and age, Mac, not everybody plays fair. There are tabloid news shows, bloggers and gotcha web sites that would be only too happy to pay for images obtained through deceptive or even illegal means—including some in Argentina."

"In Argentina?" Mac had never given that a moment's thought.

"Oh, yeah. The story's made the news there, too. You know, your ex-father-in-law, Don Roberto Rojas Morales, was pretty well known there. Admired, feared, respected, in a lot of circles."

Mac stared at his brother, surprise dawning on him. "You've done a lot of research over the years, haven't you? Into the news coverage related to my family?"

"I set up alerts after you came back from Buenos Aires, half dead and heartbroken," Hayden admitted, his dark blue eyes haunted. "That wasn't just an attack against you. Those bastards had declared war on our entire *family*. It was all Mom and your lawyer could do to keep me and Ryan both from flying down there ourselves and launching our own two-man attempt to breach that compound, take down that son of a bitch and drag back my niece and nephew."

Mac clapped him on the shoulder and cleared his throat, which had suddenly grown tight. "I appreciate the thought, man, but they surely would've killed you both—especially considering how subtle Ryan is when he's in a temper."

"The more I think about the way this jackass was supposedly hired—anonymously and online, through some app—the less I think it sounds like the way your ex-in-laws' international criminal associates would operate. Those guys are real pros."

"So you *don't* think this is a precursor to a kidnapping attempt?" Mac asked.

Hayden frowned and shook his head. "If all the facts bear out, I wouldn't think so. I'm afraid instead this is more likely to be some sleazy purveyor of ill-gotten images, wanting to peddle pictures related to your kids to sleazy blogs and tabloids to turn a fast buck."

The idea of anyone exploiting his family for a story turned Mac's stomach, but at least it was better than the thought that his home was being cased for a future break-in. "Find out whatever else you can from him," he said, "and let me know if anything changes. Meanwhile, I'll be activating the alarm system here and warning Sara to be on the lookout for any sign of anyone skulking around the area with cameras."

"Sounds good," Hayden told him. "And you might want to cover your construction materials, too. Weather's saying those storms due to blow through this evening could get a little rough."

* * *

Once Amanda left, with the twins occupied putting together their new space model set at the table, Sara found herself thinking of—and missing—Mac. That had her recalling—and regretting—the way she'd ended their earlier conversation.

She worried that, in accusing him so bluntly of trying to make things easier for himself with the children with his attempt to persuade her to stay, she might have hurt him, when he'd probably been unaware that he'd been fooling himself about his feelings for her. Certainly, it was hard to imagine going back to the easy relationship they'd enjoyed before they'd shared that kiss, when both of them were thinking only of what was best for the children.

With that worry gnawing at her, she undertook another more extensive search around the cabin for her missing e-reader, along with the undergarments that had vanished from her dresser top. But even after hunting down and turning inside out every item she recalled washing with that load of laundry in case the panties had stuck to them inside, she found no trace of the missing items. She checked the twins' drawers and closet, as well, along with every other spot that she could think of.

In the end, however, the effort only left her prickly with annoyance and wondering if one of the twins was purposely messing with her, in spite of their earlier denial about the e-reader. But she couldn't bring herself to raise the embarrassing topic of missing underwear, especially not while they were so happily immersed in putting together and playing with their model. And the only other thought that occurred to her—that *Mac* might have been the one to take her panties—was so distressing she could barely entertain it. Surely, there had to be some other explanation.

A memory returned to her, unbidden, of the movement she had spotted on the hillside after Cristo's disappearance, using Mac's binoculars. Recalling what she'd thought for a split second might have been a man wearing camouflage clothing, she felt her stomach squeeze.

What if that initial instinct—one she'd soon talked herself out of, telling herself it must have been an animal of some sort—had been right? Why on earth would anyone have been up there, months past hunting season, in the afternoon heat, dressed in that attire? Thinking back, she remembered that she'd been looking in a different direction when something—a glint of light—had caught her attention, prompting her to turn the binoculars to look toward the rock formation.

What if that flash had been the reflection off *another* set of binoculars looking back at her?

Though the thought sent a chill ripping through her, in another moment, she dismissed it, telling herself she was being ridiculous, letting her imagination, the quiet and the loneliness of this remote, rural area plant the idea that—what? Some stalker had crept down from the hillside to creep inside the cabin to steal items as intimate, but basically irrelevant, as a small electronic reader and a few pairs of women's panties?

Putting the whole disturbing subject out of her mind for the time being, she moved to the family room sofa to elevate her arm again, since it had begun to ache again slightly. There, she saw she'd missed a message from Mac earlier, possibly from during the time she'd been talking to Amanda.

Have a minute to talk? he'd written.

Heart picking up speed, she hesitated, torn between

dread at the thought of reigniting another unpleasant conversation and an even more desperate desire to find their way back to a comfortable footing—if not to the strictly professional relationship they'd at first forged, then maybe something like a polite friendship.

Or at least the pretense of friendship, though she suspected that, in reality, she would never stop aching for him to take her in his arms and finish what he'd started when he'd kissed her. But since that couldn't be, she would have to bluff her way through these next few weeks—and what she suspected would be an awkward conversation—as best as she could.

Gathering her courage, she texted back.

Sorry I missed your message before. Now a good time?

When he didn't respond, she decided he must be busy working and began checking out a web site for teachers of English as a Second Language for ideas for the twins' lessons for the upcoming weeks.

A couple of hours later, she and the children were putting away the dishes from the dinner they'd just finished when Cristo asked, "How did it get so dark already?"

Glancing at the window, Sara saw that he was right. Though normally it would have been light enough for them to take their usual after-dinner walk—something they did to avoid the heat of the afternoon—at a few minutes after seven on a mid-June evening, the sky had gone deep purple, and outside on the porch the chimes jangled discordantly, rattled by a stiff breeze.

"The rain must finally be on the way," Sara told him.

"Trueno," Silvia said, and when she listened closely, Sara heard it, too: a low groaning that sounded almost like big trucks on the distant highway. Soon, the thunder

came again, and louder, rolling long and low as the storm drew nearer, offering an explanation for the early dusk.

"We definitely won't get in our walk this evening," Sara said as rain drummed off the metal roof. Since the porches were deep, they headed outside to watch the storm, until the flashes of lightning and booming cracks of thunder went from entertaining to alarming. With the wind driving in the fat drops, they were jumping at each new boom and damp with windblown rain by the time that they retreated.

"You'd better go change out of the wet things," Sara said, pointing out where Silvia was dripping on the wood floor, "before you leave a puddle. Please leave your damp clothes on the washer."

"I will," the girl promised as she headed for the bedroom.

Behind them, the back door blew open, startling Sara and Cristo, who had managed to stay drier, as the wind flung it against the wall.

"Let's lock the doors," Sara suggested, though normally, they only did that before bedtime, "so that doesn't happen again."

Once Cristo had helped her to do so, he stood looking worriedly as he glanced toward the window.

"Is something wrong?" Sara asked him.

"I was thinking," he said, "if it keeps raining, will tomorrow get canceled? Going over to see Roxy, I mean?"

"For the barbecue at your father's? This rain's not supposed to last long." She'd checked the forecast herself.

"But what if it does?"

"I'm sure he'll call and tell us, but I'm betting he'll still want you to come over. I know he's worked very hard on getting your rooms ready," she ventured, deciding it would be better to broach the subject now, to give

Cristo time to get used to the idea, "and he definitely wants to show you."

Instead of reacting angrily, however, Cristo looked downcast. "I wish he hadn't gone to all that trouble."

"Why wouldn't he?" Sara asked. "He's your father, and he loves you."

Shaking his head, he looked up sadly. "But we're never going to live there, no matter how much work he does."

The next flash at the windows was brighter than the previous. The cracking boom that came next was loud enough to make both of them jump a little.

"¡Caramba!" he said, laughing to cover for his embarrassment at being startled.

"It's getting noisy out there," she agreed, deciding to save the lecture on his word choice for the moment, "but I need to know, what did you mean when you said that you're never going to live with your father? You do know, don't you, that you and your sister can't stay here with me forever?"

Smile souring, he shook his head. "I told you before. Abuelita will come take us home. Or she will send Abuelo's men to—"

She readjusted her arm in her sling. "Have you been talking to someone?"

Her phone rang then, and she saw it was Mac. But instinct had her hitting the button to send the call to voice mail, deciding she'd get back to him later.

"This is very important," she told Cristo, stepping closer. "I need you to tell me honestly, have you spoken to or contacted your grandmother in any way at all since we left Buenos Aires?"

"How would I do that?" he demanded, shaking his head rapidly. "You won't let me use your phone, no matter how many times I ask."

"That's true," she said, noting his defensiveness. And deciding to press even harder, while she had him separated from his sister, who tended to run interference—or tear up—when a subject became difficult. "But I still haven't found my e-reader. And I can't help wondering, with these references you keep making to your grandmother sending someone for you, if you've been using it to communicate with—"

"That's just because she loves us. We told you, we didn't touch anything except the candy. I'm sorry for that, for getting so angry about the gifts you made your friends take back, but it doesn't mean I'm some worthless thief who would steal a—"

"Even if you knew you could e-mail your *abuelita*?"

Angry tears streaked down his face. "I'm not a liar, either," he shouted at her before turning toward the bathroom. But before he could flee, another flash—brighter than any of the others—knocked out their power, plunging them into darkness as it lit up all the windows...

Including the nearest one, where Sara saw a man-shaped silhouette hurtling toward the door.

Chapter 11

"Mac?" Sara called, thinking, as thunder crashed—practically on top of them now—that he had come to check on her and the children, that he was ducking his head and running through the darkness to escape the pouring rain. Probably, that was what he'd tried to call to tell her.

But the moment's relief only lasted an instant before she saw a second man, and her scream was in her throat as he rushed toward the other door. They would have been inside in that first instant had she and Cristo not just turned the dead bolts.

"To your room!" she shouted, jerking her phone off the cord where she had had it charging. In the kitchen, she heard a chair fall, but a moment later, Cristo was back with her and she was following the boy inside the children's bedroom. In the dim light from the window, she could barely make out Silvia, who was just tugging down the hem of a dry T-shirt, staring at them in bewilderment.

"What's happening?" she asked, the whites of her eyes flashing.

"Help me!" Sara cried, trying to push the dresser in front of the door in an attempt to barricade it. With only one good arm, she couldn't budge it.

Catching on, Cristo pitched in, yelling at his sister, "There are bad men on the porch, trying to break inside!"

Silvia shrieked like a teakettle, but she joined them, helping to push the dresser.

With the door wedged closed, Sara pulled out her phone and called not 9-1-1, but Mac, her instincts telling her he was closer than the sheriff's department and wouldn't waste time with a bunch of questions. As she waited for a connection, the pounding of her heart competing with the crashing thunder, she heard deep banging thuds that sounded as if they were coming from outside. The men were kicking at one or both of the heavy wooden doors. She knew they'd be inside the house at any moment.

Then Mac's voice was in her left ear. "Storming bad there, Sara? We just had a thunderclap that—"

"We need you to come!" she shouted. "Two men—I didn't see them clearly—are trying to break in the house right now! We're barricaded in the twins' room, but I can hear them now, forcing their way inside—and I don't have any way to keep them—"

Distracted by a faint gleam, she saw Cristo between her and the door, something raised in his hands. Her gorge rose as she realized it was a small paring knife she'd used earlier to make their dinner. He must have grabbed it from the kitchen. And now the eleven-year-old meant to defend them—or at least to try.

On the phone, Mac shouted, "I'm on my way! Be right there—just don't let them take my kids."

"They aren't getting them," she vowed, a fierce determination rising to outstrip even her terror. And she knew in that moment that whatever it cost her, she would not fail these children the way she'd failed her sister's child. "Just hurry!"

As Mac fumbled to unlock the gun case, his stomach tried to force its way into his throat and memories blazed through his brain of the commandos who had ambushed him outside Buenos Aires. Remembering the utter helplessness, the humiliation he had felt when his attempts to fight back had resulted only in multiple fractures and a concussion that had left him groaning and retching on the roadside. His attackers and their AK-wielding guardians had jumped back into their SUV and roared away.

The kid this morning in the house was a false alarm. I was a fool to think even for a moment it meant the real threat, sent by the old lady, wasn't on its way. With Don Roberto dead and buried, Mac realized, Elena Rojas Morales might well have figured she had nothing left to lose. He damned well knew what *that* felt like—knew the sheer madness that could come of desperation.

But tonight, as he grabbed a Winchester rifle that had been his father's, they'd come onto *his* turf, and he would damned well see they didn't leave it. Not with his kids—and not alive, if he had anything to say about it.

Leaving the dog behind, he jumped into his truck and took off, flooring the accelerator. As he hurtled through the driving rain, he prayed to a God he hadn't been on speaking terms with in years. "Please, just let me make it there on time. Whatever it takes, whatever You ask of me, don't let me lose them—any of them—"

The insight slammed him that in pleading for Sara to protect his kids from being taken, he might have just unthinkingly named his price—in the form of her life. For the men his former mother-in-law had sent to steal his children would have no need of a translator—and would see an eyewitness as nothing but a threat to be eliminated.

Sara, he suspected, would understand the threat, as well. Yet, as devoted as she was to the children's welfare, he couldn't imagine for a moment her abandoning them, not even to save herself.

Choked with horror, he pulled out the phone, fumbled to dial Hayden. But he must have hit the wrong contact on his list of favorites, for it was his youngest brother's voice that answered, though it was tough to hear Ryan over the sound of the rain beating on the truck's roof and windshield. "What's up, Mac? I've kinda got my hands full right now, what with this weather drivin' the stock mad—"

"Damn it—" Mac said, the pickup's rear end fishtailing as he took the corner entering the subdivision too quickly. As he wrenched the truck back under control, he shouted to make himself heard over the storm's noise. "I was trying to reach Hayden. I've got trouble—big trouble—two men showed up at the Parker rental cabin in the Colt's Head neighborhood, the one up on High Meadow Road. I think they mean to snatch the kids. I'm armed and nearly there. I'm not losing them again. I can't."

A raw curse tore its way from Ryan before he pulled himself together. "On my way, and I'll call Hayden, too. Just don't go charging in and getting yourself killed—because for all you know, that's what they're hoping for, to draw you out for an execution so you won't ever threaten the old bat's custody again."

Mac realized he could be right. But it didn't change a

damned thing. "It's a chance I'm going to have to take, because if they kidnap my kids again, my life's as good as over anyway."

"Mac, listen to me! I'll only be about twenty minutes—and Hayden might be even closer, or be able to send somebody, so if you'll just wait for us to get—"

"I've gotta go, Ry. I just want you to know—I'm sorry. For all of it. I only wish we'd—"

With a flash of lightning, a crackling noise severed their connection. But there was no time to try to call back. He was almost at the gate.

Passing Sara's parked car, Mac pulled the truck as close as he dared to the cabin, not caring that he risked getting stuck on the muddy slope. Leaving the engine still running and the high beams shining toward the pitch-black cabin, he grabbed the rifle and a flashlight and bounded toward the porch. His heart fell when he found the side door, broken and standing open, the splintered wood bearing testimony to the violence of an entry that had clearly gone beyond anything even the most eager tabloid photographer would do.

Rushing inside, he shone the light around in a cabin that felt breathtakingly devoid of life. He tasted panic when he spotted a chair knocked over in the kitchen, a shattered glass on the floor. Ignoring both, he hurried to the children's bedroom where Sara had told them they would be waiting for him—

But that door was broken in, too, and when he pushed his way inside, past the partial obstruction of the dresser, he found that room empty, as well.

"Sara!" he shouted over the sound of the rain and the thunder exploding in his chest. "Silvia! Cristo, where are you?"

The white curtains fluttered around the open window, the same one his son had climbed through what now seemed like an eternity before. Had they taken the same route tonight, attempting an escape before the two men could force their way inside?

Before he could think through where they might have gone, the overhead light flickered and then came on, the sudden brilliance nearly blinding. He checked the closet, found it empty, then moved to leave the room to make a quick search of the other room when he froze in his tracks, his stomach lurching as a streak of color caught the corner of his eye.

It was blood—a long smear of bright blood on the blowing curtain.

Someone had been hurt here—cut, he realized when he spotted a small kitchen knife, its steel blade stained with red drops, on the floor below the window.

"God have mercy." He closed his eyes, his voice breaking as a wave of dizziness threatened to pull him under.

But in his weakest moment, he remembered Sara's voice crying out for him to hurry. Knowing he couldn't let her and his children down, he straightened his spine and left the knife to make a quick check of the remainder of the cabin, quickly assuring himself there was no sign of them hiding anywhere inside.

He did spot Sara's cell phone on the living room floor, where it was sticking partway out from underneath the sofa, as if it had been dropped and accidently kicked there. In her bedroom, he found her purse: another indication that she'd fled in a hurry. And since her keys were there, too, zipped inside the pocket, it told him, as well, that she'd lacked the means to either call for help or attempt an escape by car.

Heading outside, he found the rain had slacked off, the

flashing to the west indicating that the storm was moving off in that direction. Not that it mattered much, now
that he was wet already, and as he circled the outside of
the cabin, shouting the children's and Sara's names, his
pants and boots grew heavier with mud and moisture
from the grass.

Despondent to see and hear no sign of them, he started
jogging for the tree line beyond the pond, thinking it
made sense that Sara would have run with the children
toward the cover of the vegetation. Maybe she'd even
try to get them to the nearest occupied cabin—though
it was quite some distance up the road and located up a
steep hillside.

Half muffled in a distant rumble, he heard someone
calling—a voice that froze him in his tracks. There it
was again, behind him.

"*Papá!* Papá, wait!"

He turned, the beam of his flashlight catching Cristo
running toward him, wet and filthy, and deeply dis-
tressed, judging from the look on his face.

"Cristo, where's your sister?" Remembering the Spanish, Mac asked clumsily, "*¿Donde esta—?*"

"Silvia's under the porch," Cristo said, shocking Mac
with his perfectly clear English. "Sara told us to hide
there and not come out until we saw you, no matter what
we heard."

With no time to worry about the language issue at the
moment, Mac asked, "Are you all okay?"

Through the trees, he spotted the flashing red-and-
white of emergency lights heading their way on the road,
and prayed it was his brother.

"Silvia—she will be scared alone," Cristo said, looking behind himself. "We should go and get—"

"What do you mean alone? Where's Sara?" Mac's gut clenched.

The boy shook his head, his dark eyes liquid as he pointed off in the direction of the tree line. "I saw her running that way. She was shouting our names, pretending she was yelling at us not to stop until we reached the road."

Leading them away, Mac thought, his heart breaking as the nature of her ruse hit him. Tucking the rifle beneath one arm, he moved to confront Cristo, whose thin body shook with sobs.

"And then I saw the men," he choked out as Mac pulled him closer, "the men behind her—and Silvia came and grabbed my arm and made me hide under the porch with her, but we heard noises."

"What noises, Cristo? Tell me."

"Silvia tried to tell me it was only thunder." Cristo's voice was barely audible, just above a whisper. "But I know they were gunshots."

The sheriff's department vehicle rolled up the drive toward them, its lights flashing but its sirens off. As the SUV approached, Mac could see the driver wasn't Hayden but one of his deputies, Clayton Yarborough, easily recognizable with his short-cropped, prematurely white hair and somewhat darker mustache.

"*¿Papá?*" Silvia called, sounding scared behind him.

Mac swept her into his embrace, too. "I'm here, baby girl. I've got you."

"I told him about Sara," Cristo said to her, again in English. "I had to, so he knows…about us—that we've been faking—"

"You have to find her," Silvia cried, her own English as astonishingly clear as her twin's. "Find Sara for us before the bad men hurt her!"

Chapter 12

Five minutes earlier...

Of all the desperate things Sara had ever done in her life, running full-out into the storm-dark night may have been the most reckless. Spurred by the need to get the kidnappers as far from the children as she could, she'd started out with a mental image of remembered landmarks. But disoriented by both the storm and her own panic, she soon realized she had no clear idea of which way she was going.

Still, she kept moving, pausing to shout to the children as if they were ahead of her, calling out to urge them to keep heading for the road, though she couldn't be certain anyone was listening. As she lurched forward once again—praying she was not about to splash down into the pond or knock herself out by crashing headlong into a tree—she heard the low murmur of what sounded like male voices coming up behind her.

And then the shots rang out, two of them that had her heart threatening to burst itself against her ribs. She zig-zagged and picked up speed as if she might either out-run or outsmart a bullet whose path she could neither see nor guess.

The shooting ceased, but her fractured wrist, inside its cast, throbbed in time with every step. Her lungs burned and the pain of exertion dug deep into her side, yet she pushed past agony, too terrified to slow her pace. Then abruptly the ground dropped out from under her feet and she fell heavily, crashing down onto her knees and then sprawling on her belly.

As she lay gasping, too shocked for pain to catch up with her, she could feel that her head and upper body had landed somewhere well below the position of her legs and feet. Had she run into some sort of hole or off the edge of a small drop-off? Hard lumps—rocks or maybe fallen branches—littered the unforgiving ground beneath her, and she was even more uncertain of how far she'd run or in which direction the road lay.

Petrified that she'd been heard crashing down, she didn't move to get up, but merely lay there, listening to the rain come down and, presently, the deep rumbles of men in conversation. Scarcely daring to breathe, she strained her ears, desperate to make out their words.

As they jogged past, she caught only the frustration in their voices—and the angry, "Where the hell'd that *puta* go? I swear I'm gonna…"

Though she couldn't make out any more, she shuddered at the ugly Spanish slur, the threatening tone, as she recalled those awful moments as the kids were going out the window and she was standing with the knife she'd taken off Cristo out of fear he'd get himself hurt. Desperate to buy whatever time she could for the twins to hide and for her to get out, as well, she'd used her legs to shove her weight against the dresser. When the man just outside pushed even harder, reaching inside to grab at her, she'd struck once and then again, jabbing his hairy, muscular forearm with the knife.

With a howl of rage and pain, he'd withdrawn, and she hadn't wasted a moment, running to the window and losing the little knife—her only means of defense—as she'd rolled awkwardly out of the window. It was a wonder she hadn't broken a leg doing so, considering the way she'd fallen, but she'd sprung to her feet and sprinted off like a jackrabbit, certain that if the men caught her they would be in no mood to show her any mercy.

But mercy from that pair, she realized, had never been a possibility. Men such as these didn't leave eyewitnesses to what she felt certain was an attempted international abduction. The only real question was would the children stay in their hiding places if they heard her screaming if the men chose to use her pain to draw out their true quarry? Though she'd warned them against coming out, there were some things, she knew, that no eleven-year-olds had the strength to stand against. The kinds of things that would inevitably scar them forever…

So don't get caught. Just lie here, still and silent as a fawn left in hiding by its mother, and pray that they don't find the children, either. Deciding this was the wisest course, she groped around herself in the mud and found what felt like fallen tree limbs. Moving as carefully as she could so as not to make much noise, she dragged them to partly cover herself, shuddering at the feeling of the slimy leaves trailing over her wet skin.

Afterward, she lay on her side, shaking with exhaustion and aching with cold, fear and what felt like a constellation of bumps and bruises. As her ears strained for the sound of any voice or footfall, she prayed, to make out approaching sirens, or the familiar sound of Mac's truck engine, but the only noises she could hear were the dripping of the leaves and the weirdly musical trickling of water running past her.

In spite of her terror and discomfort, at some point, she found herself jerking awake then panicking. How long had she been unconscious?

It occurred to her that as mild as the weather had been, a person might still die of exposure if she lay long enough unmoving in the cool and muddy water. Her teeth were chattering already, and she found it hard to move her limbs. But what sent pure adrenaline jolting through her was the realization that she might have missed something crucial, like the children crying out for her—what if they'd been found and carried off already? She wouldn't even be able to tell Mac in which direction they'd been taken.

It was the thought of facing him that had her groaning and shaking as she rolled over and fought to push herself onto her feet. Unable to rise, she threw off the branches she remembered using to cover her body earlier—

And then screamed as the beam of light from her pursuers' flashlights caught her, and their large, silhouetted figures loomed above.

Her body felt cold as a corpse's as he pulled her against him, but still, she found the strength to fight him, her shriek barely sounding human.

Desperate to break through her panic, he called out to her. "Sara, it's me—Mac."

"I'm the sheriff, Sara. You remember? We're here to help you," said Hayden, catching a flailing wrist as they both worked to subdue her. "So let's settle down now. That's right."

Whether it was their words sinking in or exhaustion, she went limp in his arms before staring from one face to the other. "You're not—I thought you were *them*." The confusion in her eyes warred with her anguish. "But what about Silvia and Cristo? Did they find them? Are they g-gone?"

Mac shook his head at her before clutching her in a tight embrace. "They're safe, thank God—because of you. They're back at the cabin with Deputy Yarborough right now." As he rubbed circles along her back, though, he could feel her shaking violently. "Damn, Sara, are you all right?"

"Where's the baby? I have to find Promise!" she said, the glazed look in her eyes telling him that nothing was getting through. "I was asleep—I never heard her. I thought my mother was still—"

Still holding on to her so she wouldn't hurt herself attempting to get away, Mac glanced at his brother. "We've got to get her out of here. She's not talking sense at all."

Dressed in civilian jeans and a light shirt rather than his uniform since he'd been at home when Ryan had reached him, Hayden said, "Ordinarily, I'd say not to move her 'til we can get the medics out here, but that could take too long, with hypothermia setting in."

Of the same mind, Mac nodded and looked at Sara. "We need to get you inside, where it's warm and dry and you can see Silvia and Cristo. Do you think you can walk at all?"

"I don't— I'm not sure—" She staggered forward and would have fallen if he hadn't caught her arm.

"Never mind that," Mac said before thrusting his rifle

toward his brother. "Grab this for me, will you, Hayden? I've got you, Sara. Let me… There you go."

He scooped her up into his arms, his own adrenaline making light work of the burden as he carried her up from the rocky hollow she doubtless hadn't seen running blindly through the rain-soaked darkness. He'd spent the past half hour scared out of his wits that they were searching for a corpse and not a living woman— that she'd been shot down or otherwise brutalized by the men out to abduct his children. But as relieved as he was to find her breathing, he still wanted to heave. He was so painfully aware of how close she'd come to breaking her neck falling the way she must have, or hitting her head and drowning in one of the small pools of water his flashlight's beam had caught near the bottom. Even now, he couldn't be certain how badly she might be injured or whether the hypothermia she was clearly experiencing could prove a danger to her life. He only knew they needed to get her somewhere warm and dry, as quickly as they could.

Half conscious and wrapped up in blankets, Sara would later recall little more from that first night when she was transported by ambulance back to the hospital in Uvalde after first responders decided her condition wasn't serious enough to warrant the use of a medevac helicopter. She only knew that sometime the next morning she woke in a room very much like the one she'd left only days before, and she couldn't seem to stay awake for more than a few minutes at a time.

During one of those intervals, a determined-looking nurse, a short but athletically built middle-aged woman with a silver bob, readjusted the bed and badgered her to sit up.

"Just need to rest…a few more…" Sara's eyelids fluttered toward their goal.

"You can rest when we're finished. Help me out here. That's a girl. It's high time we had you up and moving."

As unlikely as *up* had seemed, *moving* struck Sara as unthinkable. She shook her head and stared in disbelief. Didn't this sadist understand that every tiny movement sent pain arcing through her stiff and battered body? "I can't."

"Come on, now," the nurse urged. "I've got you. It's a few steps around the room, and then I promise, I'll let you rest again."

"I have a broken wrist, you know."

"It's been recast while you were out of it since your cast was soggy, and anyway, I promise, I won't make you walk on it." The nurse flashed the smile of a woman who understood she'd already won this argument.

Getting up was hardest, but within a few steps, Sara began to find herself moving more easily and her head clearing. As the nurse helped her to sit again on the side of the bed, Sara admitted, "Thanks. That wasn't as bad as I thought—by which I mean it didn't kill me."

"Trust me, you're nowhere close to dying, no matter what it feels like at first."

"So what, exactly, is wrong with me?" Sara asked, still trying to fight off the fog surrounding her memory.

"According to your chart, you came in pretty out of it—hypothermic, with contusions and a few scrapes." The nurse's blue eyes were sympathetic. "In other words, you were cold, banged up and utterly exhausted. Mumbling a lot of nonsense, too, so they decided to keep you overnight for observation. We've given you pain medication, as well, so you could rest more comfortably."

"But I'll be all right?"

"Oh, yes. I imagine you'll still be very sore for some time, and before you're discharged this afternoon, I'm sure the doctor will have another listen to your lungs to make certain you didn't aspirate any rainwater that might cause issues with your lungs." She helped Sara swing her legs back into the bed.

She glimpsed the constellation of bruises dotting them before the nurse quickly covered them with the sheets. But the word *rainwater* had Sara stiffening as she remembered lying facedown in the darkness, with two men talking nearby—men she was certain had wanted to take away Mac's children.

"I just came on this morning," the nurse was saying, "and I never heard how you happened to be caught out in the storm. Were you in a wreck or...?"

Throwing off the sheets again, Sara insisted, "I need to talk to Mac, now. I have to find out if they took the twins—or hurt them."

"I don't know who—"

"I need my purse, my phone—any phone! I have to talk to him, *please.*"

And then Mac appeared in the door frame, a sight for sore eyes in spite of his unshaven and somewhat rumpled state. "I'm right here, Sara. Everything's going to be all right now," he said, pulling her, weeping, into his arms as she came to her feet. "Tell me, how are you feeling?"

Shaking her head, she said, "I'll be fine, but the children, Mac, please. I need to know if they're—"

After the nurse excused herself, he carefully explained, "They're both safe and perfectly secure, I promise—and so relieved, since I was able to tell them you're likely to be released today."

"But where are they now? Didn't you bring them?"

she asked, pushing free of his embrace to look up into his blue-gray eyes.

"Your foster care coordinator's minding them right now at her place. Hayden has a deputy keeping watch, on the off chance those two from last night figure out where we've got them stashed and take a second crack at finishing what they started."

Sara's heart leaped. "So those horrible men still haven't been caught?"

"I'm afraid there's no sign of them so far. Hayden's hoping you'll be able to help with a description. He's tied up right now at the crime scene with a search team but hopes to interview you about what happened as soon as possible. Last night, I'm afraid you weren't making all that much sense."

She grimaced, remembering only nightmarish bits and pieces. "That's embarrassing. I'm sorry I couldn't be more help—"

"You have nothing to apologize for. *Nothing*, Sara. Understand me?" he asked.

At her nod, he added, "If you had any idea how terrified I was that I was going to find you murdered—"

She saw the pain of it in his eyes, a mix of unmistakable fear and loss, regret and guilt, a look she'd seen in her own mirror after her sister's child's death, enough to know it couldn't be faked.

"I'm still here," she whispered, realizing that, impossible as it seemed, he truly did care about her as a person rather than a "convenience" as she had accused him.

Clearly overcome by emotion, he squeezed her tight until she groaned.

"Sorry," he said, loosening his hold. "It's just that— I can't believe how close those men came to killing you, to taking my kids. Surely, that's what they had to have been there for..."

Nodding, she said, "I only wish that I'd gotten a look at either of their faces. But it got dark so early, with the storm, and all I could think about was getting everyone to safety."

"That's certainly understandable. The twins couldn't describe them, either, other than Cristo saying they were big men. But did you *hear* anything, maybe?"

She struggled to think back before nodding. "I think so, yes, when they were looking for me. They sounded like they were walking not far from the spot I'd fallen."

"What were they saying? Did they use any names?"

"I really can't remember any specifics, except that they were looking for us and they sounded so angry and frustrated." She struggled to think back, but she couldn't make her brain replay the exact words, only the gut-churning terror of the moment. "My heart was pounding out of my chest. I knew they'd kill me if they found me—especially since I'd stabbed the one man."

"That blood I spotted was you—*stabbing* him?"

She shuddered at the surreal memory of the moment. "When he tried shoving his way past the dresser while the twins were climbing out the bedroom window, I jabbed the knife into his forearm two or three times to keep them out. He—he bellowed and swore. I think it might've been in Spanish, but I was so scared, I'm not sure."

He squeezed her, though more carefully this time. "I'm so sorry for what you went through—and so grateful for the way you fought for my kids. But why didn't you hide with them, underneath the porch?"

"Because they might've looked and found us then. I thought, instead, if I could lead them away from the house, give you time to make it over there..."

"The courage that must have taken." His voice thickened with emotion.

"There wasn't time to stop to think about it." She shook her head. "You would have done the same thing."

"Because I'm their father," he said. "But you—"

Uncomfortable with his praise, Sara shook her head. "We need to get back to them. Donna Milburn's a good woman, but I don't believe she speaks any Spanish at all, and they'll need to talk, after everything that's happened."

"Please sit down, will you?" He gestured toward the bed. "You're making me nervous, with that swaying."

Sighing in exasperation, she allowed him to help her back into the bed.

"There. That's better," he said. "And I have some news for you about the twins. Better hold on to your hat for this one. I'm afraid they'd been pulling one over on us for quite some time."

"What? What do you mean?"

"What I *mean* is that both of them speak and understand English quite well. Well enough for both of them to talk to me last night."

She shook her head. "That's not possible. They can't—"

"I would've thought the same thing if I hadn't heard it with my own ears. Turns out, they've been refusing to speak English as a way of avoiding being sent to live with me."

"Refusing?" She felt a wave of dizziness wash over her. "But all those lessons we did—the emotional block that's been keeping them from learning—"

"As far as I can see, the only thing preventing them from absorbing your lessons was a pact between the two never to speak English. I got them to admit as much this morning." He shook his head. "There were more than a few tears, too, I can tell you, when I got them to admit their grandfather insisted on having them tutored in the language since he considered it a business advantage. I should've realized that since he did the same with Analisa."

"I still can't believe they fooled me like that."

"They fooled *everyone*." He grimaced. "But as frustrating as it is, I can't really blame them for it."

"*Can't* you?" She suspected that most men in his position would be insulted by the deception, even angry.

Instead, Mac sighed and shook his head. "Think about it. They've been told for years that I'm a danger, the kind of man who'd hurt them if I got half a chance. They were trying to protect themselves, in the only way they knew—and stick it to me, too, for what they believed I'd done to their mother."

"When you look at it that way," she said, "it's actually pretty clever on their part. So what went wrong last night? Was Silvia too upset to keep it up?"

Mac shook his head. "Actually, it was Cristo who dropped the ruse. Poor kid was half certain you'd been shot and desperate for me to go and find you."

She closed her eyes, lifting her hand to span her forehead. "They *did* shoot at me," she said, remembering the heart-stopping sound of the loud cracks.

"Thank God, you weren't killed," he said, gently placing his hand over top of hers. "I don't know what the kids would do, what *I* would do, without you."

Too overwhelmed to respond, she fought to process not only what they'd been through but what this new information might mean. Would the children and Mac even need her any longer now that it had been discovered that language was no real barrier?

Aside from the matter of need, she was exhausted, too, as well as traumatized and battered. She hated to imagine what she must look like with her hair all tangled and body bruised and scraped. Part of her wanted nothing more than to go home, to retreat to the safe cocoon of her old life, her job and friends and the neighborhood she loved. She could call up Rachel, beg her to drive out here and rescue her from this nightmare, use her injuries as the excuse she needed to tell both Mac and her boss that she was going home.

So do it now. Tell him now you're not going back with him. You've done your part already, nearly given up your life—and your heart—for a job you never asked for...a man and a family that can never be yours...even if—especially if—he cares about you.

Because there was no way she could ever be the woman he and his family wanted and deserved.

Looking up at him, she said, "Once they release me, I'm not sure I— I don't see how I can go back to that cabin again, not after what happened."

"Of course, I wouldn't expect you to stay there again. None of you," he told her. "It's why I'm taking you all home."

"Home?" Her green eyes widened. "B-but the children—"

"Will be safe there, in their own rooms, where they can begin acclimating with you to help them. I'll be there to watch over them, and the house has a security system."

"What about me, though?"

"I'm afraid the house is only a three-bedroom, so you'll be taking the master."

"I can't put you out of your own bed, Mac. I'll sleep on the sofa or—"

"Nonsense," he said. "The sheets are fresh and clean

for you, and while you're recuperating, you'll need your privacy and comfort."

"But you—"

"The pull-out bed in the game room's not half bad, and I'll be able to hear you from there, all of you, if you need anything at all. I'll take good care of you, I promise," he said. "And more than that, I *need* to be there for you."

Sara's vision swam as her eyes filled with tears.

"What's wrong?" he asked. "Because if there's something else I can do, *anything* to make it easier, I promise you, I'll do it."

She shook her head. "It isn't that. It's— I'm scared, Mac. Scared I've already gotten in too deep. And I won't— We can't live like some sort of family, together... I just *can't.*"

"Those kids still need you, Sara. *We* all need you— now more than ever. Last night really shook them up, and without you, I can't imagine how I'll ever get them through this."

"You're a good father. I have every confidence that you can do this," she said, though inside, the thought of returning home to Austin without even saying goodbye to the twins filled her with dismay.

"If that's true, why is your voice shaking?"

"Because I'm going to miss you— all of you," she told him, "but I'm not up for this, not anymore."

"Please, Sara. Don't make this decision right now. Not when you're upset—and not when I still need you to help convince the twins they'll be safe."

"You can talk to them. I know you can—"

"I'm not so sure about that, not without you to help them see they won't be betraying their grandmother's love to go on speaking to me in English, and maybe learning, over time, to accept and even love me, too."

Her eyes burned, her vision hazing, and she knew he was right, just as she understood that she was too hooked not to see this through now—far too invested both in the family and the man who'd come to claim her.

"All right," she said reluctantly. "I'll stay for a few days because I care about your family. But you need to really get this, Mac. As soon as I can get the children settled in with you, I'll be signing off on your paperwork and heading home again…"

"Maybe— Maybe I'm *not* ready," Mac said, sounding suddenly uncertain.

"I believe you will be," she assured him. *And then you'll never have to learn why I'm not fit to be anybody's full-time mother.*

Chapter 13

With Sara dozing in the truck's front seat beside him, Mac kept his gaze on the road ahead, where bright sunshine reflected off puddles from the prior night's storm. But his thoughts kept returning to the fear he'd glimpsed earlier in her eyes all during the drive back home. As courageous as she'd proved herself the previous evening, it was obvious that she was far more afraid of her own growing emotional involvement than she was the armed men who'd tried to kill her.

Since she'd already so sharply refused his clumsy earlier suggestion that she abandon her old life to stay in the Hill Country with his family, he wasn't about to bring it up again—not when she'd made it so clear that she believed he saw her as no more than a ready-made nanny and translator for his children. At the time, he realized, there might have been a grain of truth to her argument, but last night, when he'd feared she might have been lost to him forever, the searing pain of the thought had made him more certain than ever that it was Sara herself, and not what she could do for him, that he truly treasured. And now, after learning what she'd risked for his family, he couldn't imagine ever finding another woman more worthy of his full attention. Worthy of far more than he could hope to give her, even if he could convince her to give him half a chance.

But for the time being, he understood any hopes of a future with her were a distant worry. His focus had to be on getting her well again—and neutralizing the threat to his family's safety.

By the time they made it back to Rio Frio, Sara finally woke up as he turned into the drive for the resort. Shaking her head, she blinked at him in apparent confusion. "I thought we were going to pick up the kids."

"Donna asked if I could hold off until later this afternoon. They're playing with her two girls right now. Apparently, there's a litter of kittens she's been fostering for adoption and they're all really enjoying themselves playing with them."

Sara smiled at him, her eyes brightening. "Uh-oh. You know what that means, don't you?"

"I suppose they're picking out their favorite, aren't they?"

"That's certainly how it worked when my sister and I were little girls."

"You have a sister?" he asked, pleased that she was opening to him enough to let another rare detail from her past slip out.

"Had," she clarified. "I'm afraid we lost Willow about ten years ago. Opioid addiction."

"I'm so sorry," he said, imagining how painful that must have been for someone like Sara, whose life seemed to revolve around fixing things for others. He wondered if her sister's issues had influenced her in that direction, giving her an outsized sense of responsibility for others.

"Thanks—but it's good to think back to the times when Willow put her mind toward more innocent scheming, like how we might talk Mom into letting us bring home a new kitten. And we all adored Purr-lina after we succeeded."

"Some kitten's all I need right now." Mac laughed, shaking his head, though he couldn't help thinking of his daughter and the way she'd glommed onto that teddy bear she'd been clutching like a lifeline. Though he'd taken a quick look and hadn't found anything suspicious about it, her attachment seemed to speak to a deeper need.

Sara's eyes brightened. "Well, this visit will be good for them, anyway, getting to know kids from around here who can introduce them around to others or tell them about school. Maybe it'll help to take their minds off everything."

"I thought so, too. Plus, I don't know if you heard me on the phone..."

She shook her head.

"Hayden's planning to come by later this afternoon to interview you about what happened."

"I'm not sure how helpful I can be," she said, "but I'm happy to cooperate. Oh, and speaking of phones, have you seen mine by any chance?"

He nodded. "I found it last night on the cabin floor, but I'm afraid it was broken. If you'll order a new one sent here, though, it's on me."

"That's not necessary. I have accident insurance on it."

"Maybe so, but I'm paying the deductible. I insist."

"That's very kind," she said.

"It's the least I can do, considering what you did for

my kids. And any out-of-pocket medical expenses you have, I'm covering, as well. I hope you know that."

"Since I can see that arguing would be pointless, I'll just say thanks again, Mac."

"Wise woman."

As they slowed to make the turn into the resort entrance, Sara asked, "Won't we need to go by the cabin first, to pick up the children's and my things?"

"I hope you don't mind," he said as he passed the Clearwater Crossing sign, "but I asked my assistant manager Frieda to round up her granddaughter, who works in housekeeping for us when she's off from school in the summers. The two of them packed all your belongings from the cabin earlier and brought them over here."

Sara pulled off the sunglasses he had loaned her as they entered the deeper shade. "That was very thoughtful. Thank you, and I'll be sure to thank them, too."

"I know they were glad to do it. I can't imagine you'd be eager to go back there after what you went through last night."

"You've got that right," she said, "and now maybe I'll have time to clean up and put on a little makeup so I'll look a little less terrifying before Hayden and the kids see me, too."

He smiled, remembering how she'd fussed about her tangled hair at the hospital until he'd attempted to comb it for her after the nurse had helped her into the loose sundress he'd brought over for her. "You couldn't be scary if you tried, I promise."

"Please," she said. "I tried to clean up a little before I dressed, but I still have grit in my hair and stuck to my skin from that wallow in the mud last night."

"You look beautiful to me," he said, meaning it.

"That's nice of you to say."

"No need to sound so skeptical. I'm not just blowing smoke here. You've always—from the first time I laid eyes on you—"

"Now I know you're messing with me." This time, her tone was teasing. "You were so suspicious of me that day when I first drove up, I seriously doubt you gave a single thought to my appearance."

He cracked a smile, remembering. "And you probably figured me for some kind of mad, half-dressed hermit, the way I came racing up with my ax."

"I had my suspicions," she said before admitting, "though I may've noticed the abs, too. Just a little..."

Grinning, he passed a small building whose sign marked it as the resort office before making a second turn. After threading through the woods, he pulled in front of the cedar-and-stone, lodge-style two-story he'd called home for the past six years. Though it wasn't a huge place, it was more than large enough to house his family, and he was proud of the work he'd done modernizing the older structure—mostly with his own two hands—since he had moved in.

"What a gorgeous home," Sara said, looking up to take it all in. "Those huge windows are amazing! I never would have had any idea it was tucked away back here, either."

"I got lucky that it's high enough on the bluff that it didn't sustain any damage. Don't try to get out on your own. Let me help you."

"I can do it," she insisted and, sure enough, by the time he'd left the truck and run around to the passenger side, she was stifling a groan as she slid down onto her own two feet. "I'm just stiff from the ride, that's all."

Grabbing the bag with her things, he started for the front door. Instead, however, she veered toward the deck railing near the stairway leading down to a spot where shafts of sunlight streamed through cypress boughs to illuminate the river, which chattered over the tops of smooth-worn rocks. Beyond this stretch, at the deeper bend, the river's famously clear water darkened to a deep blue-green pool. Above the now deserted swimming hole, a long rope hung beneath a thick branch, and along the bank, a rack of colorful plastic kayaks, which Mac and his staff had hauled to higher ground as the waters began to rise, awaited the visitors he hoped would soon put them to good use once again.

"I can't believe the work you've done on the property," Sara told him. "It's absolutely stunning—and Clearwater Crossing's everything you promised."

"You definitely saw the resort at its worst before, but there's still a lot of work to go to get the place back in peak condition. I have a couple of workers coming on next week to help me make the final push." Though labor was expensive, he had little choice, since he'd already begun taking reservations for the latter part of the limited tourist season, a narrow window he could ill afford to miss. "And with Frieda and her granddaughter, Mei-Li, back at work, too, I'm starting to feel like we can really make this happen."

"Maybe it'll make things easier, having the children home, too."

When Sara smiled at him, he saw how pale she was behind the mottled bruising on the right side of her face. That, along with the unmistakable stiffness of her movements, had him reaching forward to brush back a lock of blond-streaked hair that the breeze had blown across her cheek. "I'm only sorry this change has come at such a price. But I promise you, whatever it takes to keep you safe, I'm going to do it."

Her smile faded. "Do you think they'll try again?"

"Let's talk inside, where you can sit, okay?" Keys in hand, he gestured toward the door, the sight of the small sticker warning of an alarm system reminding him he had set it before leaving. It reminded him, as well, that he hadn't yet told her about Tommy's incursion into his home yesterday.

He held off for now, however, deciding she'd been through enough in the past twelve hours to have to deal with worries that some unscrupulous photographer might come looking for photos. After she had had the chance to rest, they could discuss it.

Once inside the spacious entry, he used the keypad to disarm the alarm. After stretching and yawning her way out of her bed, Roxy came wagging up to greet them.

"Hey, there, girl," Sara said, rubbing the Lab's ears as she took in the open great room whose windows overlooked the deck and river view below.

"This is quite the upgrade from the rental cabin." She eyed the massive wood beams beneath the vaulted ceiling and the loft along one side, where the children's bedrooms and another bathroom were both located on the second floor. Turning, she took in the mix of rustic woods, natural fabrics and stone that echoed the outdoor elements. "It's open, understated, comfortable, but everything blends right in with the natural surroundings You have great taste."

"You sound surprised," he said, both amused and pleased by her reaction.

"Well, you *have* been living as a bachelor for a long time."

He shrugged. "One currently working in the hospitality industry. I might've picked up a thing or two along the way."

Directing her attention away from the view she'd been

admiring, Mac pointed out the simple but thoroughly updated kitchen on the left, with several bar stools to one side of the quartz island. "There's coffee, tea, drinks—"

"I'd love some water for now. My mouth's dry from the medication they gave me."

When he brought her the glass, he found her studying a display case he'd put together, which contained lengths of barbed wire, a pair of spurs and a Rocking H-W branding iron.

"These are from your ranch?" she asked.

"They are," he said, feeling that same punch of grief he always did at the memory of the day he'd been forced to concede defeat and put the property up for sale.

"What's in that envelope, tacked to the back?"

He sighed. "Legal papers, which I might as well keep for a memento, for all of the damned good they do me. You see, back when I still could afford lawyers, I tried suing Analisa's parents in civil court for what they'd done, thinking that money might give me the leverage I needed to get my kids back. I actually won a whopping judgment against them—which felt like some kind of victory until I found out there wasn't a single person in Argentina with the guts to enforce it."

"Don Roberto had that much influence?"

"He was definitely well connected."

"But he's gone now, so maybe there's still something you can do with it."

Mac shrugged. "The money was never the real point. All I really want now is to be left alone to raise my kids."

"Do you really think that a woman desperate enough to try something like his widow did last night won't come after your family again?"

"I take your point, but I'm not following. What's this have to do with my civil judgment?"

"What if you started pushing again to try to collect the money now, since Don Roberto's no longer around to flex his muscle? Maybe going after your former mother-in-law will put her on the defensive, distract her too much to worry about the children."

"That's not a bad idea, but I can't spend tens of thousands of dollars or more tilting at windmills right now. What I really need is hard proof that she sent those men last night so Buenos Aires law enforcement can deal with it accordingly. It's the only way."

"Do you think they will?"

"I don't know. But I doubt that the governor's people will be happy with the idea of a foreign national sending kidnappers to Texas. I'm hoping we'll be able to get some help there—or maybe the feds will use their diplomatic tools to exert some real pressure."

"That would be fantastic," she said. "And if you'd like, I'll put in a call to Paul Barkley's replacement, Madeline Herrera. I'm sure that she'd be willing to lend us any help she can, or at least point us in the right direction."

He nodded. "At this point, I'm willing to try anything, but for the rest of the afternoon, Sara, I don't want you worrying about anything but resting and feeling better."

"I'll take on the world tomorrow," she agreed.

"Let me show you the rest of the place." He gestured toward a doorway just beyond the spiral staircase to the balcony. "Here's the master bedroom, and the game room, laundry and a half bath are on the other side there, leading to the back door. I don't even want you thinking about going upstairs, where the kids' rooms are, though, until you're feeling better."

"I'm not sure I could climb that staircase if I tried right now," she admitted. "I'm afraid I'll be sore for a month."

"Please sit, then, but can I get you something before I

join you? Hayden probably won't be by for at least a few hours, so we have time. A sandwich, maybe or— How about a snack?" he added when she shook her head. "I have some cheese and crackers, maybe some nuts, and I can slice an apple."

"You had me at cheese," she admitted. "Can I help you?"

"Just relax and enjoy the view. It won't take me a minute." While he was in the kitchen, he grabbed himself some water, as well, and brought it out when he had readied the plate for them.

When he sat down beside her, he said, "Hope you like smoked Gouda and sharp cheddar, too."

She gasped happily, grabbing a napkin and snagging a couple of slices and a cracker. "Definitely."

"I wanted to let you know that until we have some assurance that last night's attackers have either been captured or that the children's grandmother has called them off, I won't be leaving you and the children unprotected."

"What about the deputy Hayden sent to watch over the twins today? Will he be sticking around to help?"

He shook his head, frowning. "I'm afraid Hayden's already broken it to me that they don't have the manpower."

"But you're family. Surely, Hayden must—"

"It wouldn't matter who we are. I doubt he's managed to catch more than an hour's catnap since I reached out to him last night as it is. And he can't just conjure extra deputies out of thin air, though I do understand he's called in a search and rescue team out of San Antonio to help check out the property around the rental cabin and the hillside around the Colt's Ear where you thought you spotted movement to see if they can turn up any evidence."

"Evidence? So they don't think the men might still be hiding nearby?"

"They found a set of tracks late last night and a spot in the brush where a larger vehicle—a good-sized SUV or pickup—appeared to have been very recently driven back into the brush and hidden on the next road up the hill from the rental cabin. But there was no sign of where it might've gone, and Hayden figures they took off as soon as they realized things were heating up and they had missed their window."

"One of them was hurt, too," she reminded him. "And I promise you, that was no little scratch I gave him."

He forced a smile, though the thought made him slightly queasy. "That's my girl."

To her credit, she managed to smile back. "So maybe they had to get medical help, like I did."

"I'm sure Hayden's checking in with every clinic and ER in the region. This may be a rural county, but he's very good at what he does."

She nodded and then added, "Maybe they'll even pack up and leave, now that they've got one guy hurt and lost the element of surprise."

"It's possible," he allowed, mostly because he could see how badly she wanted to believe it, "but just in case they *are* still around, we'll keep the alarm on all the time, and I'll be armed in case of an emergency."

She lowered the slice of cheese she had been nibbling, her full attention on him.

She regarded him with an uncertain look. "You'll be careful with that gun, won't you? Around the children, I mean?"

"Definitely," he assured her. "Any time it's not on me, I'll make sure it's well secured."

She nodded, explaining, "It's not that I don't trust your

judgment. It's just, in my work, I've seen the aftermath of some horrendous firearm mishaps involving children."

"Don't worry about offending me. It's never a bad idea to be reminded to pay attention to gun safety. Especially when you have a couple of kids in the house for the first time in a long while."

They ate for a few minutes before Sara shifted uncomfortably in her seat.

"What's the matter? Do you need another pain pill?"

She shook her head. "Nothing like that. It's just that grit rubbing against my skin. If you don't mind, I'd like to see about that shower now. Or maybe a soak in the bath would be even better, if there's time."

Rising, he offered her a hand up, thinking that some tub time and a nap was the very least that she deserved after everything she'd been through. "You have plenty, so why don't you come and let me help you wrap that cast of yours in plastic for you, and then I'll show you where everything is."

A tap came at the bathroom door. Sara tried shifting to escape it and felt herself slip lower.

Abruptly remembering where she was—and how she had her left arm, in its wrapped cast, propped on a stack of towels on the edge of the tub, she jerked to a sitting position, coming fully awake barely in time to avoid dunking her wrapped arm into the water.

"Sara? You all right in there?" Mac called from outside the door. "I heard a splash."

"Oh, shoot. I'm fine. It's just—I dozed off here, and knocked all the towels right in my bath trying to keep my cast out of it." She sighed, seeing that no other towels were anywhere within reach.

"So let me grab you some dry ones," he said.

"No—don't come in! I'll… I'll find something." She tried to stand, too quickly, before her sore and tired body sent her groaning back down into the cooling water.

This was ridiculous. She was being so pathetic.

"Sara—come on. Let me help you," Mac urged. "The last thing we need is you falling."

"I'm not one of your children to be taken care of," she reminded him, frustrated enough that she felt the hot sting of tears in her eyes.

"I assure you," he said, his voice tinged with what sounded suspiciously like amusement, "I've never thought of you that way for a single second."

She hesitated, eyeing the linen closet across the bathroom. She could try getting up on her own—and risk slipping on the floor with her wet feet and making a bad situation worse. Or she could sit here stubbornly, slowly growing colder while a good man stood waiting to help her just outside.

"All right," she called, hurriedly draping her body with one of the soaked towels. "Please."

"I'm just coming in to grab the towels and hand them to you, okay? I won't look," he promised as the door cracked open.

"You're sweet, but I'm covered, more or less," she said, shivering. "I just — I'd rinsed my hair and washed, and then I leaned back in the warm water…and it was all over until you knocked."

Stepping inside the still somewhat steamy room, he grabbed a large and fluffy-looking ivory bath towel from the closet and turned toward her, studying her with an appraising look that made her stomach quiver. "You look pretty chilly there. And you've probably stiffened up, lying in one position so long."

"I'm afraid so," she admitted.

"Let me help you out of there. I don't want you falling."

She eyed him uncertainly, wondering if that was all he wanted. But it was the warmth in his expression—that same, unfailing kindness he'd extended her again and again over the short time she had come to know him— that had her wondering, was help out of this awkward and uncomfortable situation all she really wanted from what was undoubtedly the most committed, caring—not to mention mouthwateringly gorgeous—man who had ever looked her way?

Making her decision, Sara took a deep breath and reached for Mac's hand, their eyes locking as he helped her to her feet. His gaze remained steady, never straying downward, as she allowed the wet towels to slide off her and took the dry towel from him to wrap around herself.

Taking his hand once again for balance, she then stepped out of the tub onto the mat, where a charged silence fell between them. Grabbing a second towel, he looked into her face, his raised brows asking her permission.

Scarcely able to breathe, she nodded, and he dried her hair before blotting the damp skin of her arms and shoulders.

When he gently daubed her face, she whispered, "You didn't look down...when I dropped the towels..."

"Will there be a medal?" he asked, the skin crinkling at the corners of his eyes. "Because I feel like there should be a medal—but I gave my word, and I didn't want you to be any more embarrassed or uncomfortable than you were already."

"The thing is, Mac," she admitted, moving closer, "I'm *not* embarrassed with you. I couldn't be, after everything you've done for me. And you're the first man I've found myself trusting in such a long, long time."

She saw his throat work as he swallowed, heard the rasping of his breathing as it deepened. All the while, her own awareness that they were completely alone in his house, in a room just off his bedroom, with no one expected for hours, loomed in her imagination.

She swallowed hard, the fine hairs along her arms and on the back of her neck lifting from her still damp skin.

"I'm not sure that's such a great idea, Sara," Mac said, "trusting me this close right now. Because I have no idea how much longer I can keep myself from kissing you again. And I'm afraid that if I started with your lips, I wouldn't be able to keep from kissing every last one of your bruises—and everywhere else—until you were feeling better...or we both were."

"Oh..." Her skin heated as she thought of the placement of some of those bruises she'd glimpsed in the mirror. But at the moment, she couldn't look away from his mouth, couldn't stop herself from wondering how it might feel on her most sensitive places.

She raised the towel she'd taken from him, feeling the fabric catch against the peaks of her hardened nipples. And then she raised herself onto her tiptoes. Leaning close, she touched her lips to the corner of his mouth as she lifted her right hand to feather a gentle touch along his jawline.

He groaned aloud, his composure hanging by a thread an instant longer before it snapped completely and he kissed her back, his mouth hard and hot and questing as he pulled her into his arms.

She let the towels slide to the floor, allowing herself to forget the stress and doubt and all thoughts of the future to claim this glorious swirl of sensation—and the heady feeling of being desired by a man that she wanted every bit as much.

When she broke the kiss to catch her breath and more comfortably adjust her awkward cast, he asked, "Is this all right? Do you want me to stop now? Because if at any point you do, I'm willing to— I know you must be sore and tired…"

"That's not what I'm feeling now at all, not any longer," she confessed as she looked into the mirrors, thrilling to the sight of herself completely naked in his arms. "But I was thinking that, as lovely as this bathroom is, I believe I'm ready for a more thorough exploration of your bedroom. That is, if you'd be willing to give me a guided tour…"

The grin that lit his blue-gray eyes assured her he was very much on board with the prospect, as did the speed with which he removed the T-shirt he'd been wearing and reached to undo the buckle of his khaki pants.

As he stepped free of them, giving her a fine view of the extremely impressive tenting of his boxers, he said, "I believe I have some condoms in my dresser…if I'm not presuming too much."

She met his gaze before nodding and prayed she wasn't about to mess things up now, talking. But better to make certain there were no misunderstandings later about exactly what this meant. "What I said before, about leaving in a few days—that isn't changing. So this can't be— It's a *moment* that we have here. A moment we can take, if we're both willing. But right here, right now, it's everything I want."

He kissed her again, deeply, his hand sliding from her rib cage to her waist and settling on the flare of her hip. "If this moment's all we get, Sara," he said, his voice husky with desire, "then let's damned well make it count for something, because I, for one, intend to replay this in my memories for years to come."

And then he took her by the hand and led her to the bedroom, leaving a litter of forgotten towels in their wake.

Chapter 14

Mac wanted desperately to tell Sara what it had meant to him, losing himself inside her cries of pleasure—and then inside her—letting go of the bitterness and pain he'd carried so long. But try as he might, the words all knotted up inside him, too sacred to speak aloud, especially after she had warned him that this would not change anything for her.

So, instead, he tried to show her, holding her close to him afterward and gently pressing his lips to her temple. Warm and so relaxed that she felt nearly boneless as she murmured softly, "Love you." Words followed by deep, even breaths that left him no doubt that she had drifted off to sleep.

"I love you, too," he ventured, though he couldn't be certain she had meant it—or even been aware of what it was she'd said. But he didn't give a damn. The relief of opening himself to it, of admitting it aloud, felt so good.

Though others might warn him this was all too sudden, that he'd barely had time to scratch the surface of this beautiful, fascinating woman, he knew how he felt about her—how he'd been feeling for some time.

After so many years alone—years spent wondering if he had ever truly known the woman he had given his heart so many years before—the knowledge that he could feel anything again, could trust anyone at all, came as such a relief that he couldn't worry about the future. For now, he could only sink deep into the complete contentment he felt holding Sara in his arms...

He hadn't meant to nod off, too, but since he'd only managed a few broken hours of sleep earlier, the combination of the dim room, fatigue and rare contentment conspired to pull him under. He wasn't sure how much later it was when the sound of his cell phone ringing finally broke through, reminding him he had responsibilities, including two children who needed his attention.

Leaving Sara, he grabbed his pants and headed for the great room, where he found the phone sitting on the coffee table where he recalled leaving it. Though it had already quit ringing, he grimaced, seeing that it was Hayden—and that his brother had already texted him, as well.

I was hoping to stop by and interview Sara, the message read. Where the devil are you two?

There was another text below it. This one was from Donna Milburn, asking if he could come by to pick up the twins before four thirty.

Cursing at life's intrusions, he pulled on his pants and looked up to see Sara standing in the doorway, her hair tousled and a sheet wrapped around her torso.

"Keep looking at me like that," he said, stunned anew by the memory of the things they had been doing—the things a certain part of his anatomy was primed to do again, "and I'm going to completely forget I even have kids and a brother to deal with and take you back to bed."

"Judging from the regret I hear in your voice and the words you just let slip out, that's not likely," she said, her green eyes wistful.

"I'm afraid not. I need to pick up the kids from Donna's, for one thing, but before then, Hayden was hoping to come by to talk to you. Apparently, he's been trying both our phones and is wondering what we're up to."

Her grimace was quick but he caught it nonetheless.

"Don't worry," he said. "I'll tell him you were resting, and I ended up chilling on the sofa and dozed off for a little while myself."

"It's not that I'm ashamed of anything we did," she explained. "It's just— I'm a very private person. And I wouldn't want people making any presumptions about a future that isn't going to happen, or giving the children any false hopes that they're about to get a mother."

There it was, the reality she'd been so careful to warn him of before they'd made love. Still, it felt like biting down on a cold iron nail while enjoying a bite of warm, rich, chocolate pudding.

"So when you told me 'love you' afterward, you didn't really mean it, did you? That was just the afterglow talking— or was it the drugs they'd given you?" Even as the question came out, he knew he was being an ass, throwing such a statement in her face like this so soon after she'd given him her trust. But he couldn't help himself. The pain of what felt like a betrayal was too great, sending him straight back to that day he'd heard his wife's voice on that tape...

Try as he might, he'd never been able to shake off his initial jolt of recognition, despite the recording's poor quality and the fact that the accusations had been in Spanish, along with every doubt his attorney and their hired expert had cast upon the cassette's authenticity. It *had* been Analisa, accusing him of the most heinous of crimes against her, though for years he'd been unwilling to admit the truth of her betrayal, even to himself.

Sara's eyes flared wide with shock, welling with tears an instant later. "I—I don't remem—" Then she frowned, her forehead furrowing with concentration before she shook her head and stared at him in wonder. "You're only angry because you said it back to me. I heard you, but don't worry, Mac. I won't hold you to it."

"I *meant* it," he insisted. "If I weren't head over heels in love with you, I would never, for the first time in more than eight years…"

Her eyes softened. "You—you've been *celibate* this whole time? Oh, Mac."

"I don't want or need your pity," he said, his voice little more than a growl. "I've had my focus elsewhere. And there've been— I'll admit, I've had some issues trusting."

"I could never pity you," she said, going to him and reaching out to lay her hand above his heart. "But I am honored that you opened up enough to let me inside—"

"But did you *mean* those words?" he asked, hated how pained his challenge sounded.

She hesitated, her eyes avoiding his as she turned away. "Maybe we should talk about this later. You should let Donna know you'll be picking up the kids and tell your brother I'll be ready for my interview as soon as he wants to drop by."

"I'll do that," Mac said sharply, "but as far as I'm concerned, your refusal to discuss it has already told me everything I need to know."

While Mac went to pick up the children, Sara, who'd hurriedly dressed and neatened up as well as she could manage, struggled to focus as she explained to Hayden as much as she could recall about the events of the previous evening. With his darker, wavy hair combed straight back and his deep blue eyes shadowed by fatigue but shrewd, he sat across the resort unit's dinette table from her, a small recorder between the two of them. Though he shared his brother's strong, masculine jawline and broad cheekbones, he was a bit shorter as well as stockier than Mac, almost burly in comparison—the kind of man she could well imagine taking down criminals with a minimum of effort.

Provided he could identify and find them.

"I only wish I could be of more help," she told him after answering the questions he'd used to tease out more information, "or that I'd actually seen their faces."

"It's probably best you didn't," he said, his expression softening. "If you'd gotten any closer, I can't imagine they'd've let you get away from them alive."

"I don't think it was their idea to *let* me escape as it was," she said, shuddering. "At least, it didn't feel that way when I heard them shooting at me."

"We're all grateful you had a bit of a lead on them and darkness in your favor," Hayden said, sounding sincere. "And, speaking strictly from a personal standpoint, I can't imagine picking up the pieces if Mac lost another woman that he clearly cares for."

She shook her head, her cheeks burning at the thought of how angry Mac had been with her only a short time before. But it was only because she'd hurt him badly, refusing to admit that the words that had slipped out when she'd let her guard down had been the absolute truth. "How did you…? Did he say something to you out there, something about the two of us?"

The brothers *had* spoken outside, alone for several minutes after his arrival, before Mac had left for Donna's.

Hayden shook his head. "He didn't have to. We're not really close—or, at least, we haven't been in recent years—but I know my brother well enough to know the fear I saw in him last night while you were missing was personal. It wasn't just on the children's behalf, either."

"I care about them, too," she admitted, darting a worried glance at the recorder. "About all of them, very much, but this isn't— I don't want anyone to be hurt, especially the children."

"Don't worry. I won't mention anything to anyone about you and my brother," he assured her, moving to shut off the recorder. "But can I say this one thing to you?"

Drawing a deep breath, she nodded and braced herself for whatever plea or warning he felt obligated to give her on Mac's behalf.

Instead, he smiled at her. "I'm honestly not sure what any woman would ever see in that bullheaded, antisocial brother of mine, but after hearing the details of what happened with what I absolutely believe was an attempted kidnapping last night, there's no question in my mind whatever as to what he sees in *you*. What you did for my niece and nephew—"

"It was what any decent human being would do, that's all. I was only—"

He held up a hand, cutting off her protest. "Let me finish, please. It was a good deal more than most would, at great risk to your personal safety. As far as I'm concerned, you saved my family a whole lot of grief, and we owe you big-time for it."

"Thanks," she said, uncomfortable with the praise, "but I was only doing my job."

He smiled, nodding his approval. "Speaking of your job, I've been a little curious about your background."

Caught off guard, she felt herself tense, wondering, had he been digging into her past for some reason? As a law enforcement official, how much access would he have, she wondered, to records of investigations that had taken place in other counties? Including the investigation of her niece's death—and her own role in it.

"Are you all right?" He frowned as he studied her face. "You're looking awful pale all of a sudden."

"It's…it's nothing. I just— It's a long day, that's all. For you, too, I imagine."

"Maybe, but I'm not the one just out of the hospital. Would some cold water help? Or something else?" Standing, he grabbed her empty glass and went to the refrigerator.

"The water would be fine, thanks."

"Out of the way, dog," he scolded Roxy, who had risen from her bed in one corner of the dinette when he'd gotten up, only to tangle under his feet. "Go lie down, will you? Good girl."

The sound of ice clattering from the door dispenser was following by the trickle of water. "Anything else, while I'm up?" Hayden asked.

"That'll be great. Thanks." When he gave her the glass, she fought to steady her hand after noticing how hard it was shaking. "Now, what was it you wanted to know before?"

"I was just wondering how a social worker out of Austin ends up getting sent to Argentina to escort two kids back to the US, not to mention sticking with them here for a whole extra month. That's surely pretty out of the ordinary for someone in your position, isn't it?"

"Definitely," she said, relieved that he'd asked something she could easily answer. "It's kind of an odd story. After meeting with several of my Spanish-speaking clients after their release from a juvenile facility, I brought what sounded like a pattern of abuse to the attention of their superiors. When they didn't seem inclined to listen, I kept right on rattling cages—until I reached Paul Barkley at the governor's office and the bad apples were not only fired but charged."

"Good for you, sticking up for those kids," Hayden said approvingly.

"Anyway, Barkley remembered my work on that and thought of me when they needed someone bilingual who was good with kids."

"Good to know that all Mac's calls and letters to anyone in politics who'd listen didn't totally fall on deaf ears," Hayden said.

"Speaking of Paul Barkley, though, are you aware that he was struck and killed in a hit and run right after the children's return?"

"I heard something about that, but I have to admit, since it happened so far from my jurisdiction, it hasn't really been on my radar."

"I can't help thinking, what if it should be? After all, Paul *was* instrumental in arranging to have the children brought back here to this country."

Hayden's dark brows lifted. "So you're thinking, what? Retaliation by the children's grandmother—against a government official?"

"Why not?" Sara asked, not missing the skepticism in his voice. "If she'd be upset enough to send two men to try to grab the children, why *not* also send a message about what will happen to anyone else who tries to interfere with what she sees as her family?"

"You don't think it's more likely Barkley was just accidently hit in traffic? Because if that evil old woman was going to have someone eliminated, I'd think she'd more likely send hit men after my brother. With Mac dead, she might even figure there'd be nobody left from here to fight to bring those kids home. Not that she'd be right about that…"

Catching his meaning, and his loyalty to the children he also considered family, Sara nodded and decided he had a good point about Mac being a more likely target than Paul Barkley.

"I'll tell you what, though," Hayden continued. "I'll touch base with the investigating officers on the Barkley case and lay out the theory that what happened here last night was no random home invasion, on the remote chance there could be any connection."

"Thanks for humoring me," she said.

"I wouldn't be," he told her, "if I didn't figure you might possibly be onto something. And if there's even the slightest chance the investigators there in Austin might have some information that could help point me in the direction of our suspects from last night, it's well worth pursuing."

"Speaking of those suspects," Sara said, "Mac mentioned your search around the cabin area. May I ask if you found anything?"

Hayden nodded. "We did come across signs they'd parked a vehicle off of the next road over."

"He told me about that. He said the suspects were long gone, though."

"I'm afraid so. We found this, as well, though." He pulled out his cell phone and fiddled with it, bringing up a photo. "I've bagged and taken the item into evidence to be processed for prints or other trace evidence, but maybe you'll recognize—"

"My missing e-reader!" Leaning forward, she tapped the screen when he turned it so she could see. "It disappeared from the cabin sometime before I broke my wrist. I was afraid one of the twins might've taken it to try to use it to message their grandmother. Where did you find it?"

"Near the spot off the road where the truck or SUV had been hidden. One of them may've dropped it before they were leaving."

"That means—" a shiver of revulsion crawled over her skin "—at least one of them was inside the cabin at some point, maybe while we were making a grocery run or out taking a walk together."

"Anything else you notice missing?"

She made a face. "A few pairs of my panties. I'd been sort of hoping they'd gotten lost in the wash or— I really didn't want to think too hard about alternatives."

"I can see why that might be unsettling, especially as isolated as that place is. But they didn't take anything of the children's?"

"Not that any of us noticed," she said.

"That's odd. Almost makes me wonder if the kids were ever the real targets in the first place."

"I don't understand," she said.

"Since it was only *your* things that were taken, unfortunately, I can't rule out another motive. A motive more focused on you and not the children."

Feeling her skin crawl, she shook her head in disbelief.

"Tell me, Sara," he said, since, already, she had asked him twice to use her first name, "is there perhaps someone you've dated—or anyone who's shown an unhealthy fixation on you? Someone who's had trouble taking no for an answer, called or texted repeatedly and inappropriately?"

"You're…you're talking about a stalker? No," she said, answering her own question. "Of course, like any woman alive, I've occasionally received inappropriate attention, but no one I couldn't just block and ignore, and nothing in quite a while, and it's not like I have any especially persistent exes pining away for the scraps of my attention."

She thought how the last man she'd dated had been so focused on his fitness and career goals that he'd scarcely seemed to noticed when she'd broken off the relationship. "I'd think it was more likely their taking *my* stuff was just impulsive."

"But both items taken were personal and, in the case of the underwear, even sexual—to the wrong kind of man."

"So maybe one of these would-be kidnappers is a perverted creep, too, and grabbed my stuff on impulse while he was checking out the cabin entrances to come back later to snatch the kids."

"That could very well be. Taking the items could've just been a power trip for the guy, unrelated to the end goal," Hayden said, though he didn't look as if he was fully on board with the theory.

"That reminds me," she said. "One of the doors was messed up earlier, popping open even if it was locked. I wonder if they'd done something to it and that was why they thought they would be able to easily force their way inside."

"Lucky for you, it didn't work out that way."

She shook her head. "Oh, it wasn't luck at all. Mac fixed it after we noticed it came open, the morning I came home from the hospital after my wrist was set. If he hadn't made sure those doors were solid…"

"Good thinking on his part."

"Did you find anything else?"

"Nothing of much interest—"

The front door opened, the twins racing through it.

"Sara! Sara, *mira*!" both of them called, running as Sara, lifted to her feet by her own excitement, erupted in a cry of pure joy. In a moment, all three of them came together in a flurry of mingled voices, hugs and tears, as Mac walked in behind them, a tiny orange-and-white kitten in his arms.

Chapter 15

"I can't believe you're such a sucker." Snorting, Hayden shook his head as the two of them stood in the kitchen watching the children and Sara in the great room, where they'd spent the past five minutes speaking in a rapid-fire mix of Spanish and English that Mac could barely follow, except to note their obvious relief to be reunited. At the moment, however, they were all sitting on the sofa, fawning over the ball of fluff that crawled and scampered from one to another.

"Not a sucker, a strategist," he assured his brother, tapping at his temple.

"There's an actual *strategy* involved in getting yourself bogged down with another animal you could be stuck with for up to twenty years?" Hayden scoffed, taking his typical attitude toward long-term personal commitments. As committed as he was to his career, at thirty-six, he still limited his romantic entanglements to women who lived outside of the county and insisted on breaking things off the moment he caught the slightest hint that his partner of the moment might be coming down with what he referred to as a "bad case of expectations."

"Let's be realistic here, bro," Mac said. "With eleven-year-old twins, a dog, and a resort property in need of constant tending, I'm never going to be the footloose bachelor anyway, so what's one more furry creature? Especially one living in the very house I'm hoping they'll quickly start thinking of as home—a home where they don't have to be watched like prisoners to keep them from escaping."

Though he would never admit as much out loud, the fact that Sara obviously liked kittens had also nudged him in the direction of surprising his children with a furry distraction from last night's trauma.

"In other words, the thing's a bribe."

"Come on, man. We always had a dog and a cat or two around the house as kids, and as I recall, you *loved* them." Just as Hayden had been head over heels for his old high-school girlfriend, once upon a time. "Do you even own a *houseplant*?"

"I've got a *cactus*." Hayden scowled.

Mac laughed, shaking his head. "Figures. But I wouldn't bet against it being plastic."

"You sure are in a good mood. That *nap* of yours must've done you a world of good." His mocking tone was one more reminder that he hadn't bought Mac's story about his and Sara's supposed separate rest times.

Mac gave him a warning look over the cheap shot before asking, "Why *wouldn't* I be in a good mood? Sara's home from the hospital, I've finally got my kids where I want them, and they're actually speaking to me in a language I can understand."

"They *did* want something from you, though, right?" asked Hayden. "Back when we were all kids, even you and Ryan and I could quit fighting long enough to act like angels when we were trying to con Mom or Pop into a new—"

"Do you *always* have to act like such a killjoy?" Mac asked irritably, reminded of his brother's penchant for ramming uncomfortable truths down his siblings' throats.

"As I remember, you're the one who's spent the past eight years so miserable that people could hardly stand to be around you," Hayden reminded him.

"I've done fine by my guests," Mac argued, though he delegated as much of the warm-fuzzy duties as possible to Frieda and focused on logistics and facilities.

"You've faked it well enough to get by when you had to put in face time, you mean," Hayden countered. "But I *am* excited to see those kids of yours finally starting to come around. And it's refreshing as hell to finally hear what sounds like actual optimism from you for a change."

Mac couldn't help but look over at Sara, who was taking photos of the children cuddling the kitten. "I know there are still a lot of challenges to come, but I *am* feeling hopeful…"

When his brother said nothing in response, he glanced over to catch the look in Hayden's eyes. A look that didn't match up with what he'd said before about Mac being damned lucky to have such an incredible woman watching out for his kids.

Had something happened in the interview between them, or was it only his brother's naturally suspicious nature coming out?

"Is something wrong?" Mac asked, his gut tightening with apprehension.

Hayden glanced back toward the living room, where

Sara's tone had turned more serious as she asked the children why they hadn't felt they could tell her that they had studied English.

"Let's step outside for a few minutes, give them a little privacy," he suggested.

Mac's gut clenched, his pulse bumping faster. But whatever it was, ignoring it was not an option.

Outdoors, they headed for the same railing where he'd stood earlier with Sara, looking down over the river. But it was another conversation with his brother that haunted Mac, a conversation they'd had only hours after he had learned of Analisa's drowning…

What was she even doing there, on an overnight trip to some snorkeling spot, while she was supposed to be visiting her parents in Argentina? And leaving the kids behind with them in Buenos Aires—that doesn't sound like her.

What does it even matter? Mac had asked his brother, his voice ragged with his devastation. *Her parents said it was some old girlfriends she went to school with, but… but she's gone now— I just can't believe— I have to get down there, bring the kids back.*

But Hayden hadn't been content to leave things at that. Much later, long after Mac had returned, beaten bloody, his brother had once more broached the subject, asking, *Has she ever talked about these old school friends before? And have you ever* heard *from any of them—or could there be someone else, maybe?*

His implication had been as clear as it was devastating. And though, with the passing years Mac had begun to ponder the same question and to wonder if, just maybe, Analisa could have said the terrible things heard on the tape to her parents out of a desire to free herself to be with some lover from her youth, he'd immediately shut down Hayden and had never quite forgiven him for daring to voice the questions he'd been afraid to ask himself.

"First off," Hayden said now, staring out over the water, "I needed to tell you, Tommy Dinshaw, the kid you caught taking those pictures at your house, has been released. I couldn't squeeze anything more out of him, and since he was in custody during the home invasion, he clearly wasn't one of the abductors."

"Great. So now I have to worry about him showing up to try to score another quick buck."

Hayden shook his head. "Not likely. Kid's father came to collect him, and he's given me his word that we won't see Tommy's face again in Real County—or have any more trouble out of him ever."

"And you believe that?"

"Oddly enough, I do. Guy reminded me a lot of Dad."

Mac smiled at a memory of their father, who'd been hell on the three of them when they'd messed up. "In that case, I expect Tommy's not going to have a real fun summer. But that's good to know. So what else was it you wanted to tell me…about Sara?"

Hayden didn't bother denying that that was the real reason he had dragged Mac out here. "She was a pleasure to talk to. She's clearly very concerned about your family, and she's as smart as she is brave."

"So why do I have the distinct impression you're about to warn me off her for some reason?" Mac asked. "You're not suspicious she could be somehow involved, are you? Not after she was hurt trying to lead those men away from them?"

Hayden was quick to shake his head. "I don't think she would ever intentionally do anything to endanger your family. Absolutely not, but—"

"Whatever you are trying to say, just say it," Mac demanded. *So I can tell you how wrong you are.*

"Her e-reader had been taken, along with several pairs of underwear, before this. She told me there was no one she was worried about, no stalker or ex-boyfriend, anything like that, but—"

"She's not a liar, Hayden."

"But earlier, she'd looked like she was going to be sick when I started to ask about her background. Which makes me wonder exactly what's in her past that has her so—"

"Her *past*? Are you serious? The woman's been through hell. She's probably just not feeling well—or shaken up." Or maybe troubled, wondering how she could have made love with such passion when she'd only meant to break his heart.

"That's not it, Mac. I've been interviewing witnesses— and suspects—long enough to know when someone's hiding something."

"Sara's no damned *suspect*. She's the woman I've trusted with my children—the woman who *saved* my kids, and taught me how to—" *Love again,* he nearly said before realizing that his brother would likely only view such a statement as an unfortunate weakness to be forever avoided in his own life. Perhaps, in part, because he'd witnessed the utter wreckage Analisa's death—and, Mac reluctantly admitted, at least to himself, her betrayal— had wrought in all their lives. "Never mind. I'm sure you wouldn't understand."

"I just don't want to see you hurt again, blindsided by a woman's secrets. You have enough challenges, getting your kids used to a whole new life."

"If it makes you any happier, Sara's heading back to

Austin as soon as we get the kids settled. She'll be gone from our lives before I know it."

Hayden laid a hand on his shoulder. "You've lived through worse, man. You can live through losing her, too."

"I suppose I'll have to, for the kids' sake, won't I?" Mac answered, reverting to the gruffness he'd worn like armor for the past eight years.

But underneath, his chest felt like an open wound, the scarred territory cracked wide open by his second failed attempt at love.

Over the next two days, Sara decided that the good thing about having children and animals around—especially a furry young one still mastering the basics of life without its mother—was that they definitely tended to root a person in the immediate needs of the present. From getting the children acclimated to their new home to helping them get their new pet situated, she had plenty of pressing mundane tasks to keep her mind off of worries over the kidnappers returning—or perhaps more photographers like the young man Mac had told her he'd caught taking pictures in the children's rooms before. She also had the opportunity to talk to Silvia and Cristo about their earlier decision to speak Spanish only.

"I can see why you might have been afraid…" she said, now speaking English as the three of them cleaned out the dishwasher while a pot of water on the stove boiled for the potato salad she planned on making for their long-delayed cookout later. Since her hip and back remained sore, the children were taking turns bending over to hand plates and flatware up to her to put away.

If Mac were here, he would undoubtedly fuss that she shouldn't be doing so much, but he'd gone out to the patio area, with Roxy at his heels, to clean the grill in preparation for the burgers.

"Afraid to be alone with him, I mean," Sara continued. "Is that why you pretended?"

"Sí," Cristo admitted, tugging at a curl. "He looked so big and tough and angry, and I thought—"

"No, Cristo. We can tell the truth now," Silvia told him before looking at Sara. "It was *my* idea. I thought maybe he would send us back if he thought we couldn't understand each other, that we'd be too much trouble for him."

Sara sighed and shook her head. "For a while, you two had me thinking I was the worst teacher in the whole world."

"Or we were the most hopeless students ever!" Cristo said with a mischievous grin. "Sometimes, it was so hard, pretending we couldn't remember anything, like babies. One time your face turned *so* red!"

The twins' brown-eyed gazes came together and the two of them burst out laughing. Relieved their ruse was over, Sara couldn't help but join them, though her heart ached to think these precious moments would soon be coming to an end.

I should tell them, tell them right now, that tomorrow Rachel and Evan will be driving out again. Only this time, Rachel would be driving Sara home in her car. Sara had already used the house's landline to clear it with Judge Cartwright after forwarding a final—and glowing—report on Mac's fitness as a father and the twins' positive progress toward accepting their new living situation.

But she couldn't make herself spoil their mood or the day ahead, so instead she found herself asking, "Did you finally pick a name for the little fellow?" when the kitten looked up at them from where he'd been sleeping, curled on a seat cushion. Adorably rumpled from his slumber, his orange-and-white fur stuck out from his face in clumps as he yawned. "Or are you still narrowing down your list of choices?"

Not surprisingly, the twins had decided to go with a space-themed name for their new pet. So far, the top contenders were Apollo, Rocket, and their dad's suggestion, Pluto—though the children had been eager to inform him that, scientifically speaking, that celestial body had lost its status as a planet. These two, Sara had discovered, were very serious about their space facts.

"His name is *Comet*," Silvia announced, "because of his long, orange tail."

"And because he's always streaking under someone's feet?" Sara asked.

Cristo shook his head and frowned. "I think you're confusing comets with meteors. Those are the ones that blaze across the sky as they enter the atmosphere."

As Silvia nodded vigorously and explained how comets differed, Sara felt a pang deep inside her at the thought of how much she would miss this bright, engaging duo—these children who had come to feel like an extension of herself.

And breaking away from Mac, she realized, was going to be even harder. She was still haunted by the disappointment she'd seen in his eyes last night when she had told him, even though, to his credit, he hadn't tried to argue with her.

Instead, almost more painfully, she'd watched as the tiny flame of whatever hope he'd been nurturing that he might change her mind flickered and died—especially when she'd told him that while his family would always hold a special place in her heart, she thought it best for everyone that they make a clean break rather than extend the pain with further contact. Since then, he'd retreated to a cool politeness, keeping their conversations brief and focused on the children…and making her both dread and wish for tomorrow to hurry up and arrive, so she could escape the guilt and awkwardness consuming her…

Along with the hollow ache of loneliness she felt each time she imagined a return to an old life that had somehow lost its appeal.

As she put away some plates, Mac poked his head in the door. Frowning at her, he said, "Sara, I told you not to worry about any of that. You're still supposed to be resting."

"Turns out that I'm incapable of being completely useless for more than one day," she said as Roxy came in to lap some water. "Besides, I have my helpers."

"I see that," he said, flashing an approving smile at the twins, who beamed at their father's recognition. "And you're hardly useless. But I was wondering if you might come outside for a few minutes. Hayden's come by to talk to us."

"Uncle Hayden?" Cristo asked with obvious interest. "He said he would show me his sheriff's SUV."

"I'm afraid the grown-ups are going to need to speak in private first," Mac said, his expression serious. "How about if you two go watch a little TV or hang out with your kitten until we're through? Then I'll remind him and see if he has time."

It was either a measure of how much more comfortable they had gotten with their father or how much they'd been enjoying the kid-friendly channels he'd introduced them to that they scooped up the newly christened Comet without argument and headed for the game room, with Roxy trailing after them. After checking the potatoes once more with a fork, Sara turned the heat off on the stove and then headed outside. Once there, she nodded hello to Hayden, who looked sharp today in a fresh uniform, his deep blue eyes bright and alert.

"Good to see you, Sara," he said. "Great to see you up and around and looking more rested."

"I'm sure we're all a lot less exhausted than we were the other day," she said, though nightmares of the kidnappers returning had punctured her sleep again last night. But before rising, she'd dreamed, too, of making love with Mac—a dream that had weakened her resolve to the point where she'd been on the brink of slipping from her bed and into the game room where he had been sleeping when she'd heard the early rising children stirring. "Can I grab anyone a drink from inside?"

"I've got one already," said Mac, who, despite his casual attire—shorts, tennis shoes and an old T-shirt— looked tense and more than ready to hear whatever it was that his brother had come to tell them.

Hayden shook his head. "No thanks. I just stopped by because I have some news I wanted to share with both of you in person." A smile spread across his handsome face. "*Outstanding* news."

"Please tell me you've locked up both of those bastards," Mac said, his voice a low growl.

"Sorry, but with so little for us to go on, I'm afraid those guys are in the wind somewhere—most likely gone for good."

"Why would you think that?" Sara said. "Wouldn't they more likely be lying low somewhere nearby, waiting for their next chance to strike?"

"Not once they got word," said Hayden, "that the woman who was paying them has been arrested."

"*A-arrested?*" Mac sputtered. "Are you— You'd better not be messing with me, bro."

"I'm dead serious," Hayden insisted. "I told you I'd set up news alerts following the family years ago, and I saw that Elena Rojas Morales, the widow of Don Roberto, was taken into custody. But it wasn't until I reached out to Paul Barkley's replacement, Madeline Herrera, that I was able to get the details as they were relayed to the governor's office."

"So what happened?" Sara asked, mostly because Mac seemed stunned speechless.

"She's been charged in the assassination of the undersecretary who authorized the twins' return to the US. Apparently, it was all quite gruesome, with some kind of stuffed animal left on the scene," Hayden explained. "But surveillance footage led investigators to the killer, who quickly admitted she'd hired him to avenge what she thought of as an outrage against her husband's memory."

"So does that mean my theory about her arranging Paul Barkley's death was actually right?" Sara asked, disbelief straining her voice.

"I had that same thought," Hayden said, "but when I called the Travis County Sheriff's Department detectives handling his death investigation, I got my second big surprise this morning."

"No need to keep us in suspense," Mac said.

Hayden explained, "An area resident, an eighty-three-year-old man whose daughter claims has been diagnosed with dementia, was brought in by family members after they discovered blood, human hair and significant front-end damage on the front of a van he'd kept parked in his garage."

"Oh, no." Sara winced, briefly squeezing her eyes shut, as if that might dispel the awful image. "But what on earth was he doing driving in the first place?"

"I didn't get that part of the story," Hayden said, "but

it happens more often than you think. Family'll take one set of keys, only to find out the elderly family member has another hidden. Or more often, no one wants to hurt poor Grandpa's feelings—or they fool themselves into thinking he'll go no farther than the corner store."

"Now they'll all have to live with knowing that he killed an innocent man." She hugged herself. "For me, that guilt would almost be worse than any legal and financial consequences they end up facing."

Hayden nodded. "That's because people like us have an actual conscience. Unfortunately, some folks never think past how things impact their own interests."

"At least Barkley's family have some answers now," Mac said, "and I'll be able to breathe a whole lot easier, knowing that my family's going to be safe."

"But what about the twins?" Sara frowned at Mac as a new worry hit her. "Have you thought of what you'll tell them…about their grandmother?"

Mac shook his head, his forehead creasing. "I've hardly had time to let this news sink in myself. But I can't tell them—can I?—that their grandmother could be going to prison?"

"There's no *could be* about it," Hayden assured them. "Turns out that the official who was killed is a cousin to some big-name actor down there, so the family's calls for justice are getting tons of media attention. Nobody's going to just let this gruesome hit job in the capital complex go."

"I don't know that I'd tell the children right away," Sara told Mac, "but I would recommend you work with a family therapist and let them help guide you on how much and when it's best to share. I can get you a referral."

Mac's longing look served as an unspoken reminder that he'd far rather have her help than that of any stranger.

"Listen, you two," Hayden said. "As much as I'd love to hang around and help you hash all this out, or better yet, help celebrate the good news with whatever it is you're planning on cooking up—" He gestured toward the open grill behind Mac.

"Hope you'll take a rain check on that and join us another time for a *proper* celebration," Mac invited, sounding sincere. "Although you might need to bring along a designated driver, because there might be a beer or three cracked open."

Hayden smiled and offered his hand. "We'll see about those beers, but I wouldn't say no to the chance to formally welcome my niece and nephew back home where they belong. Please tell Cristo I'll be glad to show him my sheriff's vehicle then—I'll even let both kids work the lights and sirens—next time that I see them."

Once the two men shook and Sara thanked him for everything he'd done, Hayden touched the brim of his hat before his phone buzzed. Answering on his way to his SUV, he murmured an acknowledgment to the speaker and then added, "So what's the location on that wreck? All right. On my way."

As he jogged off, clearly in a hurry, Mac said, "That's what I'll have to remember when inviting him and Ryan, to always make it about the kids. Then maybe eventually…"

"They'll provide the bridge you all need to start really talking," Sara finished for him, agreeing with his assessment. And seeing in his face how much his relationship with his brothers meant to him. "But first, I think you're going to have to learn to forgive yourself for whatever mistakes you might've made while navigating grief and trying to get your kids home."

"That could be the toughest part," he admitted. "And

even harder if I don't have you around to rely on for excellent advice."

"Please, Mac," she said, hating the weakness she heard in her own voice. "Don't make this any tougher than it is already, especially right now, when we should all be enjoying this day—and this amazing news."

"And we will—because it's a big deal, knowing that we're safe now, that I won't have to worry every minute about my kids being violently snatched, and that I can start easing them into a normal life. But don't you understand the hole you'll leave in our lives—and in my heart—when you leave? Have you even told them yet?"

She shook her head, admitting, "I couldn't. I know they'll be upset, and that they've come to depend on me—"

He frowned. "They're not just dependent on you. They *love* you. Last night…when I was reading to them, they interrupted me to ask if I would marry you, so we could all be a family together."

"That's just what I didn't want to happen," she said, her throat thickening. "Them getting ideas that I might—"

"I've done my best, but I can't hide it from them. They can see I love you, Sara, that I'm hopelessly gone on you, and nothing would make me happier than having you as my wife."

Blinking back tears, she blurted, "But I can't ever— I can't be anybody's mother. Don't you understand that?"

"No, I absolutely don't. Because, as far as I'm concerned, there's no one on this planet I'd ever trust more with my children. And it's obvious you love them, too. So help me understand, please. What is it that's holding you back, Sara? What happened in your past that makes you imagine you can't—"

She felt the dampness on her cheek as the ragged truth

tore free. "I—I can't live through it again. I can't love another child like my own and then lose her!"

As she stood trembling before him, he stepped closer. Blue-gray eyes filling with compassion, he laid a hand on her upper arm. But it was the gentleness of his words that completely broke down her defenses. Broke down the walls she'd built up over more than a dozen years.

"Who did you lose, Sara?" he asked quietly. "Tell me, who was she?"

"My…my older sister's child. She named her Promise… before she took off with a boyfriend."

She was shaking so hard now that Mac took her into his arms, practically supporting her as he stroked her back.

Relying on his strength, she somehow found the courage she needed. The courage to finally tell him the one truth that could convince him she wasn't fit to love.

The low chatter of the river, rippling over the rocks below, formed a backdrop to a living tapestry of June bird and insect song, but Mac's full attention was on the woman in his arms.

"My parents were divorced," she said, "and my mom wasn't up for taking responsibility for another of Willow's 'mistakes.' That was how she saw her. But I only saw a baby, a tiny miracle I loved enough to make any sacrifice, promise anything, to keep from being given up to strangers."

"Just how old *were* you, at the time?"

"Fifteen, but you have to understand, I'd been the peacemaker in that house, as well as the closest thing we'd had to a functioning adult, for years. My mother— she turned so *angry* after Dad left her for a younger woman, and my sister, Willow, was always stirring up some drama, trying to get a rise out of her—or maybe to do something so awful that Dad would *have* to run back to the rescue."

"Except he never did, I take it?"

She snorted. "He'd washed his hands of us completely, other than sending the support checks. But *someone* had to make sure the meals were cooked and the bills got paid on time—and keep things calm enough so the neighbors wouldn't keep calling the police when my mom and sister got into another shouting match."

It killed him to think that she'd been forced to do that. "So, at fifteen, you took on the care of your sister's child, too."

"Not legally, but for all intents... I was so certain I could handle it. Promise went to day care while I was at school, but otherwise..."

"I'm sorry, but your parents were both dead wrong to let that happen," he said, a rush of anger heating his voice. "You were still a kid yourself, for heaven's sake, no matter how mature you had to act. And for you to give up everything that should've been part of your teenage years while the child's own grandparents ignored her—"

"I *chose* it, Mac, and for the first year and a half, we more or less made things work. Promise was talking more and more and toddling, getting into everything—and Mom had really started to come around with her. She'd always bought what she needed, but she'd even watch over Promise sometimes, or help out when she wasn't too busy with her job or socializing."

"When it didn't inconvenience her too much, you mean..." he grumbled, beginning to understand why Sara might be estranged from such a woman.

"But during the fall of my senior year, I got sick," Sara

said. "I tried faking my way through it, but I ended up in surgery for appendicitis."

"My youngest brother had his appendix out, too," Mac said. He still remembered Ryan curled up in agony, alternately retching or howling all the way to the hospital the night he'd fallen ill.

"I was released a day later, but I was still groggy and nauseated from the pain meds. I was resting on the sofa when Mom got a request to show this property a client had been trying to unload for ages."

"Don't tell me, she left you there, alone with a toddler, right after you'd had surgery?" he asked, something in her voice filling him with dread.

"She…she *did* tell me she was going out. Or, at least, she said she did. I really can't remember. All I know was when I woke up, the house was way too quiet and…when I went to look, I f-found…"

Shaking harder, she began to weep in earnest, shaking so hard that he helped her to a bench, where he sat down beside her.

"I'm such a mess," she said, wiping uselessly at her face. "I'm sorry."

He moved to grab the paper towels he had been using to clean the grill and tore off several for her.

As she blotted her face, he said, "Don't be. Best to lance this wound and drain all of the poison. And something tells me it's been festering in secret for a hell of a long time inside you. You haven't talked about it, have you?"

"Rachel knows that Promise died," Sara said, her voice barely above a whisper. "But she has no idea it was my fault."

Mac saw it in her face, the remorse and devastation. The guilt that she'd been carrying for all these years.

"Why would you believe that?" he asked her, struggling to keep his voice and his expression neutral.

"The back door should've been locked, but it was—it was open. My mother had run out in a hurry and had her hands full. She'd called me to catch it for her."

"When you were sleeping on the couch, you mean?" he asked, recalling how Sara had said before she didn't actually recall the conversation with her mother. "Still half out of it from surgery?"

Instead of responding, Sara's face drained of color as she continued with her story. "I ran to Promise's room, but she...she must have climbed out of her crib. She'd done that a couple of times already, but this time I... I couldn't find her anywhere inside and I knew—I absolutely knew—even before I saw the pool gate was unlatched and..."

When she disintegrated into tears again, he pulled her onto his lap, holding her like the child she had been. The half-grown child who had struggled so bravely to be a mother to a broken family.

"I'm so sorry for what happened," he said, not needing to hear any more, "but it's obvious to me—painfully clear—that what happened was a terrible, tragic accident. Not something you should blame yourself for, or continue punishing yourself for, when all along, your mother was the one who should've—"

"But don't you see, she was right from the beginning. And right to point out that if I hadn't stubbornly insisted I was mature enough, that I could handle Promise, she could have gone to a *real* family, a good family where she could have grown up safe and healthy."

Shocked, he felt a rush of fury. "Your mother put that on you—after what happened?"

"She was right, though, wasn't she? I messed up everybody's lives, and after my sister found out, she only got worse. It wasn't a year later that Willow was gone, too."

"And I suppose your mother blamed you for that, too?" Mac felt furious on her behalf.

Sara didn't answer, but her pained look spoke volumes.

"I'm sorry your family was so much less than you deserved," he said. "But, Sara, don't you see? Your mother was just covering up for whatever guilt *she* was feeling, blaming you. She probably never told you in the first place that she was going or to lock the back door for her. But even if she did, there's no excuse for just shouting out something so important to a drugged person and running out the door. She should've taken time to put her things down and locked the door herself."

"I—I know that," Sara said. "In my head, I really do. But it was never my mom's idea to raise Promise in the first place. And it was *my* responsibility."

"But she had legal custody, right?"

"She had legal custody of me, too." Sara's voice went bitter. "It didn't make her any kind of mother. And I knew that. Don't you see? I screwed up…and there's no chance in this world I'm ever permanently putting myself in that position again."

Chapter 16

After their conversation, Sara had gone to lie down in the darkened bedroom, telling Mac she had a headache. It hadn't been a lie. Thanks to the flood of tears, her sinuses had throbbed to the point where she'd felt she might be sick. Or maybe it was only the shame and horror she felt facing him after exposing that, in reality, she had no business giving him or anybody parenting advice.

Mac had been kind, doing all he could to comfort her and struggling to convince her that, in his eyes, she was still the same woman who had, as far as he was concerned, saved his family. Other than his clear anger with her mother, whom he'd called downright abusive, Sara wasn't surprised by his attempts to convince her this made no difference in the way he viewed her. *Except I'm more in awe than ever of the person you've always been, even when your family failed you.*

But in Sara's heart, no one else's mistakes were, or

ever had been, the point, only her own, along with the vow she'd made the first time her sister had left Promise in her care so she could go out and party. *It's just you and me, little girl. I swear, we'll get each other through this.*

After washing her face, she took something for her headache and lay down for a while, the cool washcloth across her forehead. After a time, she heard voices in the great room—Mac speaking to the children in hushed tones. But, to her relief, they left her to herself and, after a time, she drifted off to sleep.

Sometime later she heard a light tap at the door, before Mac cracked it open and stuck his head inside.

"I'm sorry to disturb you," he said quietly when she moved aside the cloth to peer at him, her vision bleary. "It's just— The kids and I put together some food for you from our cookout… I thought it'd give me an excuse to come check to see if you're feeling any better."

"A little, I think," she said hoarsely as he came in, carrying a paper plate that trailed the smoky scents of the grill. "I'm still half out of it, though, so… I'm not sure I'm up for company. Not yet, anyway."

He set down the burger, baked beans and potato salad on the nightstand. From his shirt pocket, he plucked a napkin wrapped around a plastic flatware set and laid it down, as well, before reaching up to smooth her hair down near her temple. "Take whatever time you need. But promise me you'll at least try to eat a little to feel better."

"I can do that, I think," she told him, mostly because she didn't want to make him worry.

"Good. Can I bring you a fresh drink?"

She shook her head, gesturing to the insulated water bottle she'd filled before coming in to lie down. "I still have plenty, thanks."

"If you'd rather eat out in the dinette, we'll be heading back outside in just a minute. I promised to show the kids how to kayak."

"But they don't have any swimsuits," she reminded him.

Shrugging, he said, "So, we'll all get our shorts and T-shirts wet. Hot as it is out there, that'll be half the fun. And before you ask, we've already put on sunscreen."

She pushed herself to a sitting position, a fluttering in her stomach. "You really think it's safe now, going to the river?"

"You're still worried about those men, aren't you?"

She blew out a breath, rubbing at arms suddenly pebbled with gooseflesh. "I keep having these horrible dreams about them coming back to get them."

"But with the woman paying them arrested—"

"What if they haven't gotten word yet? Buenos Aires is a continent away," she argued. "If they've been hiding out in the hills, without internet service or a good cell phone connection…"

"I really can't imagine them hanging around this rural area for days on end without making their move, not without at least checking in with their boss, especially with Hayden's people combing all the river camps and rentals for suspicious activity. But if it makes you feel any better, we'll stay right out here at the swimming hole, where you can watch us from the deck if you like. Since the kids are just learning to paddle, there's no need to go far anyway."

"All right," she agreed. "I'll eat some dinner—it smells delicious, by the way—and then I'll head out on the deck to watch."

He flashed a handsome smile. "We'll be sure to wave. And, Sara?"

"Yes, Mac?"

Leaning close, he cupped her cheek in his hand. "I love you. That's a fact that's not going to change, whether or not you give yourself permission to accept it."

She closed her eyes and nodded as he pressed his lips to her forehead, her heart overflowing with the realization that she could live a hundred years and never meet a better man. When she opened her eyes again, he'd left, leaving her to wish things could really be as simple as he had suggested. But if Mac was fighting his own battle learning to forgive himself for losing the family legacy in his attempt to recover his children, her own struggle felt like an unwinnable war.

Still, she couldn't stop thinking how, when she had told Mac her darkest secret, he hadn't turned from her in disgust—or demanded that she leave his sight forever. Instead, he had returned to offer kindness, to try to convince her that nothing that she'd said had changed his heart about her. Was he simply saying so because he knew that she was leaving tomorrow with Rachel and Evan? That he wouldn't have to worry about the impact of her flawed judgment on his family?

Or was it possible that he imagined her as worthy of the same understanding and compassion she had willingly shared with clients who had shared equally scarring early traumas with her? She pictured herself sitting with an older veteran she'd worked with, holding the man's gnarled hand and asking, *What good is continuing to punish yourself endlessly doing anyone at this point?*

But this was different, wasn't it? Her vow to devote her life to serving others, rather than selfishly pursuing the dream of having her own family, *was* about more than just self-flagellation.

"You're helping others all the time," she reminded herself, "so many people, every single day, with your work."

And she'd continue doing so, once she was back on the job in Austin—though she'd never again allow herself to fall into the trap of becoming so emotionally entangled with one family, as she had here. Instead, she'd find satisfaction in being a good social worker—and a doting surrogate aunt to the newborn her best friend would soon be bringing into the world...

And, whenever she felt lonely, she'd remember what it had felt like, having the love of a man and a family that she had helped, in her small way, to heal.

Giving up on her plate of food, she buried it in the trash can, where Mac wouldn't see how little she had eaten. Deciding he might worry if she didn't put in an appearance on the deck, however, she headed to the bathroom to run a brush through her hair and make sure her eyes weren't still too puffy.

After splashing a bit of water on her face, she dried off and then headed for the patio door leading to the deck. Just before she reached for it, the doorbell rang. She paused, thinking of her replacement cell phone, which was due to be delivered.

Realizing she might need to sign for it, she ran to the door, utterly bewildered when she checked the peephole and saw, instead of a uniformed driver, a familiar but completely unexpected face. Hurrying to unlock the dead bolt, she opened up to ask, "What are *you* doing here now? And where's— Wait! What's that? Oh, my—"

Scrambling backward, she tried to slam the door and turn the dead bolt in time to prevent the new arrival from pushing inside. Tried and failed, shock making her react too slowly to the unfolding threat.

Mac stood in knee-deep water between his children, each of them bobbing atop a plastic kayak. Though each wore a fluorescent life jacket, their grins glowed even brighter as they awaited the slightest opportunity to renew their earlier splash war, using their paddles to soak one another once again.

"Are you two going to pay attention or am I going to have to drag you out of those boats and toss you in with the catfish?" he threatened.

"I'd like to see you catch me!" Silvia sassed, giggling as she paddled her red kayak away, with Cristo hooting encouragement as Mac went into shark mode, swimming after them. Roxy even got into the fun, swimming around and barking happily.

Soon, however, he found himself joining the Lab on the shoreline while the twins resumed their splashing war. As he watched, he couldn't help thinking how far they'd come, from Cristo's quick side hug last night to Silvia's newfound spunkiness—a sharp contrast from the days she'd clung so desperately to the teddy bear she'd found at the cabin.

Reminded again of its sudden appearance, Mac thought of something Hayden had mentioned about the murdered Argentinian government official having been found with a stuffed animal.

"Why the hell didn't I check that toy of hers more closely?" he murmured, a chill ripping through him. Though he'd squeezed and felt the teddy when she'd left it unguarded days earlier, he'd been unwilling to risk damaging or destroying something she treasured when he'd felt no hard pieces inside. But what if he'd missed something: a miniature microphone or speaker—or even a GPS locator tag—hidden inside?

Nausea hit him at the thought, his skin going hot as he called for the kids to paddle their kayaks to the bank.

"Already?" protested Cristo, his curls dripping from the dousing his sister had just given him.

"Comet will be lonesome if he's cooped up too long alone in the bathroom—and there's something I need to take care of, too. But if you listen now, we can come on out again tomorrow."

"Can Sara come, too?" Silvia asked. "You could wrap her arm, maybe, and put her in the two-man kayak and we could—"

"We'll talk about it later," he said, unwilling to explain without her what she should have told them both already—that this time tomorrow she would be gone.

"Who's *that*?" Silvia asked a few minutes later as he lifted the last of the kayaks into the storage rack.

Looking over, Mac spotted Frieda's eighteen-year-old granddaughter, whose thick, black hair hung in a single side braid over the shoulder of the Clearwater Crossing Resort T-shirt she wore with a pair of shorts and the ratty tennis shoes she reserved for days when she came to clean the cabins. Though she was as delicately built as her Chinese American mother, she scrambled nimbly as a mountain goat down the rocks rather than go out of her way to get to the easier staircase.

"Kids, this is Mei-Li." Not surprisingly, the children had immediately taken to his grandmotherly assistant when they'd met two days before, but Mei-Li hadn't been around then. "She works for me, too, and Miss Frieda's her grandmother. Mei-Li, it's great to see you back. Meet Cristo and Silvia."

Though she was often shy around adults, Mei-Li smiled warmly at the children. "I'm so glad to finally meet you. My grandma's been going on and on about you. She insisted on baking brownies. I was wondering if you two might come over with me to the office and sample some? And then I'll send you back with some more for you and your dad."

"And Sara, too," Silvia said. "She would have been out here with us, too, but she has a bad headache."

"In that case, we'll have to make her a personalized goody bag," Mei-Li told them. "And I have a package that was delivered to the office for her. You can take it home to the house with you, as well."

"Go ahead and take them with you," Mac said, deciding they could change clothes when they got back. "But do me a favor, will you, Mei-Li? I want you to walk them home yourself, all the way."

"We're *not* babies," Cristo argued. "We know the way back from the office."

"I understand that," Mac said before grinning at him, "but how else am I supposed to be sure there are any of Frieda's famous brownies *left* for Sara and me by the time you two get home?"

Fortunately, the twins only giggled at this, and Mei-Li, who caught his eye, nodded and mouthed the words, *I'll do that. That* clearly meant that Frieda had impressed upon her his reasons for being extra vigilant with the children's safety.

As he headed alone back up to the house, it occurred to him that, very soon, he was going to have to learn to let his guard down with them, if he wanted his kids to be able to enjoy a normal childhood. He suspected the effort would be nerve-racking as hell, at least until he grew used to the miracle of their return to him—and confident that no one was trying to steal them away or leak photos to the unscrupulous press.

With a towel draped over his shoulder, he let himself inside the sliding door on the deck, wondering where in the house Silvia might have left her stuffed bear. Deciding it was most likely in her room, he took two steps toward the staircase before going still at the sound of Sara speaking. Figuring she must be talking on the landline, he took another step before stopping again, his muscles tensing as he realized how upset she sounded. Besides, it came to him a second later—there *was* no extension near the front entryway, where her voice was coming from.

Moving as quietly as he could, he edged in that direction, his heart pounding like a jackhammer as he realized that she wasn't alone inside the house.

"I told you, they're not home," Sara insisted, struggling to maintain eye contact and force her voice back to something approaching her normal register. Fighting tears as her mind scrambled to think of some way out of this, not only for her own sake, but all of theirs, including Mac and the children—and the best friend she thought of as a sister…

Because it would kill Rachel if she ever learned of this, or if she saw her husband—the man she'd supposed was flying back home from his training session in Seattle this very evening so the two of them could drive to the Hill Country together tomorrow afternoon—standing in the entry, pointing a gun straight at her best friend.

"He—he took them to his brother's, the sheriff's, for the afternoon," she lied, praying that Mac and the children wouldn't walk in on this nightmare before she found some way to defuse it, "but it doesn't even matter, because this…this crazy scheme of yours—ransoming the kids to their grandmother—it's not you, Evan! None of this is you!"

"Don't tell me who I am," he shouted, a wild-eyed stranger wearing an old friend's face. Twitchy and thinner than he'd been when she'd last seen him, Evan barely looked like himself now, his face and clothing grimed with dirt, as if he had been sleeping rough for days, and his normally meticulously styled hair sticking up in unruly patches. "You don't know. I have to deliver what I promised. If I don't, I'll—we'll lose the house, the cars—everything I've worked for."

"I don't understand. How? You earned millions—tens of millions—when the company went public—"

"Which I got conned into investing. I thought I was so smart, putting everything we had into a foolproof workaround to avoid the huge tax hit. Instead, it was a freaking scam and I… I lost— I can't lose— I can't go back to scraping and clawing for every dollar like a—"

"You lived without the giant house before," she reminded him, "and you've never gone hungry, neither of you. Rachel—she doesn't care about the rest, not really. All she cares about is having the man she loves by her side." As well as a best friend to help support her. But Sara very much feared that Evan—and a former employee, whom he claimed had abandoned their joint plan after the stab wounds to his forearm grew infected—had been behind the break-in at the cabin, and would see no other choice except to kill her to keep her from identifying the man she'd known so long…

Unless she could somehow remind him of the friend he'd been before the pressure to maintain his newfound lifestyle had twisted him into something she no longer recognized. Into someone who would kidnap children. Her stomach flipped as it occurred to her that he—this man she'd known forever—had very likely been the person who'd taken her personal belongings, as if on some sick level it had excited him, knowing that in the end, her life would be in his hands.

"This way, Rachel *will* have me," Evan insisted.

"She'll never have to know what happened—and our child will never want for anything—"

"But listen to me," Sara pleaded. "There *won't* be any money. This is all for *nothing*, I'm telling you. There won't be any ransom. There can't be. We just got word from the sheriff, the children's grandmother has been arrested in Argentina. I can show you on the computer where she's in jail for ordering a hit on a government—"

"Enough with the lies!" he shouted, raising the gun's muzzle as he advanced on her. "Now just tell me where those kids really are!"

She heard the rage, the desperation, but in his reddened eyes she saw exhaustion and a shadow of the sweetly awkward, insecure and perpetually broke nerd who'd trailed Rachel with puppylike devotion until he'd finally come into his own and won her heart.

Looking into his face, she said, "Come on, Evan. Stop this nonsense right now. Come with me and let's call Rachel." Heartbeat booming in her ears, she pushed the wrist pointing the gun at her away—or tried to.

"Damn it, *don't*!" he said, panic transforming his expression into that of a man she didn't recognize. One she belatedly realized would do anything to regain control—and keep her from contacting the one person whose judgment he feared above all others.

Realizing how dangerously she'd miscalculated his mental state, she twisted, instinct prompting her to avoid—

"No!" shouted another voice—Mac's—rushing up behind her…

Just as the shot exploded in the entryway and a red mist filled the air.

Chapter 17

A searing pain slammed his upper right chest, so fierce, Mac couldn't draw breath. But it was the shock of it that took him down, his legs crumpling underneath him and his vision blackening around the edges. He might have gone under right then if Sara hadn't screamed his name, anchoring him to the necessity of remaining conscious. Remaining alive so he could help her—and neutralize this threat before his kids and Mei-Li walked straight into danger.

With the sound of his own breath loud in his ears, he struggled to raise the handgun he'd retrieved from the master bedroom closet after hearing the voices in the entry. But Mac couldn't find the strength to lift his arm—or even make out his target, as Sara dropped sobbing to her knees to block his view.

"Where are they?" shouted the man behind her. "Where the hell are those kids?"

"Mac, you can't die on me!" Sara cried. "Please, Evan, it's not too late! We can call an ambulance! You're not a murderer! I know you aren't!"

As slowly as his mind was churning, it got through to Mac finally that Sara was calling this man by name. That she somehow *knew* the shooter.

An instant later, he placed the name—it was her friend's husband, the supposedly wealthy one who'd shown up with his wife with the expensive but forbidden high-tech gifts last week. But who he was mattered far less than the fact that he was still clearly hell-bent on getting his hands on the twins—and Sara was Mac's only hope of stopping him before it was too late.

Don't pass out, his mind screamed as the blackness chewed away at his field of vision.

"I freaking asked you, where *are* they?" Evan demanded, coming up behind Sara.

As he did, Mac used his ebbing strength to shove the gun toward her hand. Gaze flicking downward, she spotted it and met his eye, a desperate message passing between them before she grabbed at it—only to let it tumble from her hand when Evan grabbed her by her hair, eliciting a yelp as he dragged her to her feet.

Pushing the muzzle of his gun to her head, he said, "Last chance, or so help me, I'm blowing her brains across the—"

From the kitchen area near the patio door, Mac heard Mei-Li call out cheerfully, "Brownie delivery!"

"Want to see Comet?" Silvia asked her.

"I'll go get him," Cristo said.

"Run!" shrieked Sara, shoving her full weight against her captor as he released and attempted to rush past her, distracted from killing her by his desperation to reach the children before they could escape.

Mac's children—whose safety gave him the final blast of adrenaline he needed to lurch forward, grab the pistol Sara had dropped and pour every ounce of will he had into turning to aim and pulling the trigger once, twice, and finally a third time. Firing until Evan fell facedown, his back blossoming with bright red spangles as the sounds of screaming—Sara's, Mei-Li's and both twins'—rent the air.

Mac had no idea how long he was unconscious, only that when he came to, he was lying on what he supposed must be a stretcher in the middle of the great room. There seemed to be a number of people milling around, mostly uniformed.

When he tried to raise his head, a freckled EMT who barely looked old enough to shave said, "Mr. Walker? Can you hear me?"

Mac tried to answer, but the pain in his side was enormous, and there was something over his face, maybe an oxygen mask.

Apparently noticing his struggle, the EMT shook his head. "It's okay. Don't try to speak. We've got a medevac helicopter en route. Should be here in about five minutes."

"You're awake. Thank God." It was Hayden, moving in to command Mac's field of vision, his face etched with worry. "It's gonna be all right, man—*you're* going to be, I swear it."

Mac wasn't so sure about that, but he nodded and squeezed his brother's hand when Hayden took it.

"The guy who shot you—the kidnapper—he was DOA," Hayden assured him, "and we've got the other one, some employee of his that got caught up in this, in custody. Guy wrecked his truck trying to drive to the hospital after passing out from infected stab wounds to his forearm. So, your children are safe now. They'll be safe, I swear to you, no matter what."

Mac forced himself to reach up, to push the mask aside to say, "My kids—"

"They're in the master, scared to death—I won't lie to you about that. Sara and Mei-Li are trying to calm them down."

Of course, they would want Sara. And, of course, she'd see to them, though she must be half out of her mind with shock and worry now herself. Because that was who she was: a woman who would always put others' needs before her own. Who loved his children as she'd loved her own niece, as if she'd given birth to them herself. "Hayden—listen to me... I want Sara to—to be the one to raise them. If I don't make it..."

"Quit talking like that, brother. You're going to make it." Hayden scowled down at him, looking angry that he would dare to suggest otherwise. "You *have* to. Those kids need their—"

"*Listen* to me. They *need* Sara. They love her. You have to—make this happen—" Mac gasped, fighting to sit up against the youthful EMT's restraining hand and pushing away the mask when he tried to return it to his face. "I don't give a damn how. M-marry her if that's what it takes to make it legal."

"I'm gonna forget you said all this, big brother."

"No, Hayden, please. I need to know. Need to know that they'll be taken care of... The children, Sara—the money the Rojas-Morales family owes... It's all on you now to try—get back...family legacy..." As pain twisted through him, Mac squeezed his brother's hand, hard enough to make him wince. "On you..."

The words morphed into a moan of pain—a moan that fell silent as the darkness overwhelmed him.

Four months later...

As she looked down from the upstairs window of Silvia's bedroom—borrowed with the girl's enthusiastic blessing for this occasion—Sara's stomach fluttered at the sight of the deck below, lit up with solar torches and decorated informally with an array of flowers in the rich autumnal hues. The sunset played its part, as well, illuminating ribbonlike wisps of low clouds above the horizon in a wash of orange, gold and scarlet that reflected off the river below.

Since the assembled guests, who sat facing the opposite direction, were missing these moments of perfect beauty, she took it as a private gift instead...a blessing on her decision from the tiny girl she'd loved and lost so many years before.

"We're about to have a family, Promise," she said. "A dad, a brother and a sister to share our memories and make new ones." Last night, for the first time, she had dared to open the old photo albums her mother had mailed to her—perhaps a signal that, eventually, the two of them might find a path to healing. As she'd shared the images with Mac and the children, some of the memories had brought tears, but many had sparked joy, too, reigniting memories of a love that had utterly transformed her.

A tap came at the door, signaling that it was time to write another chapter in that story. When she called out, somewhat nervously, "Come in," Hayden, strikingly handsome in his dark suit, stepped in to offer her his arm.

Looking up at him, she smiled, honored that he was taking on this role on behalf of her and the children. Knowing of his years-long cold war with his brother, she considered his participation nothing short of a miracle— and a measure of how deep his commitment to his family ran. Still, he looked slightly awkward as he gazed down at her.

"There's still time for you to make a break for it," she told him, "if that's what you're thinking."

He shook his head. "Never crossed my mind. I was just thinking that you make an awful pretty bride." He eyed the tea-length ivory dress and simple veil she wore over the updo Amanda Greenville had helped her with before rejoining the other guests, with obvious approval. Admiration warming his handsome face, he added, "Almost makes me wish I'd taken up my idiot big brother on that offer of his and bribed the medevac crew to shove him out of the chopper over the mountains somewhere."

She burst out laughing. "*Ha!* Mac and I were talking about that the other day, and we decided that, as allergic to commitment as you've always been, you'd've run for the border before rigor mortis had him fully stiffened up. Now walk me down that aisle like you promised, Sheriff, before my groom gets cold feet, too."

Grinning, he snorted. "Sara, you could leave my brother standing out there all night, and he would just keep waiting for you. He'd wait until the end of time, because you're the only woman for him. The damned *right* woman, this time."

Though her eyes were damp, she managed to fire back, "Well, as long as he doesn't try pawning me off on any *other* siblings…"

As they descended the stairs, the children, waiting along with their wranglers, Mei-Li and Frieda, at the bottom, jumped up and down in excitement, clearly more than ready for their star turn. "*¡Que bonita!*" they both exclaimed at once, excited to finally get a look at the wedding dress, which had been shrouded in secrecy for months.

"You look amazing, too!" Sara whispered as they approached the open patio door, impressed at how grown-up they appeared in their festive clothing. "Ready?"

All smiles, the twins nodded, giving her two thumbs-up.

As the music outside the open patio door began to play, they walked ahead of her and Hayden, arm and arm, to where their father waited with the preacher.

Standing tall and strong, now that he was fully recovered from the gunshot that had come within less than an inch, according to his surgeon, of ending his life, Mac's gaze dialed in on Sara's. And in those handsome bluegray eyes of his, she saw no hint of past heartbreaks or whatever lingering struggles the family might face in the future as they pursued the restoration of their legacy...

Instead, she saw only the memory of how love and trust had allowed the two of them to pool their strengths to survive violence, grief and, in Sara's case, the loss—at least for now—of an important friendship. And how that same bond had opened her heart to shades of joy she had never guessed existed in this world.

* * * * *

Don't miss these other exciting stories from
Colleen Thompson:

First Responders on Deadly Ground
Deadly Texas Summer
Lone Star Redemption
Lone Star Survivor

Available now from Harlequin Romantic Suspense!

#2175 COLTON'S DANGEROUS REUNION
The Coltons of Colorado • by Justine Davis

When social worker Gideon Colton reports a parent for child abuse, he never thought he'd put his ex—the child's pediatrician—in harm's way. Now he and Sophie Gray-Jones are thrown back together to avoid danger...and find themselves reigniting the flame that never really went out.

#2176 FINDING THE RANCHER'S SON
by Karen Whiddon

Jackie Burkholdt's sister and nephew are missing, so she returns home to their tiny West Texas hometown. The boy's father, Eli Pitts, might be the most obvious suspect, but he and Jackie are helplessly drawn to each other. As secrets come to light, it becomes even harder to know who is responsible—let alone who it's safe to have feelings for.

#2177 BODYGUARD UNDER SIEGE
Bachelor Bodyguards • by Lisa Childs

Keeli Abbott became a bodyguard to *avoid* Detective Spencer Dubridge. Now she's been tasked with protecting him—and might be pregnant with his baby! Close quarters force them to face their feelings, but with a drug cartel determined to make sure Spencer doesn't testify, they may not have much time left...

#2178 MOUNTAIN RETREAT MURDER
Cameron Glen • by Beth Cornelison

When a mysterious death finds Cait Cameron's family's inn, she enlists guest Matt Harkney, father to a troubled teenager, to help investigate recent crimes. Love and loyalty are tested as veteran Matt risks everything to heal his family, catch a thief and save Cait's life.

SPECIAL EXCERPT FROM

⊕ HARLEQUIN

ROMANTIC SUSPENSE

*When a mysterious death finds Cait Cameron's family's
inn, she enlists guest Matt Harkney, father to a troubled
teenager, to help investigate recent crimes. Love and
loyalty are tested as veteran Matt risks everything to
heal his family, catch a thief and save Cait's life.*

Read on for a sneak preview of
Mountain Retreat Murder,
*the first book in Beth Cornelison's
new Cameron Glen miniseries!*

He paused with the blade hovering over the crack between
boards. "Are you sure you want to keep prying up planks?
Whoever did this could have loosened any number of
boards in this floor."

The truth of his comment clearly daunted her. Her
shoulders dropped, and her expression sagged with sorrow.
"Yes. Continue. At least with this one, where I know
something was amiss earlier." She raised a hand, adding,
"But carefully."

He ducked his head in understanding, "Of course."

An apologetic grin flickered over her forlorn features,
softening the tension, and he took an extra second or two
just to stare at her. Sunlight streamed in from the window
above the kitchen sink and highlighted the auburn streaks
in her hair and the faint freckles on her upturned nose. The

bright beam reflected in her pale blue eyes, reminding him of sparkling water in the stream by his cabin. A throb of emotion grabbed at his chest.

"Matt?"

"Do you know how beautiful you are?"

She blinked. Blushed.

"What?" The word sounded strangled.

"You are." He stroked her cheek with the back of his left hand. "Beautiful."

Her throat worked as she swallowed, and she glanced down, shyly. "Um, thank you. I—"

"Anyway…" He withdrew his hand and turned his attention back to the floorboard. He eased the pocketknife blade in the small crack and gently levered the plank up.

As he moved the board out of the way, Cait shined the flashlight in the hole beneath.

She gasped at the same moment he muttered, "Holy hell."

In the dark space they exposed was a small plastic bag. Cait moved the light closer, illuminating the contents of the clear bag—a large bundle of cash, bound by a white paper band with "$7458" written on it.

When she reached for the bag of money, he caught her wrist. "No. Don't touch it."

When she frowned a query at him, he added, "Fingerprints. That's evidence."

Don't miss
Mountain Retreat Murder *by Beth Cornelison,*
available April 2022 wherever
Harlequin Romantic Suspense
books and ebooks are sold.

Harlequin.com

HARLEQUIN

Heartfelt or thrilling, passionate or uplifting—Harlequin is more than just happily-ever-after.

With twelve different series to choose from and new books available every month, you are sure to find stories that will move you, uplift you, inspire and delight you.

SIGN UP FOR THE HARLEQUIN NEWSLETTER

Be the first to hear about great new reads and exciting offers!

Harlequin.com/newsletters

Love Harlequin romance?

DISCOVER.

Be the first to find out about promotions, news and exclusive content!

f Facebook.com/HarlequinBooks

Twitter.com/HarlequinBooks

Instagram.com/HarlequinBooks

Pinterest.com/HarlequinBooks

You Tube YouTube.com/HarlequinBooks

ReaderService.com

EXPLORE.

Sign up for the Harlequin e-newsletter and download a free book from any series at **TryHarlequin.com**

CONNECT.

Join our Harlequin community to share your thoughts and connect with other romance readers!
Facebook.com/groups/HarlequinConnection